AGENT MOOSE

MOOSE ON A MISSION

WITH ART BY

Mo O'Hara Jess Bradley

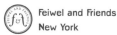

Feiwel and Friends
New York

To my brother Matt, who introduced me
to comics and graphic novels and is my hero.
—M. O.

For Emma, without whom my childhood
would have been far duller (but also
with far less NKOTB). Miss you.
—J. B.

A Feiwel and Friends Book
An imprint of Macmillan Publishing Group, LLC
120 Broadway, New York, NY 10271
mackids.com

Our books may be purchased in bulk for promotional, educational, or business use. Please
contact your local bookseller or the Macmillan Corporate and Premium Sales Department
at (800) 221-7945 ext. 5442 or by email at MacmillanSpecialMarkets@macmillan.com.
Library of Congress Control Number: 2020919294

First edition, 2021
Book design by Liz Dresner • Color by John-Paul Bove • Lettering by Micah Myers
Feiwel and Friends logo designed by Filomena Tuosto
Printed in China by RR Donnelley Asia Printing Solutions Ltd.,
Dongguan City, Guangdong Province.

ISBN 978-1-250-22222-0 (hardcover)
1 3 5 7 9 10 8 6 4 2

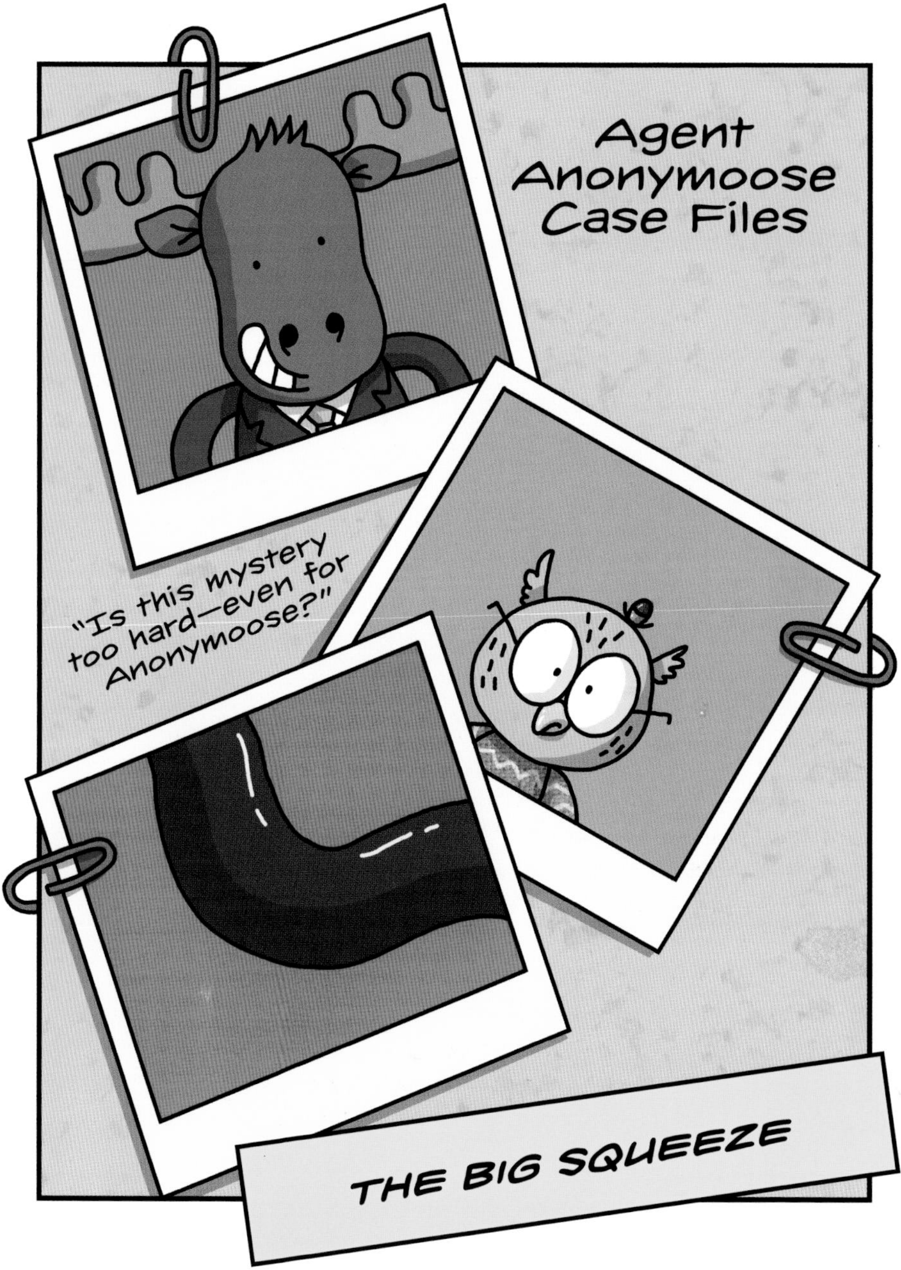
Agent Anonymoose Case Files
"Is this mystery too hard—even for Anonymoose?"
THE BIG SQUEEZE

Special Agent Anonymoose
Personnel File

Size: Extremely large

Distinguishing features: Antlers, dark brown hide, small birthmark that looks a little like North Dakota

Talents: Master of disguise, spying, investigating the strange (and possibly strange) goings-on in Woodland Territories, world-renowned Twister player

Favorite item of clothing: Snazzy investigating suit with lots of important pockets for spy stuff

Clearance for spying: First Class Spy Clearance for secrets

Clearance for height: About seven and a half feet

Not-Quite-So-Special Agent Owlfred Personnel File

Size: Small enough that he can fit in a moose's pocket

Distinguishing features: Gray, feathery, can do that crazy owl thing where they twist their head most of the way around (but it makes him slightly motion sick)

Talents: Very precise analysis of clues and data, calm attitude in a crisis, patience in a crisis (also very good at just avoiding crises)

Favorite item of clothing: Exceedingly tiny bowler hat that he's been told accentuates his fetching feathery ears

Clearance for spying: Third Class Spy Clearance for secrets

Clearance for height: Irrelevant due to flying and all

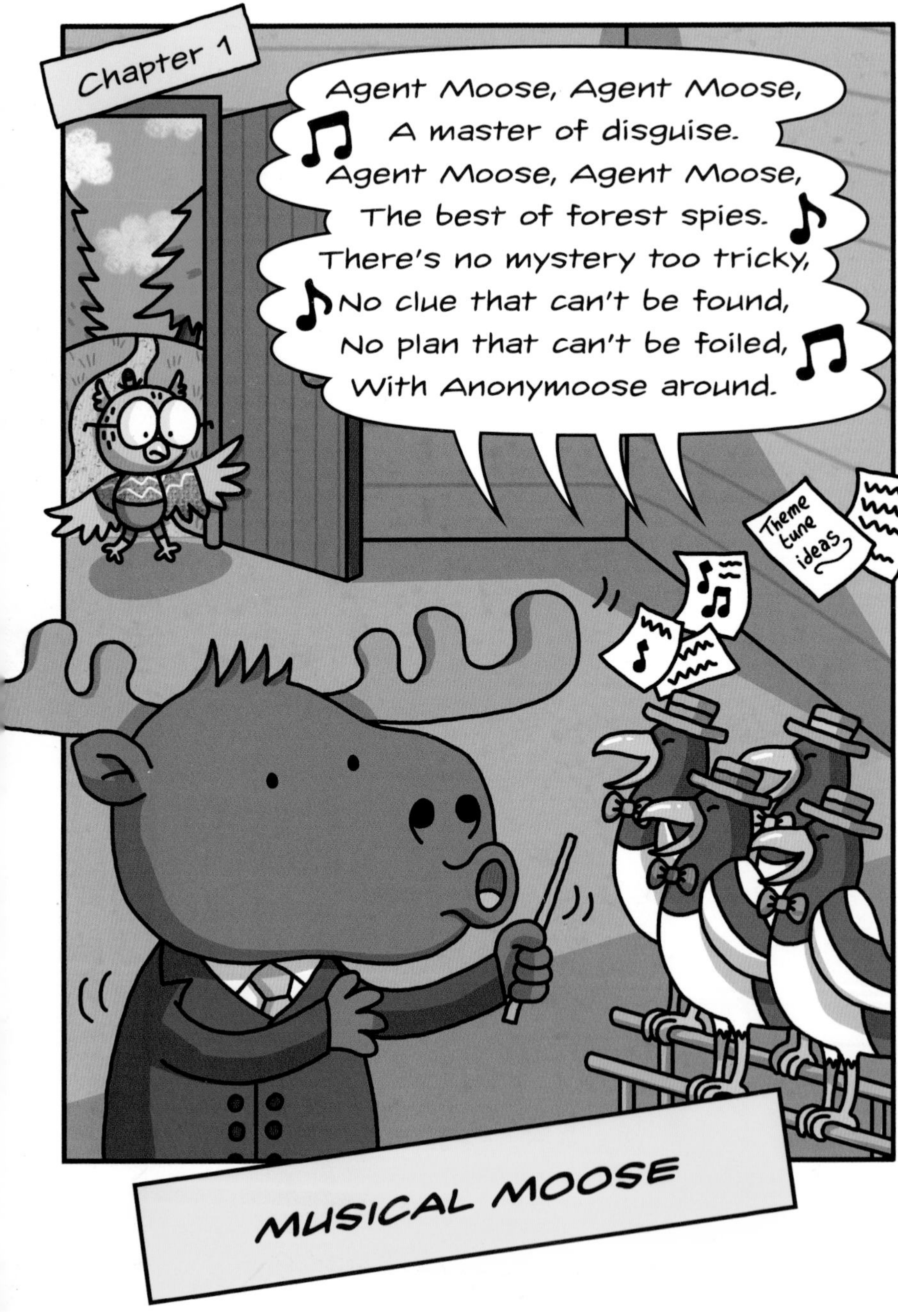
Chapter 1
Agent Moose, Agent Moose,
A master of disguise.
Agent Moose, Agent Moose,
The best of forest spies.
There's no mystery too tricky,
No clue that can't be found,
No plan that can't be foiled,
With Anonymoose around.
Theme tune ideas
MUSICAL MOOSE

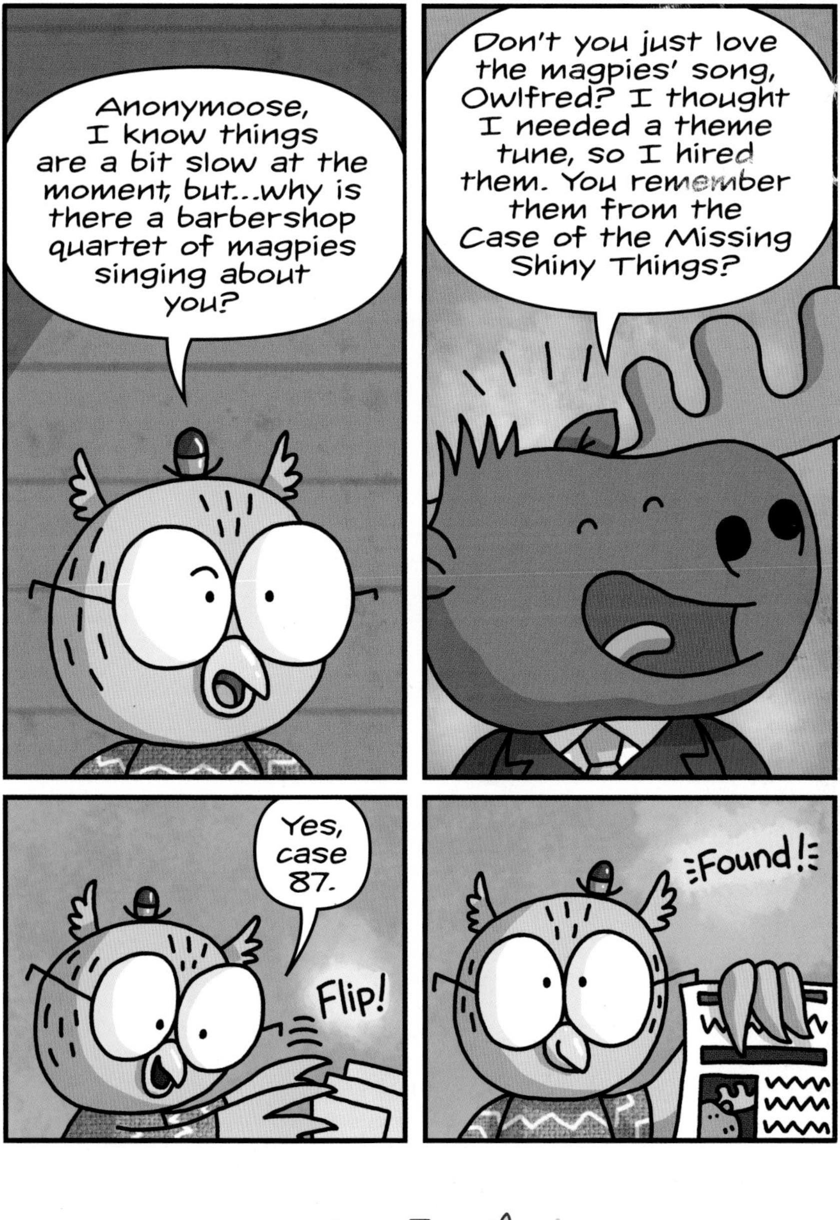
Anonymoose, I know things are a bit slow at the moment, but...why is there a barbershop quartet of magpies singing about you?
Don't you just love the magpies' song, Owlfred? I thought I needed a theme tune, so I hired them. You remember them from the Case of the Missing Shiny Things?
Yes, case 87.
Flip!
Found!

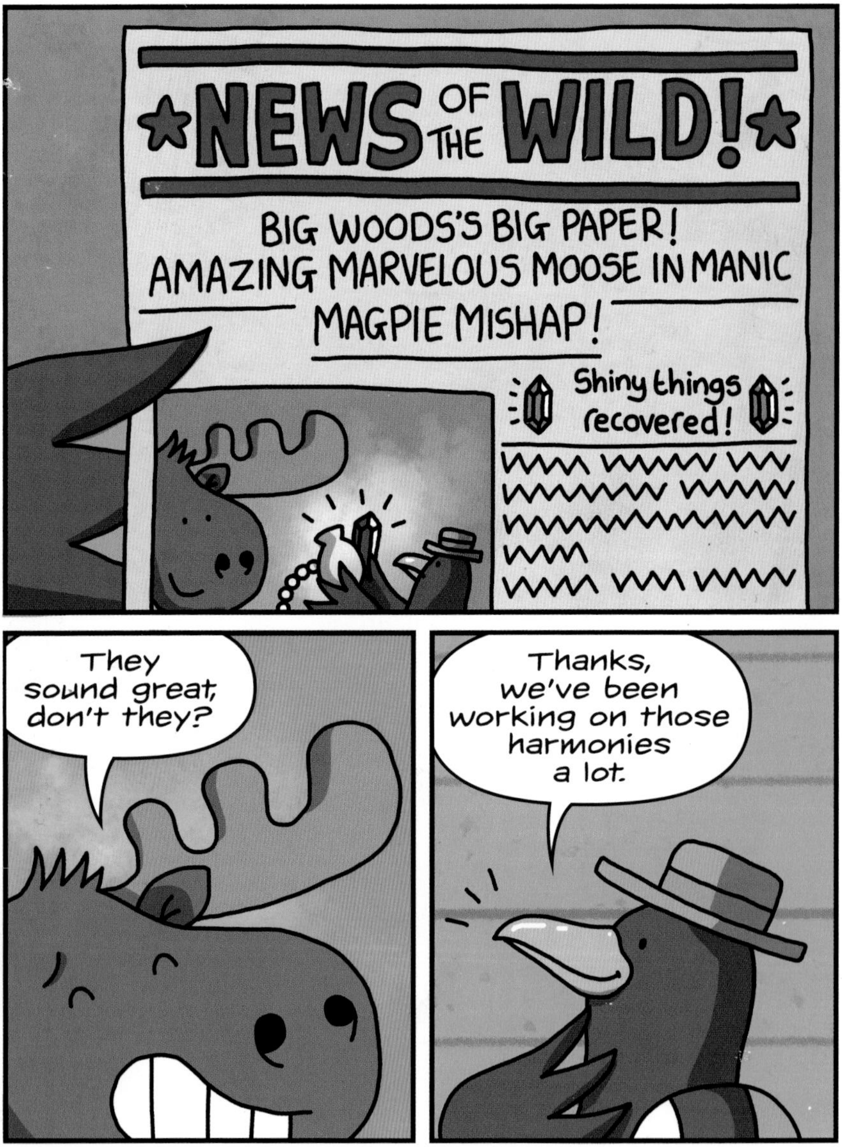
NEWS OF THE WILD!
BIG WOODS'S BIG PAPER!
AMAZING MARVELOUS MOOSE IN MANIC MAGPIE MISHAP!
Shiny things recovered!
They sound great, don't they?
Thanks, we've been working on those harmonies a lot.

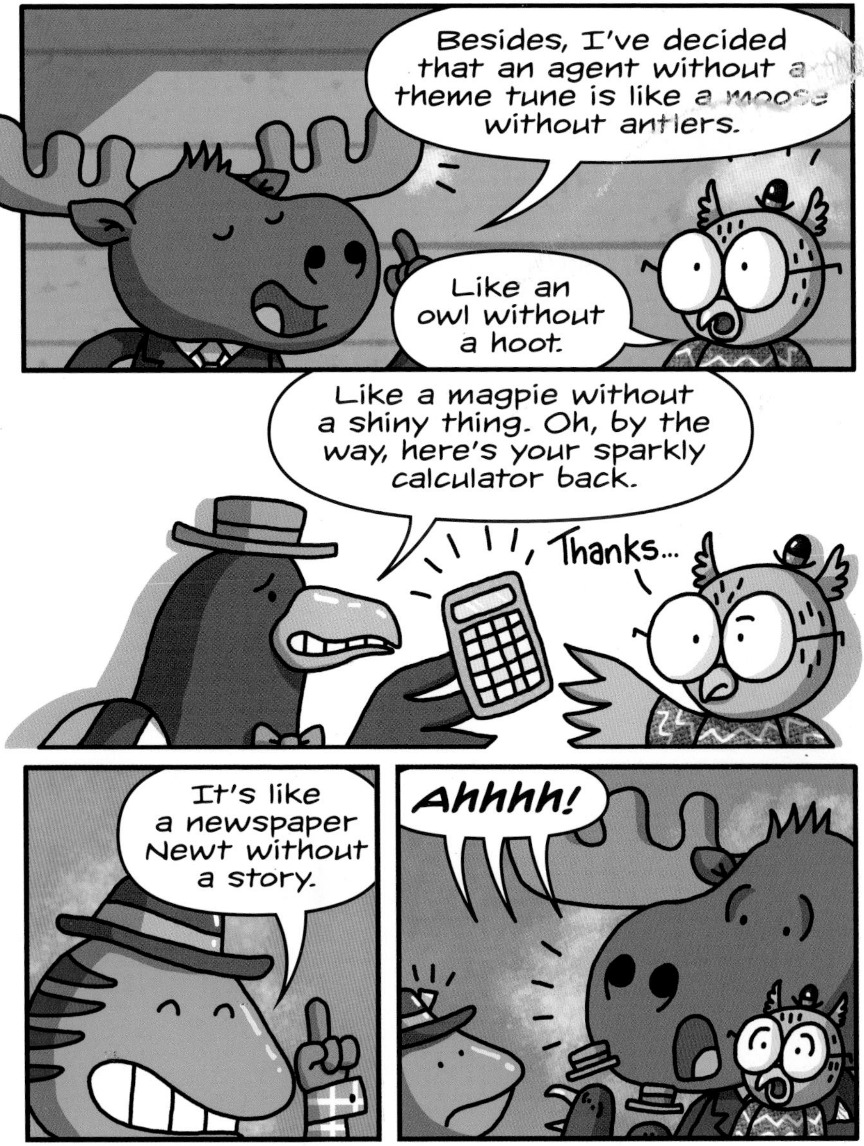
Besides, I've decided that an agent without a theme tune is like a moose without antlers.
Like an owl without a hoot.
Like a magpie without a shiny thing. Oh, by the way, here's your sparkly calculator back.
Thanks...
It's like a newspaper Newt without a story.
Ahhhh!

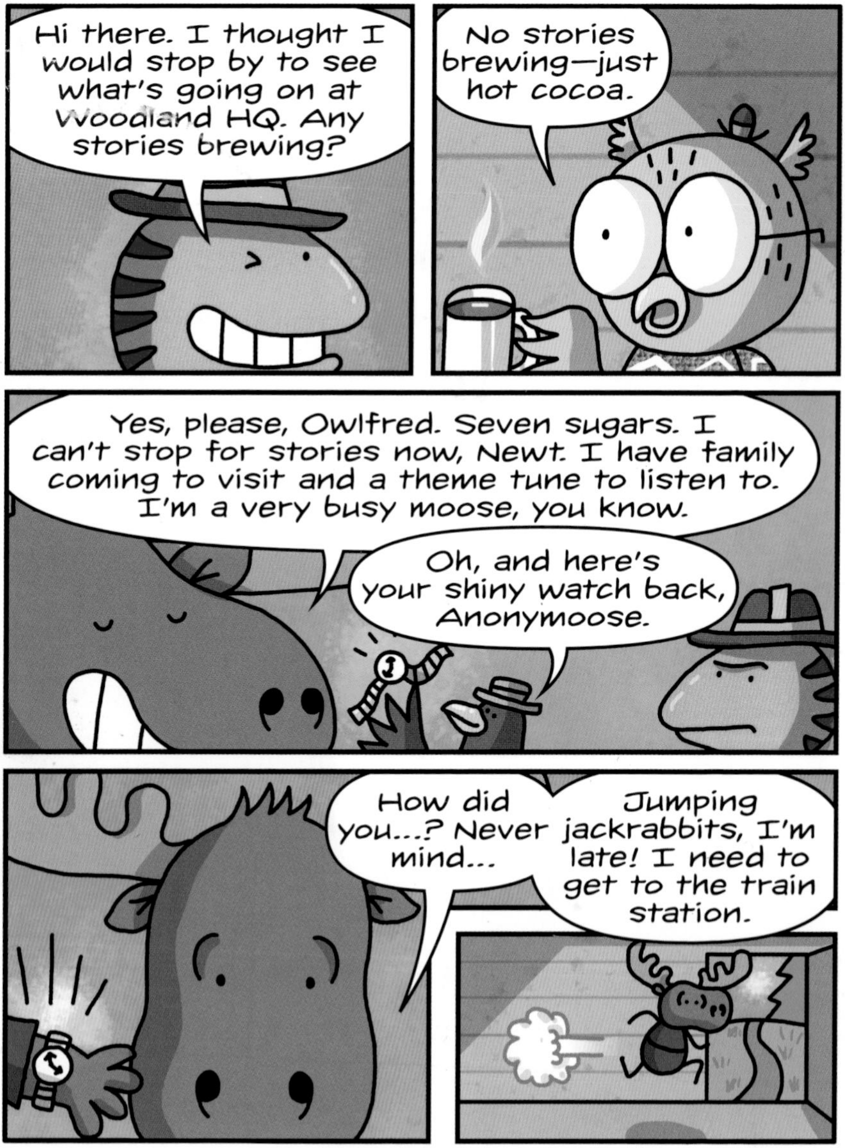
Hi there. I thought I would stop by to see what's going on at Woodland HQ. Any stories brewing?
No stories brewing—just hot cocoa.
Yes, please, Owlfred. Seven sugars. I can't stop for stories now, Newt. I have family coming to visit and a theme tune to listen to. I'm a very busy moose, you know.
Oh, and here's your shiny watch back, Anonymoose.
How did you...? Never mind...
Jumping jackrabbits, I'm late! I need to get to the train station.

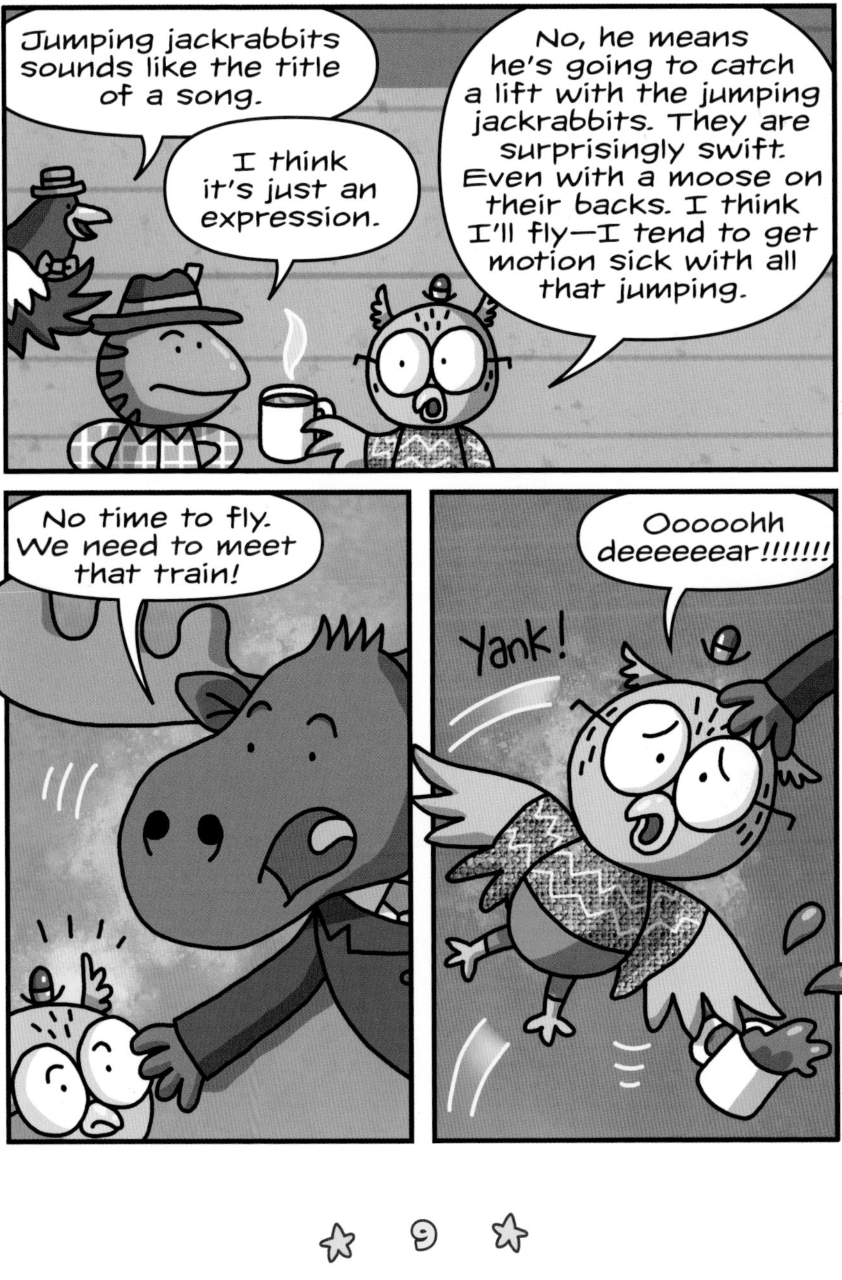
Jumping jackrabbits sounds like the title of a song.
I think it's just an expression.
No, he means he's going to catch a lift with the jumping jackrabbits. They are surprisingly swift. Even with a moose on their backs. I think I'll fly—I tend to get motion sick with all that jumping.
No time to fly. We need to meet that train!
Ooooohh deeeeeear!!!!!!!
Yank!

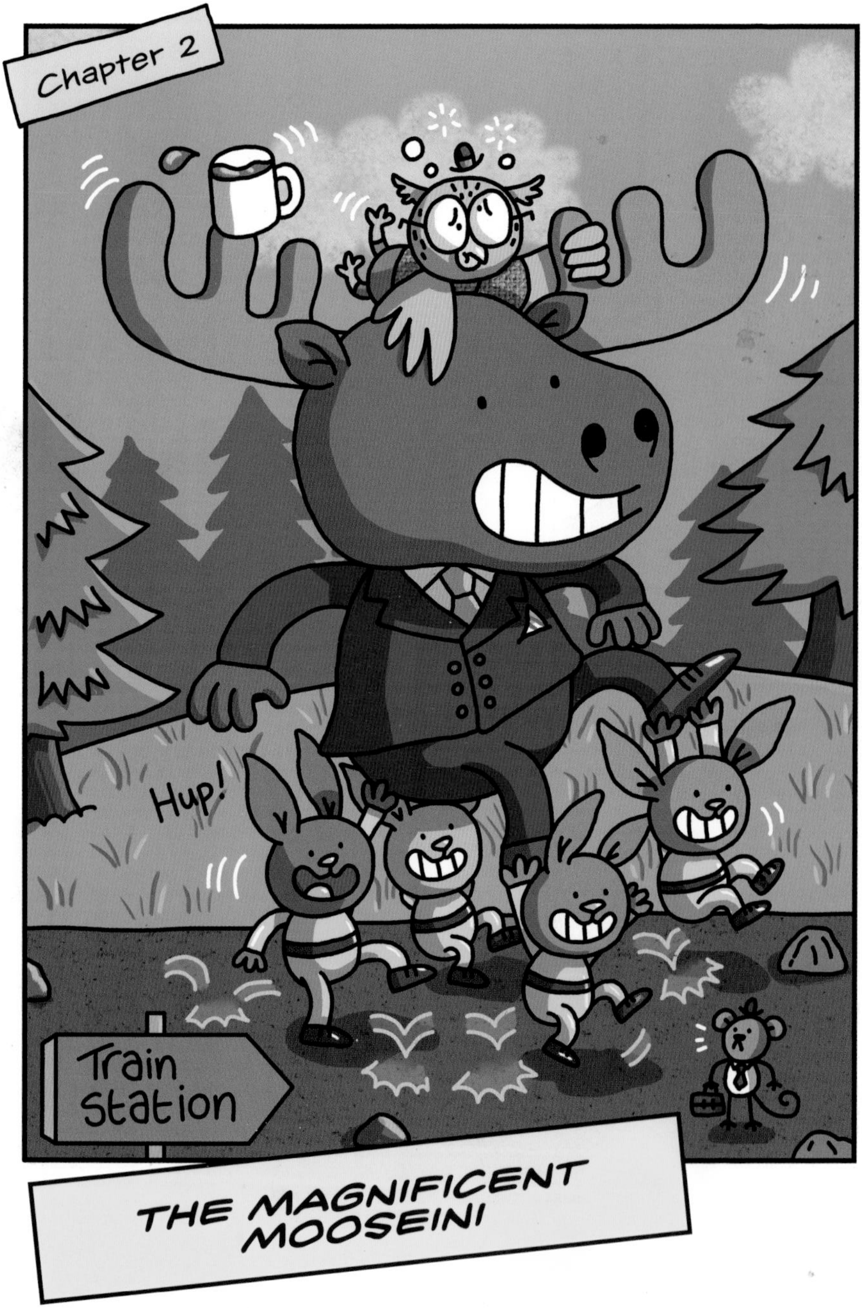
Chapter 2
Hup!
Train Station

THE MAGNIFICENT MOOSEINI

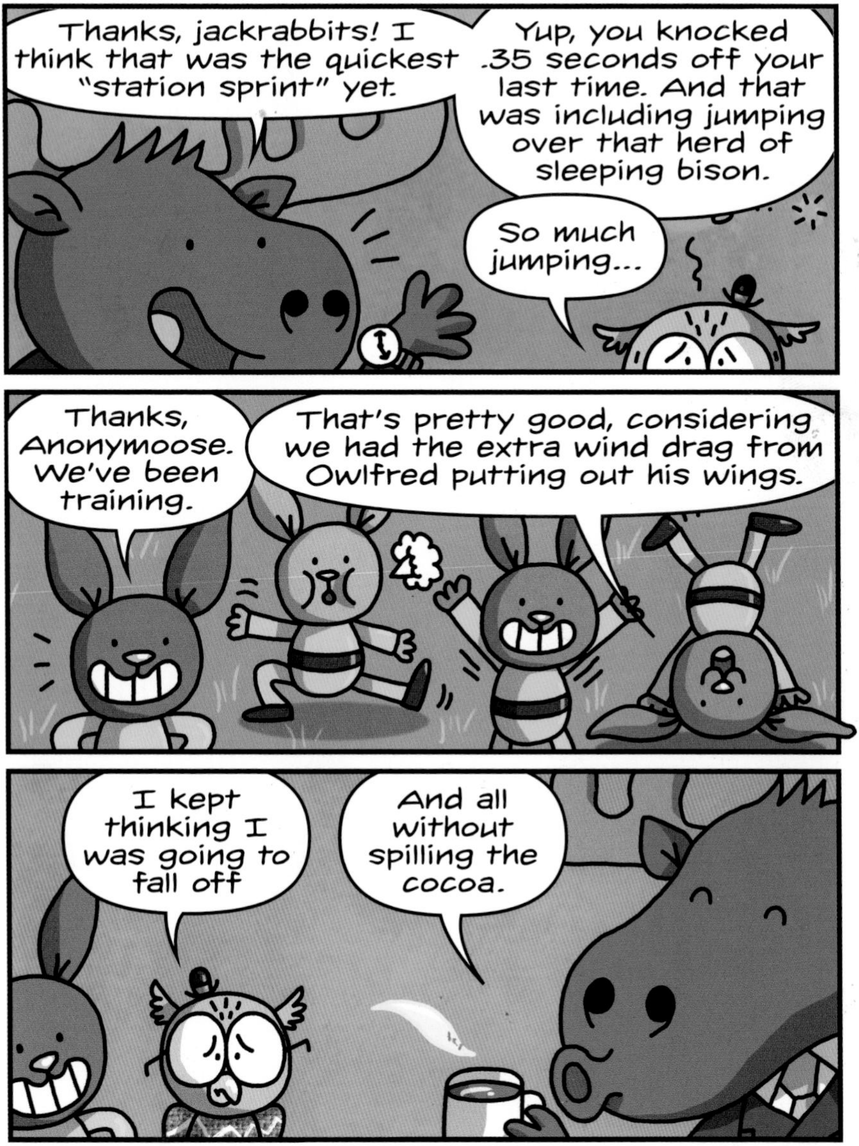
Thanks, jackrabbits! I think that was the quickest "station sprint" yet.
Yup, you knocked .35 seconds off your last time. And that was including jumping over that herd of sleeping bison.
So much jumping...
Thanks, Anonymoose. We've been training.
That's pretty good, considering we had the extra wind drag from Owlfred putting out his wings.
I kept thinking I was going to fall off
And all without spilling the cocoa.

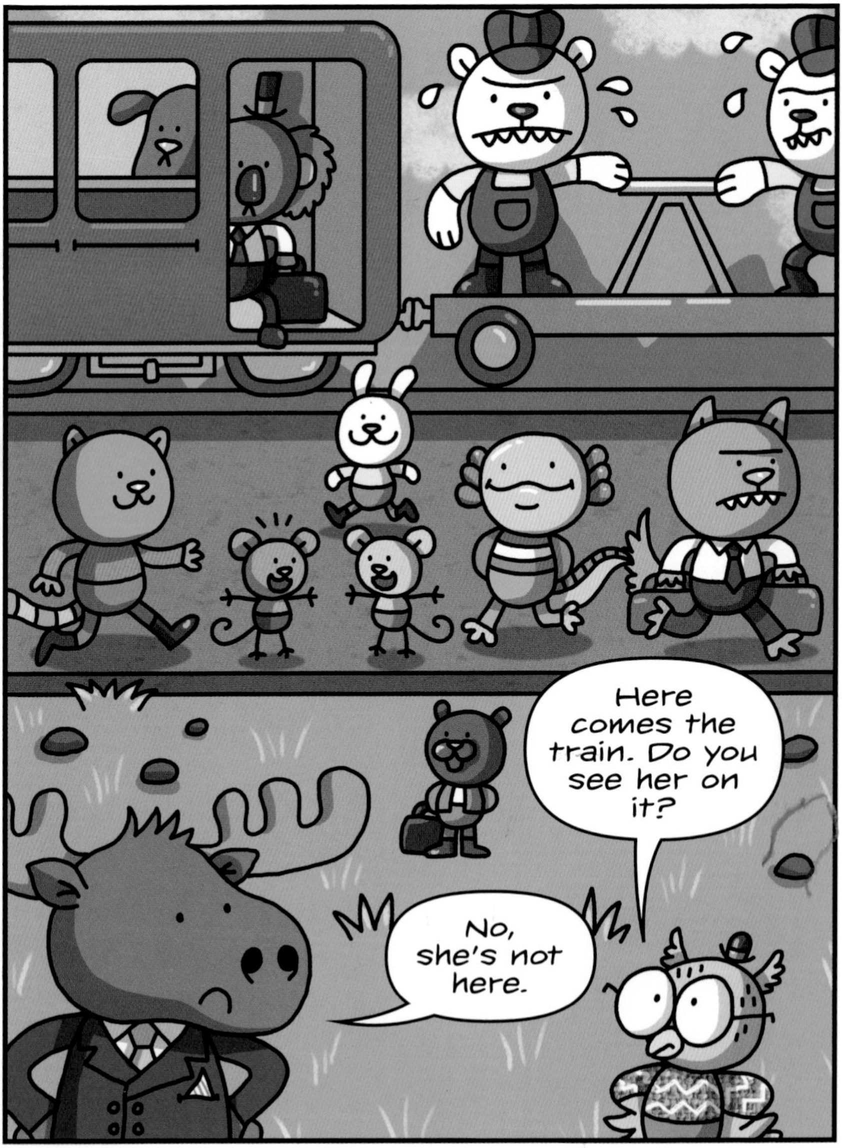
Here comes the train. Do you see her on it?
No, she's not here.

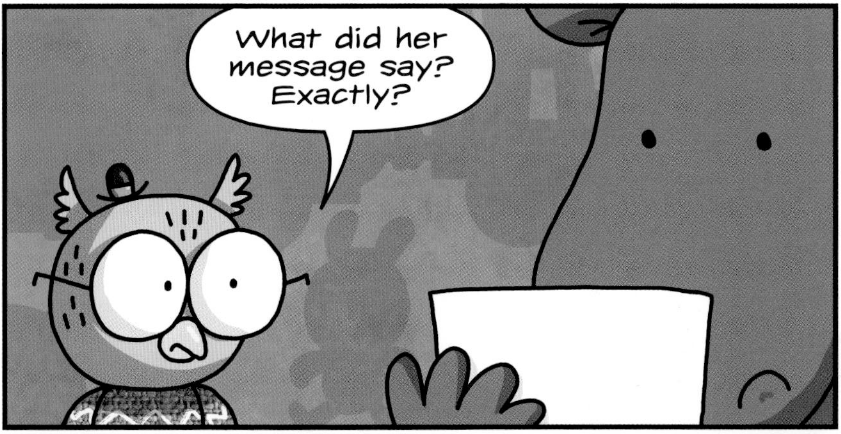
What did her message say? Exactly?

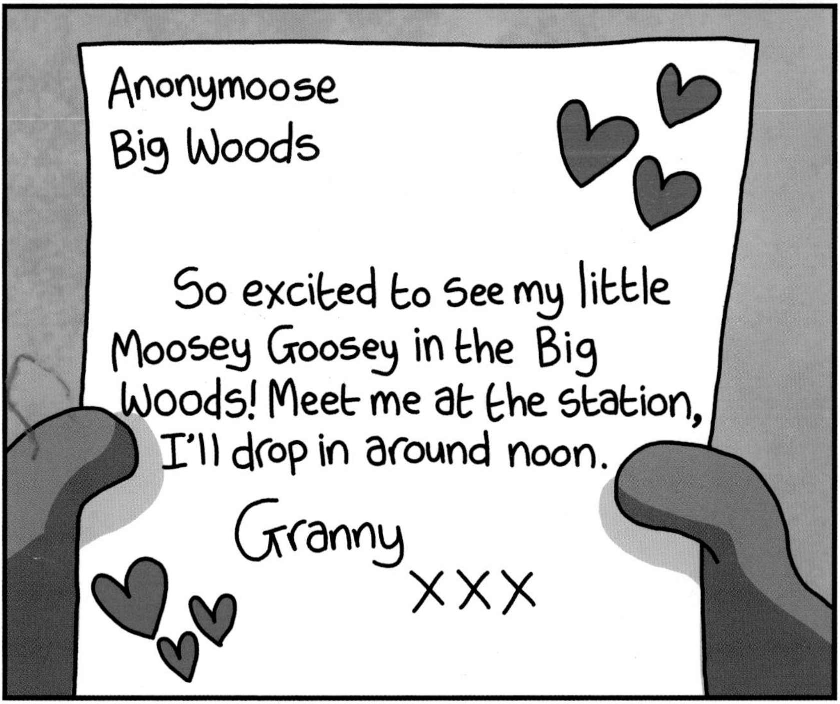
Anonymoose
Big Woods
So excited to see my little Moosey Goosey in the Big Woods! Meet me at the station, I'll drop in around noon.
Granny
XXX

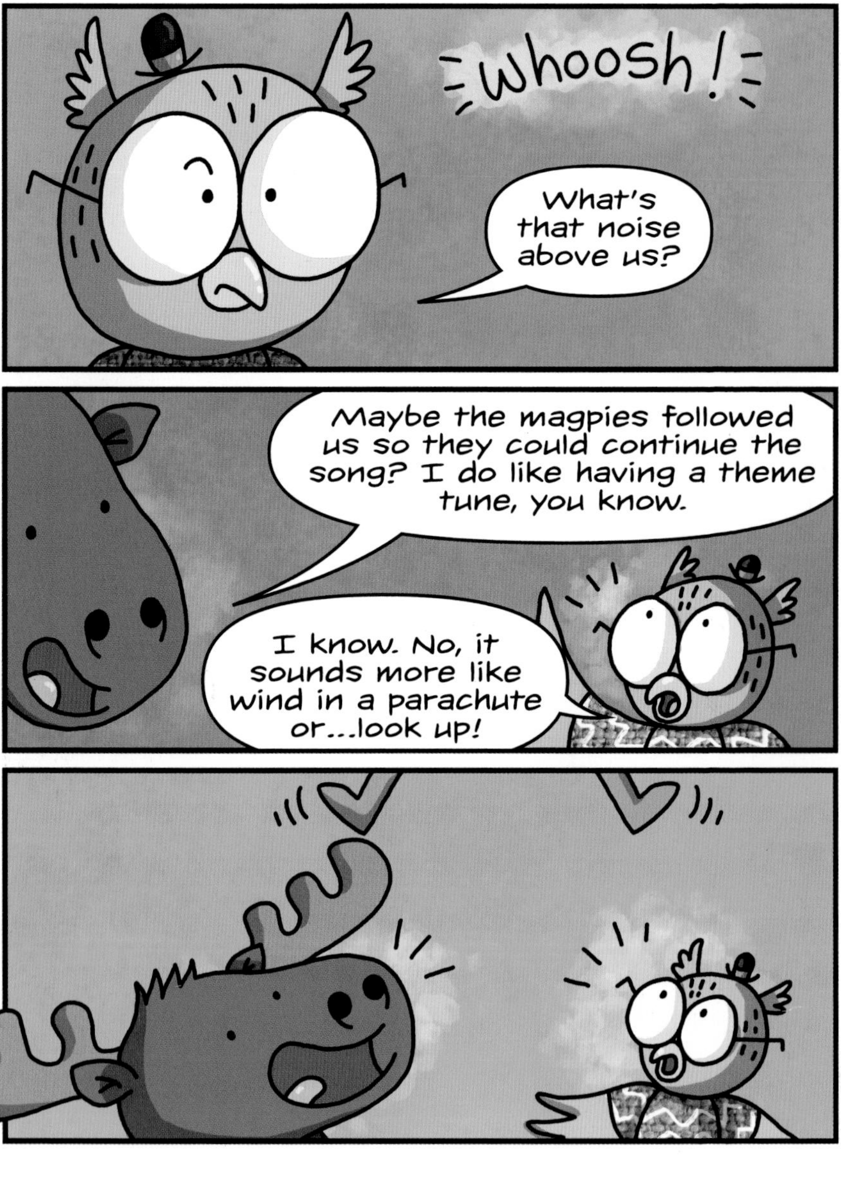
whoosh!
What's that noise above us?
Maybe the magpies followed us so they could continue the song? I do like having a theme tune, you know.
I know. No, it sounds more like wind in a parachute or...look up!

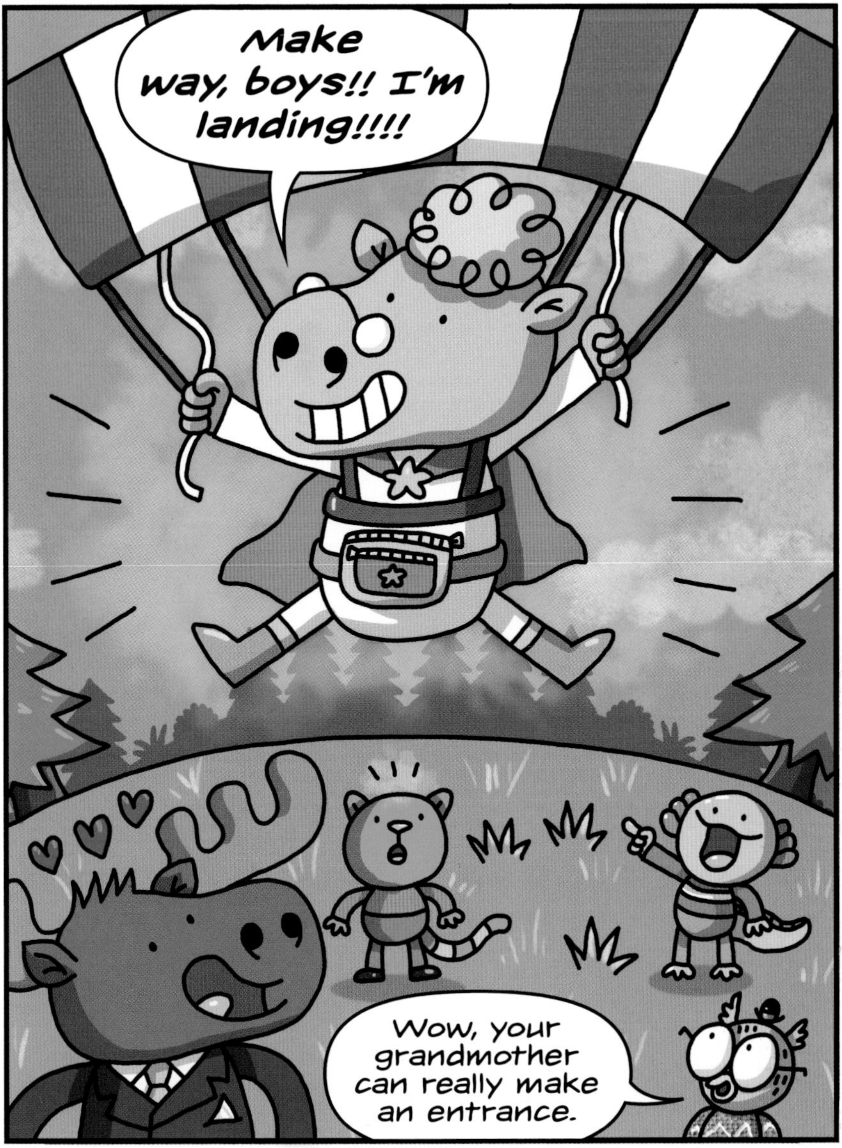
Make way, boys!! I'm landing!!!!
Wow, your grandmother can really make an entrance.

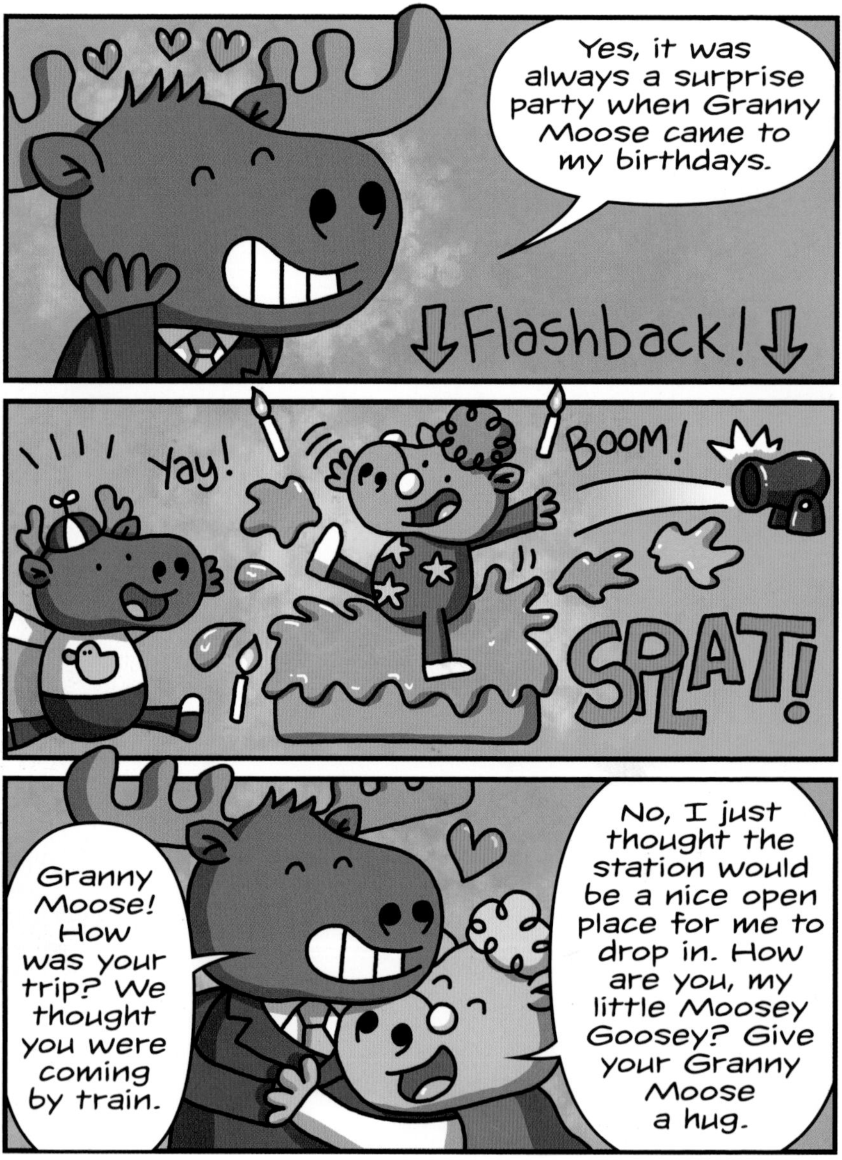
Yes, it was always a surprise party when Granny Moose came to my birthdays.
Flashback!
Yay!
BOOM!
SPLAT!
Granny Moose! How was your trip? We thought you were coming by train.
No, I just thought the station would be a nice open place for me to drop in. How are you, my little Moosey Goosey? Give your Granny Moose a hug.

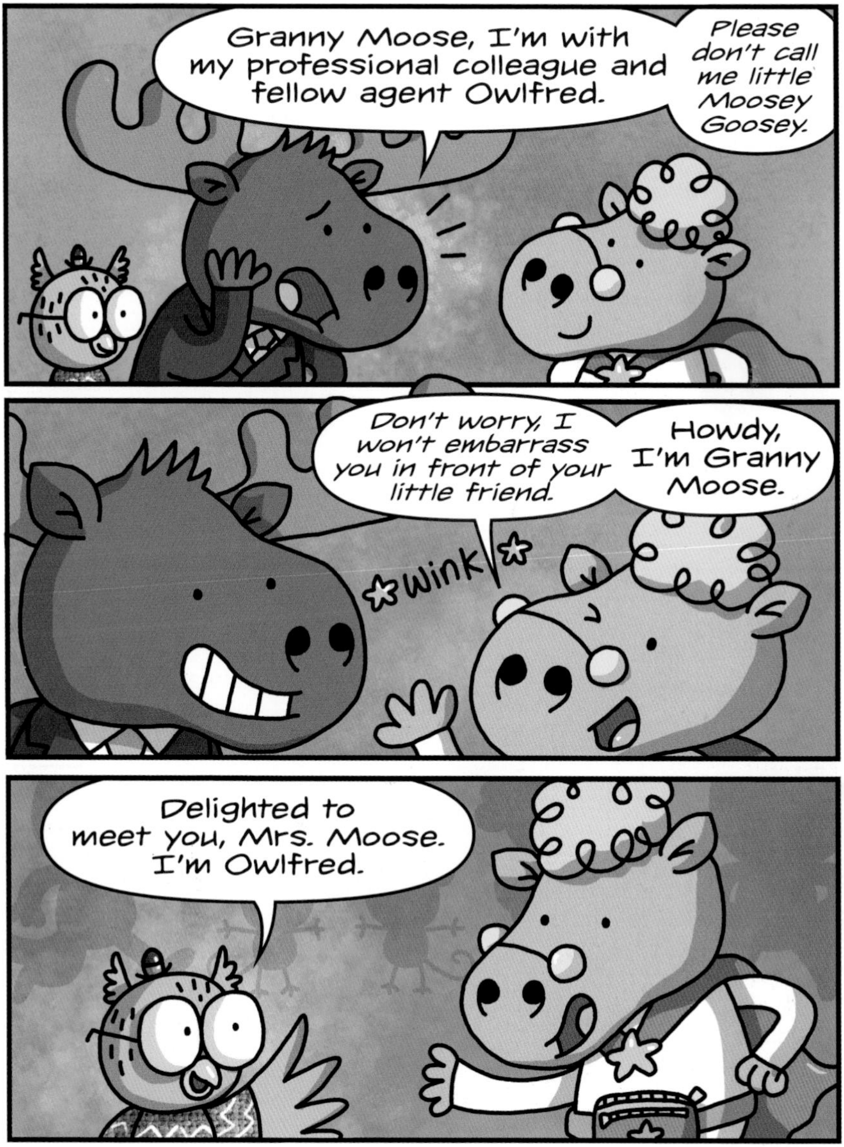
Granny Moose, I'm with my professional colleague and fellow agent Owlfred.
Please don't call me little Moosey Goosey.
Howdy, I'm Granny Moose.
Don't worry, I won't embarrass you in front of your little friend.
Wink
Delighted to meet you, Mrs. Moose. I'm Owlfred.

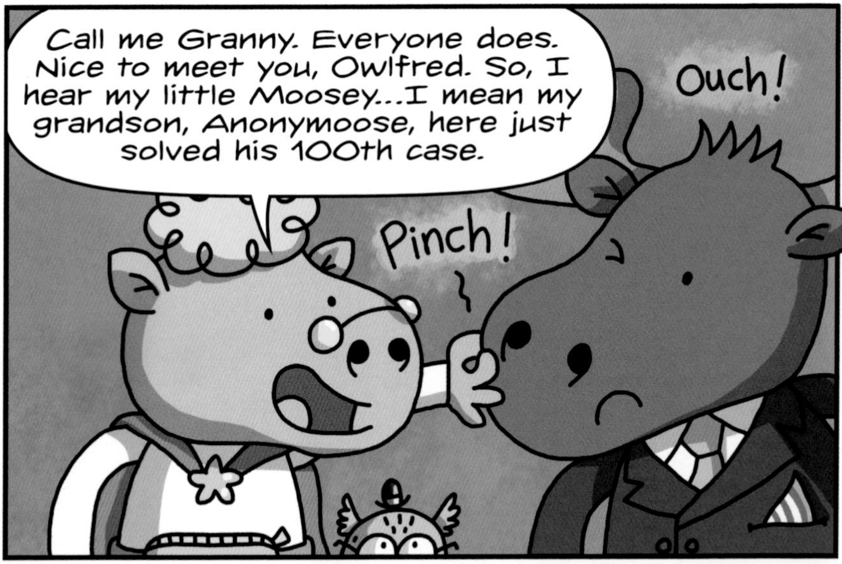
Call me Granny. Everyone does. Nice to meet you, Owlfred. So, I hear my little Moosey...I mean my grandson, Anonymoose, here just solved his 100th case.
Ouch!
Pinch!

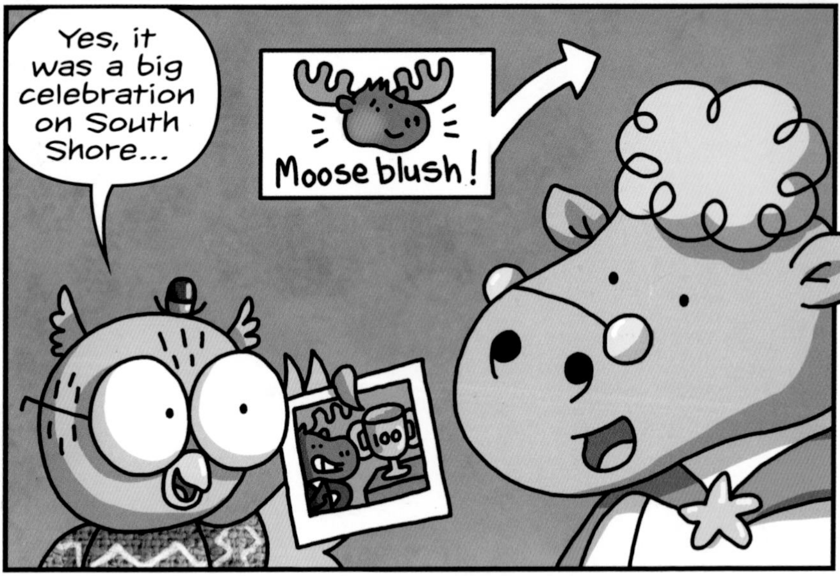
Yes, it was a big celebration on South Shore...
Moose blush!
100

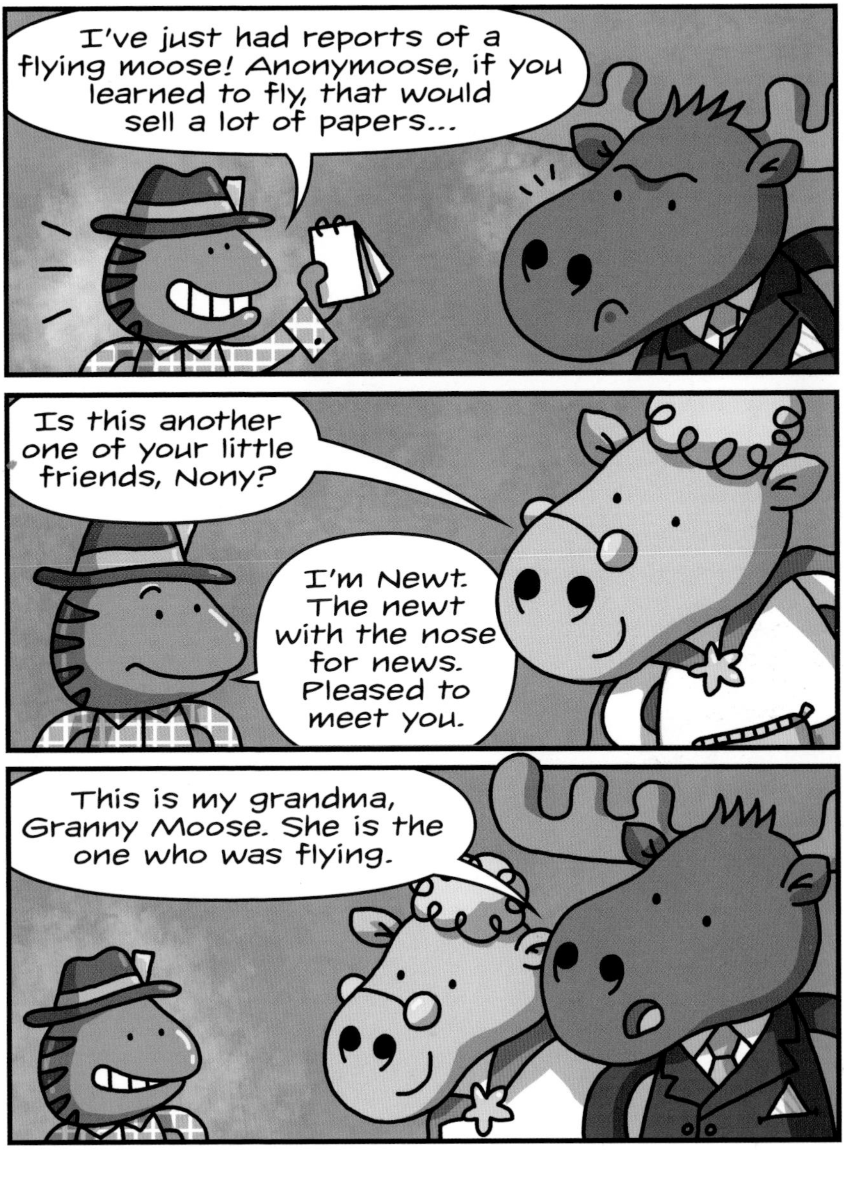
I've just had reports of a flying moose! Anonymoose, if you learned to fly, that would sell a lot of papers...
Is this another one of your little friends, Nony?
I'm Newt. The newt with the nose for news. Pleased to meet you.
This is my grandma, Granny Moose. She is the one who was flying.

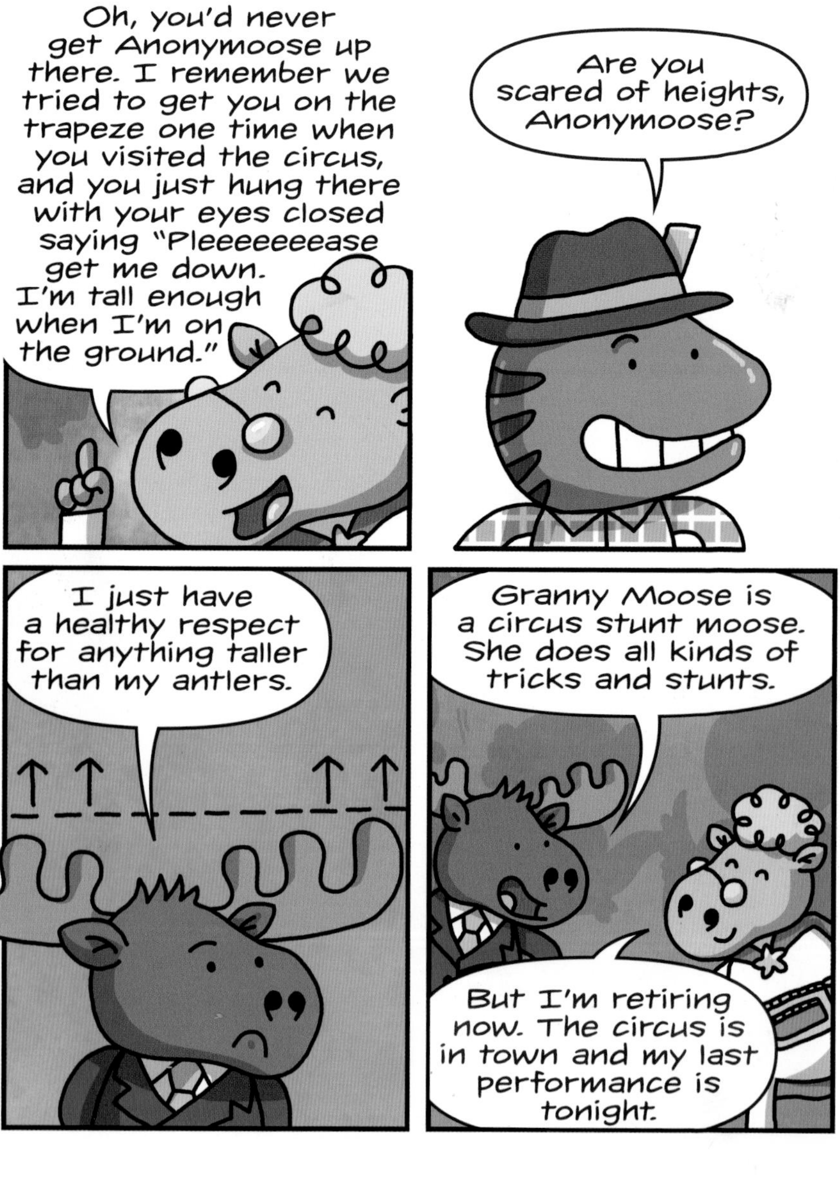

Oh, you'd never get Anonymoose up there. I remember we tried to get you on the trapeze one time when you visited the circus, and you just hung there with your eyes closed saying "Pleeeeeeease get me down. I'm tall enough when I'm on the ground."
Are you scared of heights, Anonymoose?
I just have a healthy respect for anything taller than my antlers.
Granny Moose is a circus stunt moose. She does all kinds of tricks and stunts.
But I'm retiring now. The circus is in town and my last performance is tonight.

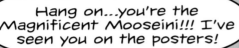

Hang on...you're the Magnificent Mooseini!!! I've seen you on the posters!

MAGNIFICENT

MOOSEINI!!

Oh, are they still using that old picture? Gosh. I just wanted some family time with my grandson. I didn't know you would bring all these friends to meet me, Nony. Who's this dashing anteater, then?

I don't actually know any anteaters, Granny.

WAVE!

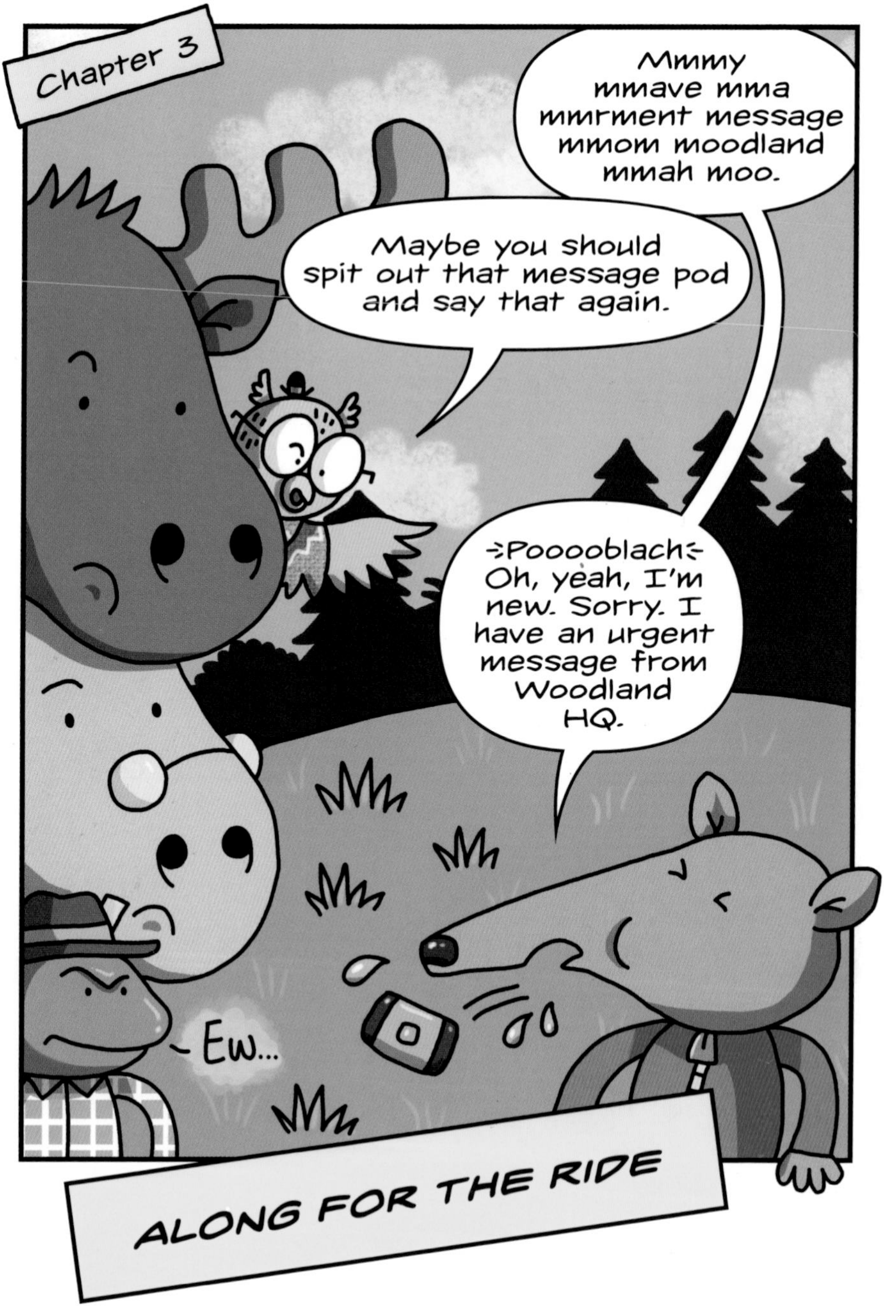
Chapter 3
Mmmy mmave mma mmrment message mmom moodland mmah moo.
Maybe you should spit out that message pod and say that again.
Poooooblach Oh, yeah, I'm new. Sorry. I have an urgent message from Woodland HQ.
Ew...

ALONG FOR THE RIDE

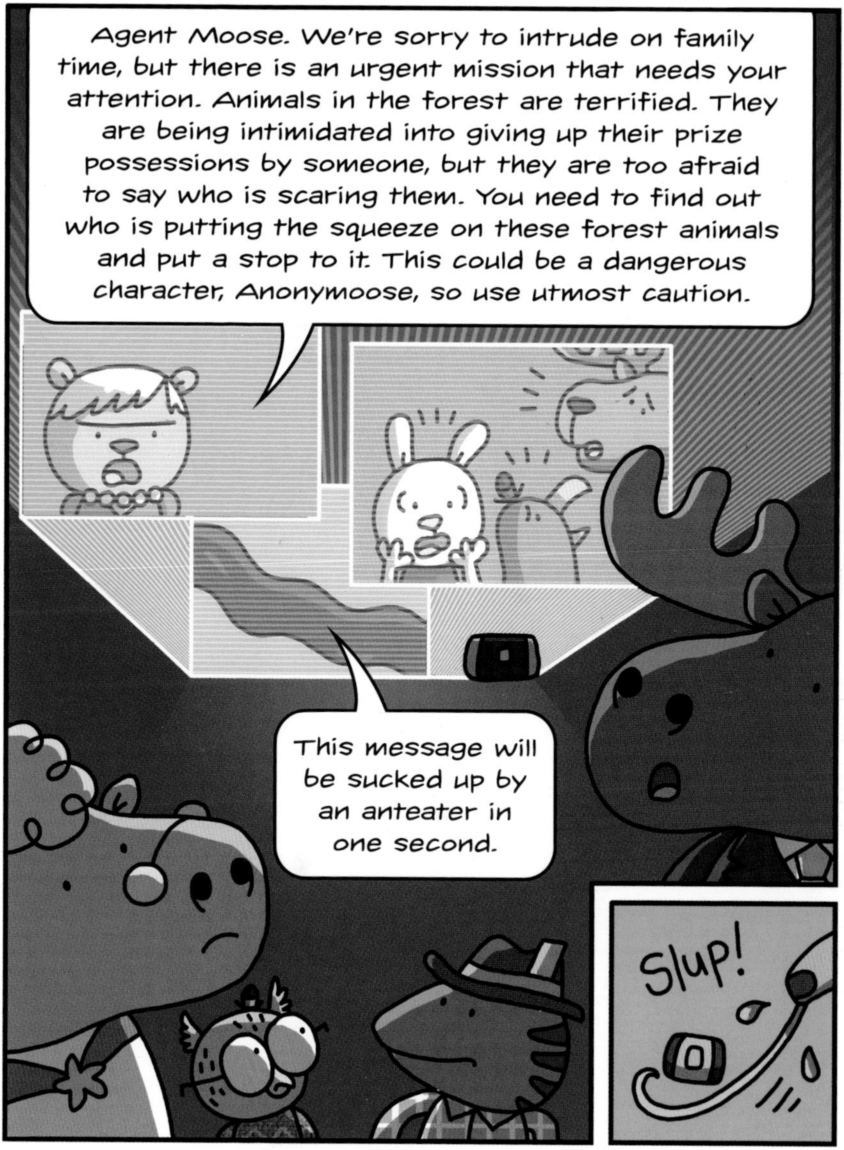
Agent Moose. We're sorry to intrude on family time, but there is an urgent mission that needs your attention. Animals in the forest are terrified. They are being intimidated into giving up their prize possessions by someone, but they are too afraid to say who is scaring them. You need to find out who is putting the squeeze on these forest animals and put a stop to it. This could be a dangerous character, Anonymoose, so use utmost caution.
This message will be sucked up by an anteater in one second.
Slup!

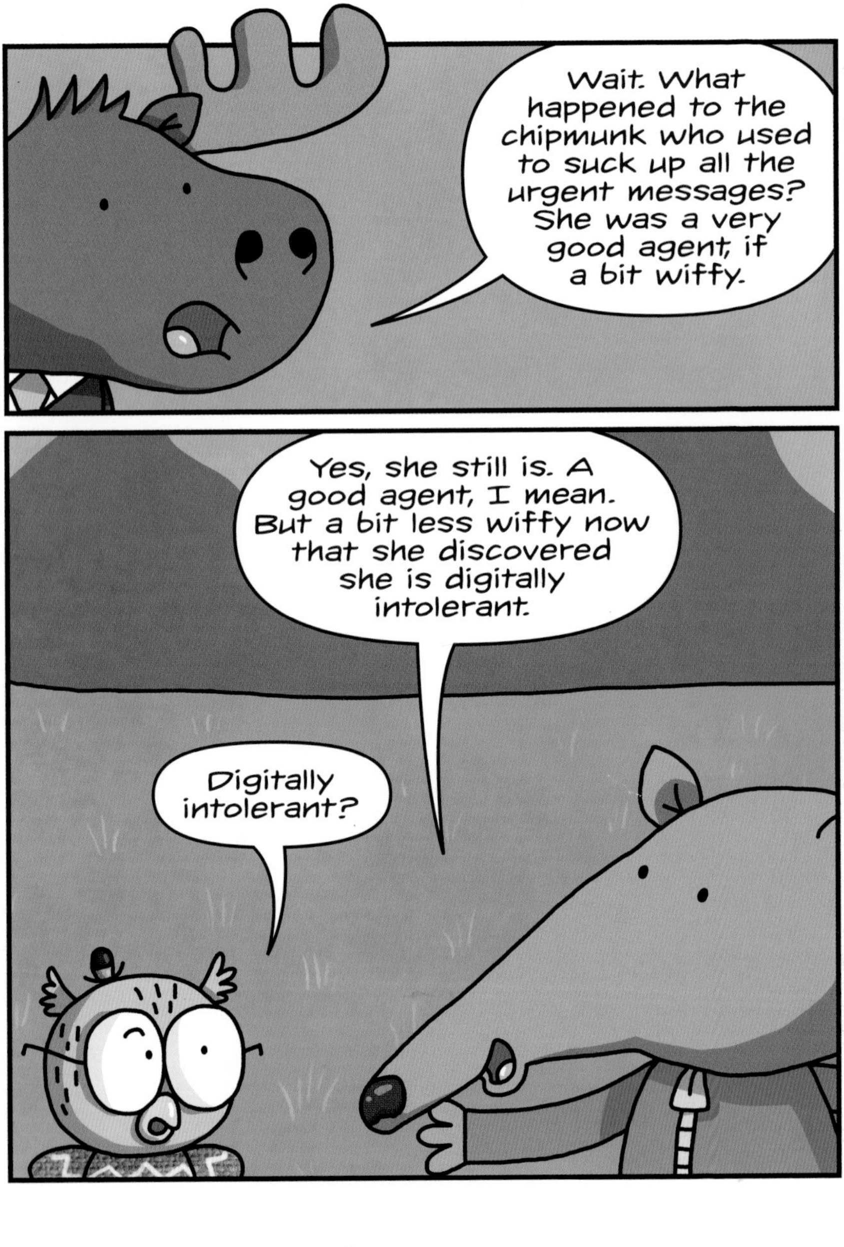
Wait. What happened to the chipmunk who used to suck up all the urgent messages? She was a very good agent, if a bit wiffy.
Yes, she still is. A good agent, I mean. But a bit less wiffy now that she discovered she is digitally intolerant.
Digitally intolerant?

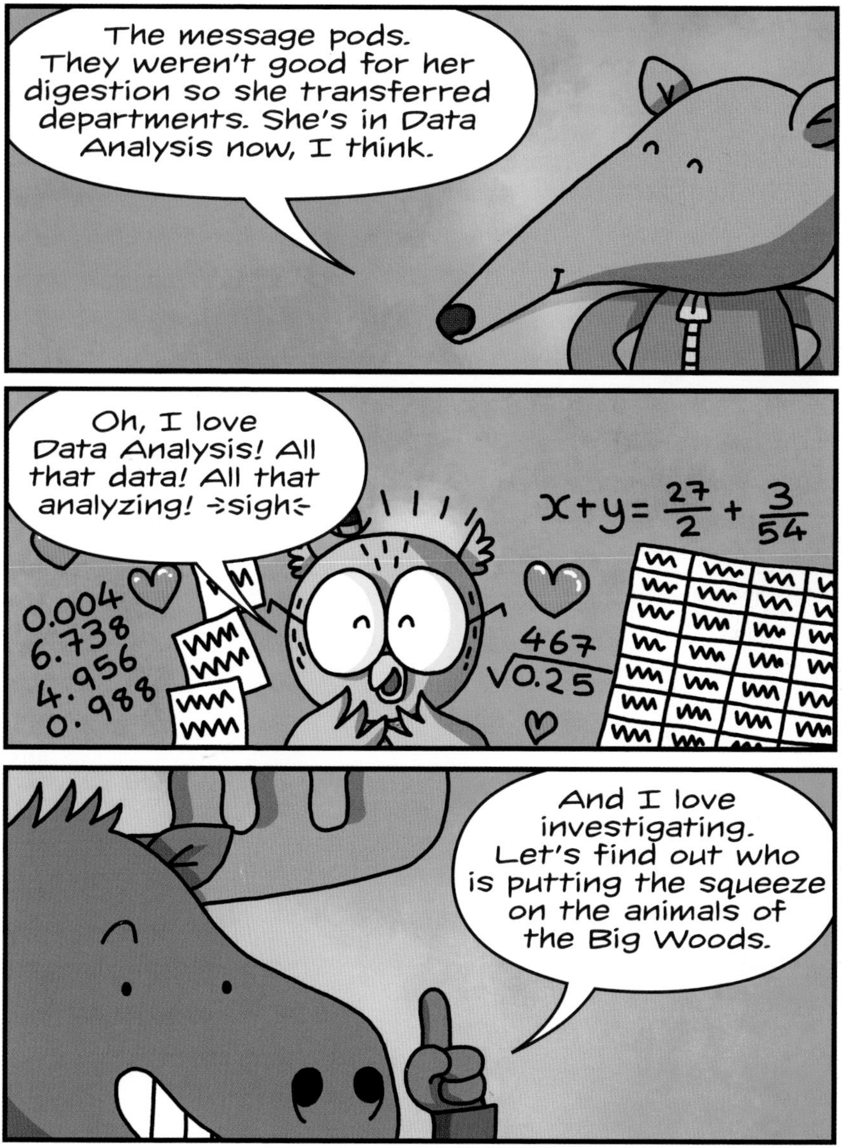
The message pods. They weren't good for her digestion so she transferred departments. She's in Data Analysis now, I think.
Oh, I love Data Analysis! All that data! All that analyzing! ⇁sigh↽
x+y= 27/2 + 3/54
0.004
6.738
4.956
0.988
467
√0.25
And I love investigating. Let's find out who is putting the squeeze on the animals of the Big Woods.

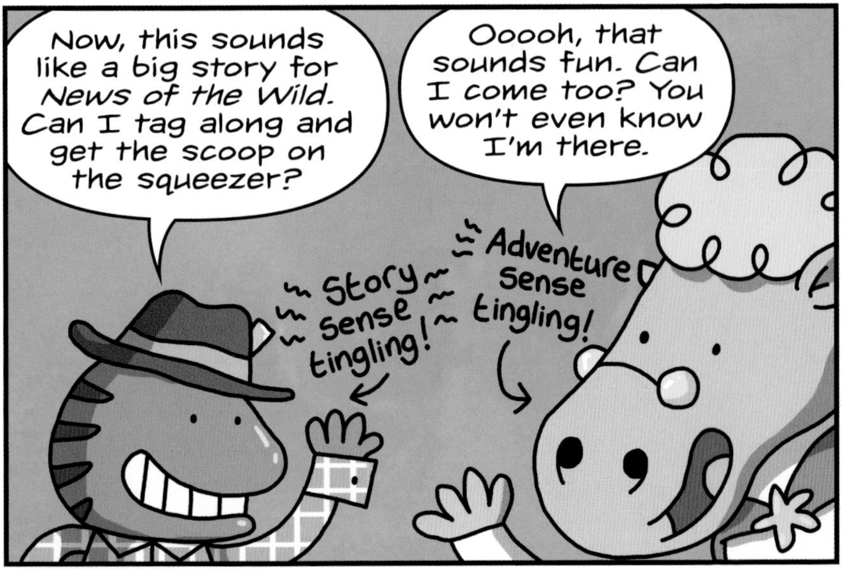
Now, this sounds like a big story for *News of the Wild*. Can I tag along and get the scoop on the squeezer?
Ooooh, that sounds fun. Can I come too? You won't even know I'm there.
Story sense tingling!
Adventure sense tingling!

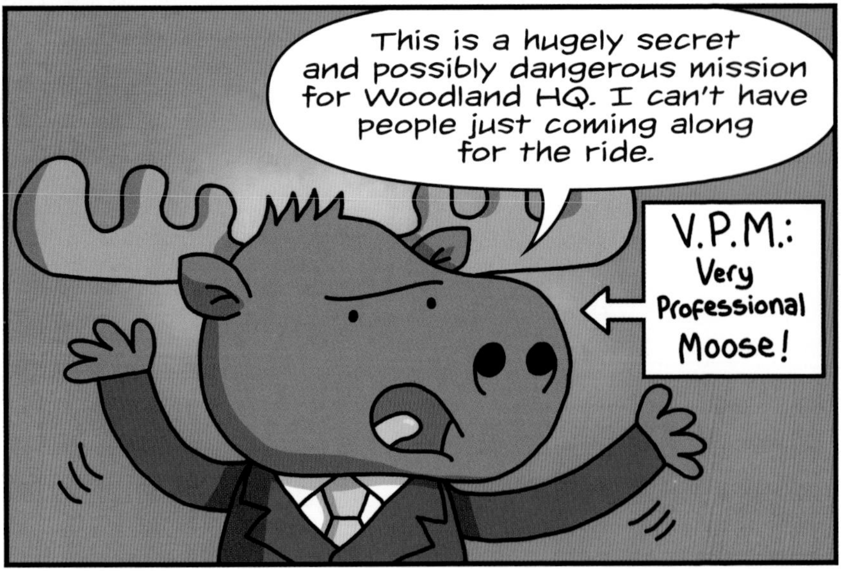
This is a hugely secret and possibly dangerous mission for Woodland HQ. I can't have people just coming along for the ride.
V.P.M.: Very Professional Moose!

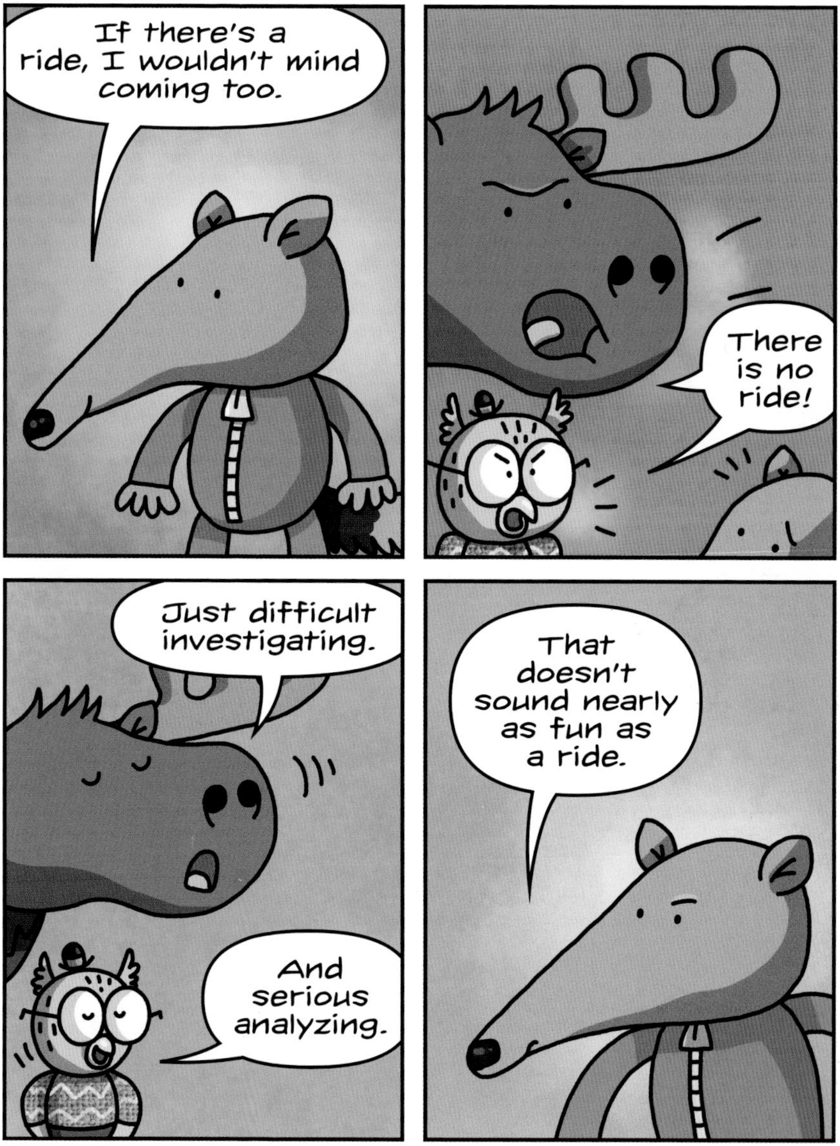
If there's a ride, I wouldn't mind coming too.
There is no ride!
Just difficult investigating.
And serious analyzing.
That doesn't sound nearly as fun as a ride.

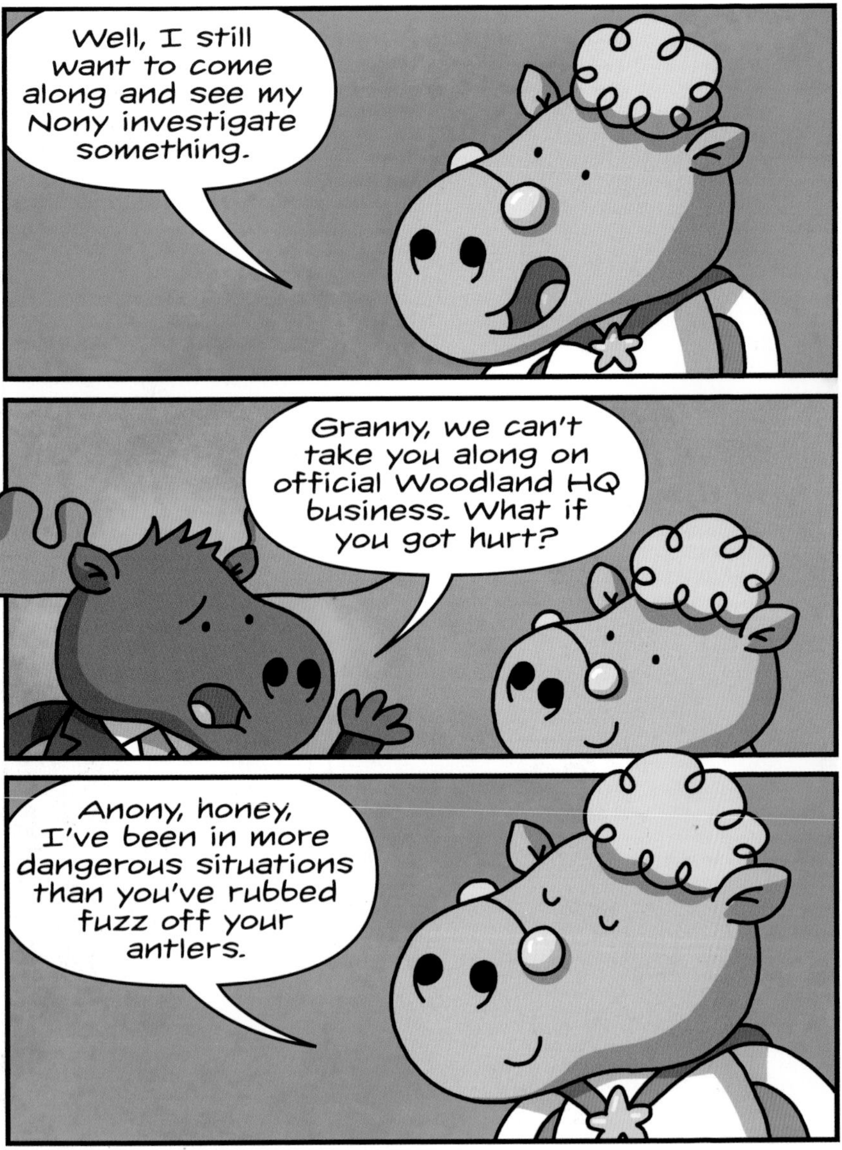
Well, I still want to come along and see my Nony investigate something.
Granny, we can't take you along on official Woodland HQ business. What if you got hurt?
Anony, honey, I've been in more dangerous situations than you've rubbed fuzz off your antlers.

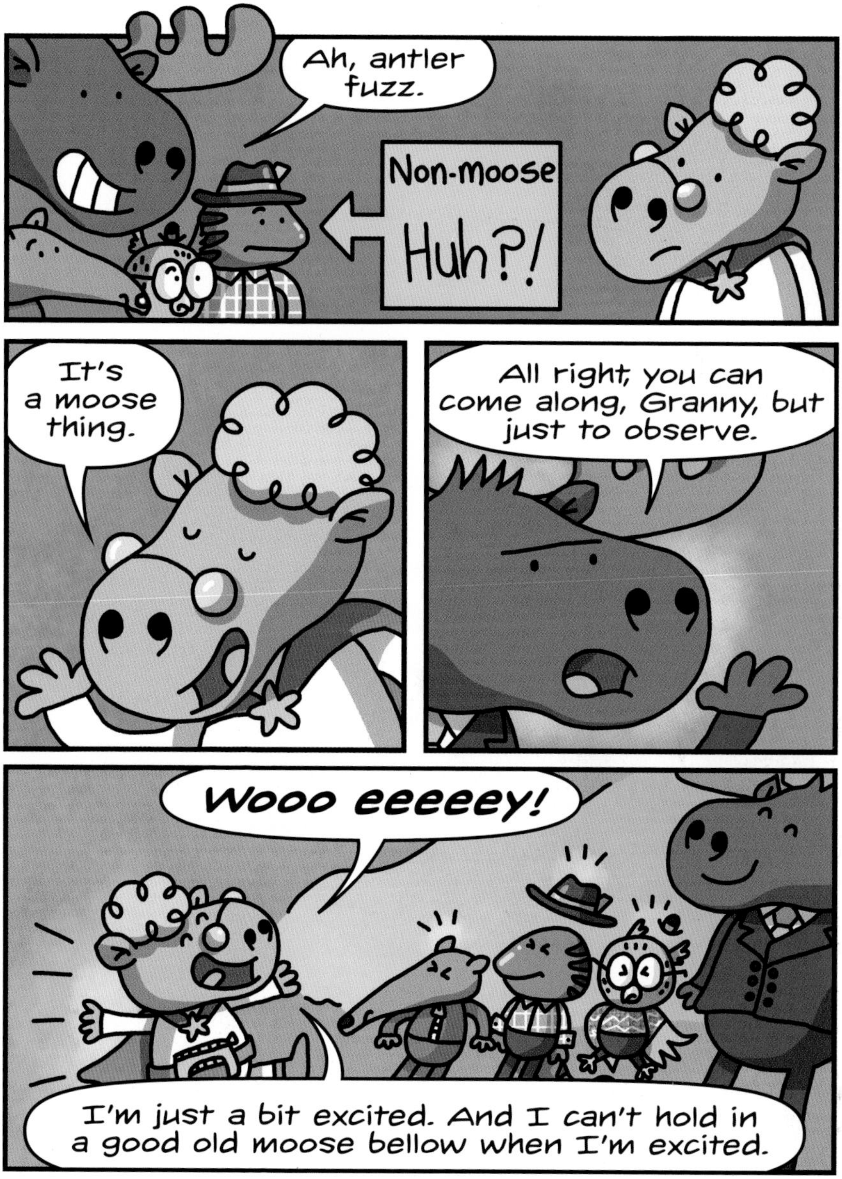
Ah, antler fuzz.
Non-moose
Huh?!
It's a moose thing.
All right, you can come along, Granny, but just to observe.
Wooo eeeeey!
I'm just a bit excited. And I can't hold in a good old moose bellow when I'm excited.

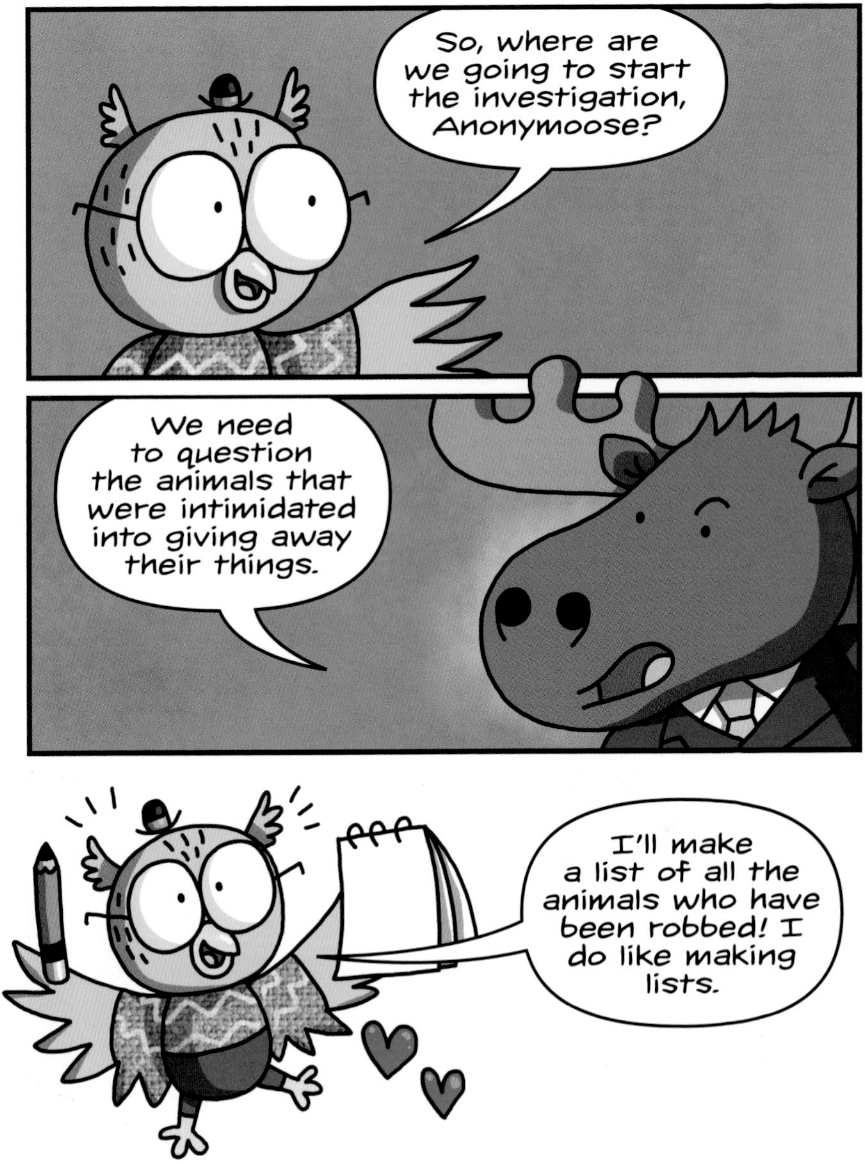
So, where are we going to start the investigation, Anonymoose?
We need to question the animals that were intimidated into giving away their things.
I'll make a list of all the animals who have been robbed! I do like making lists.

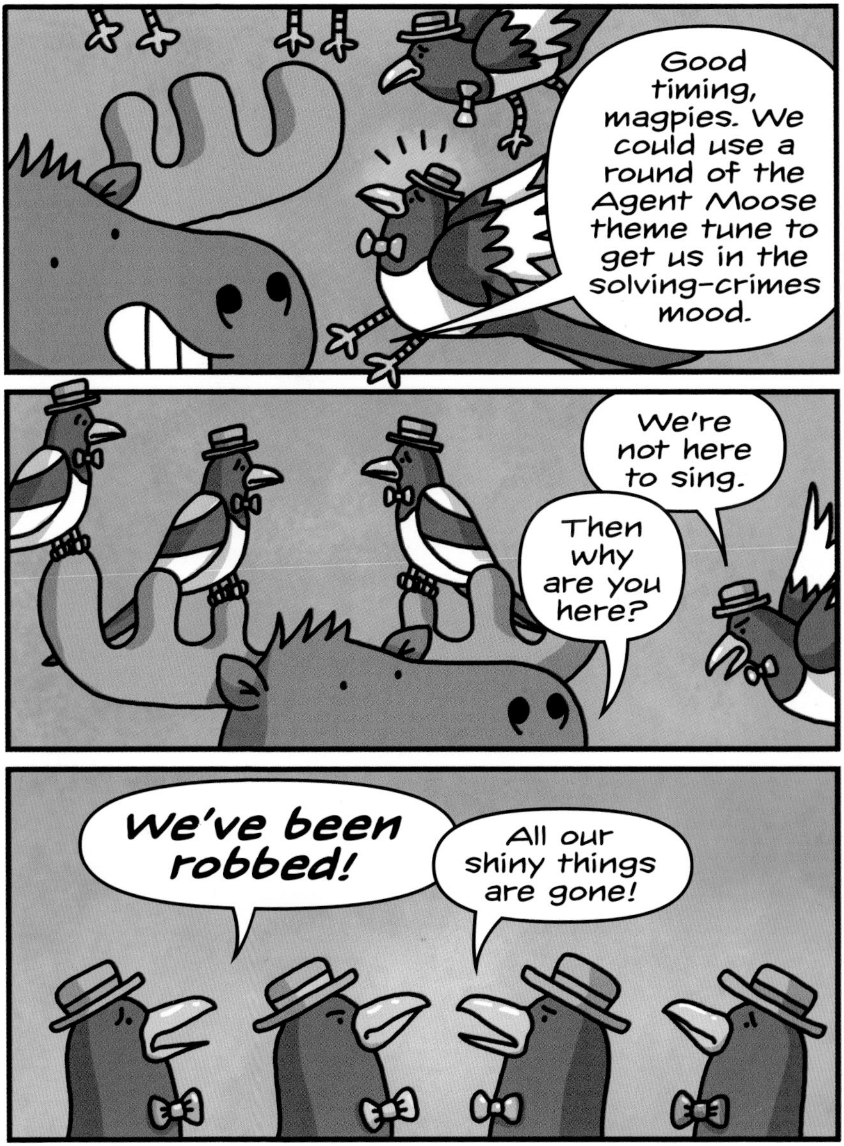
Good timing, magpies. We could use a round of the Agent Moose theme tune to get us in the solving-crimes mood.
We're not here to sing.
Then why are you here?
We've been robbed!
All our shiny things are gone!

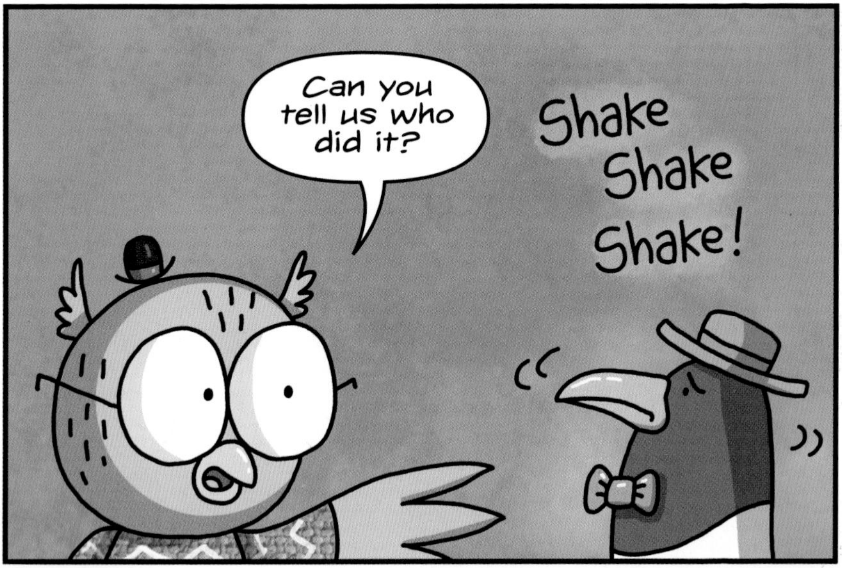
Can you tell us who did it?
Shake Shake Shake!

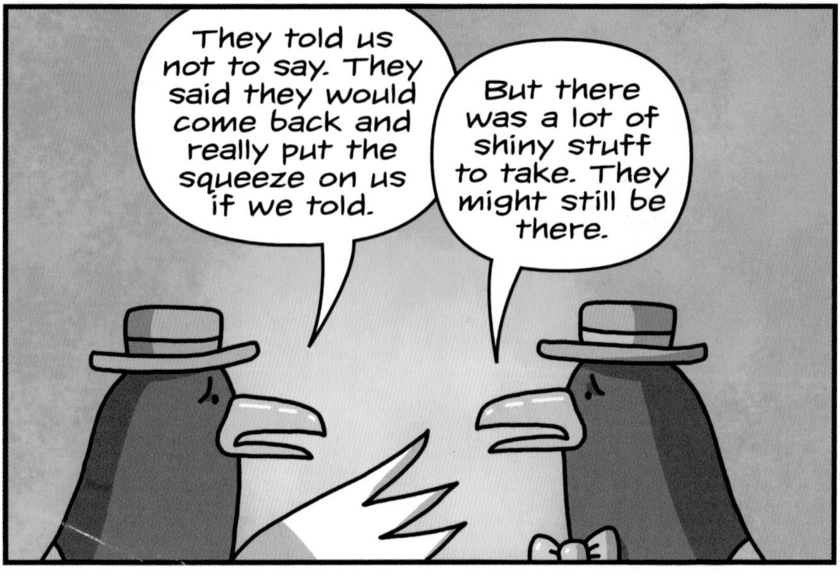
They told us not to say. They said they would come back and really put the squeeze on us if we told.
But there was a lot of shiny stuff to take. They might still be there.

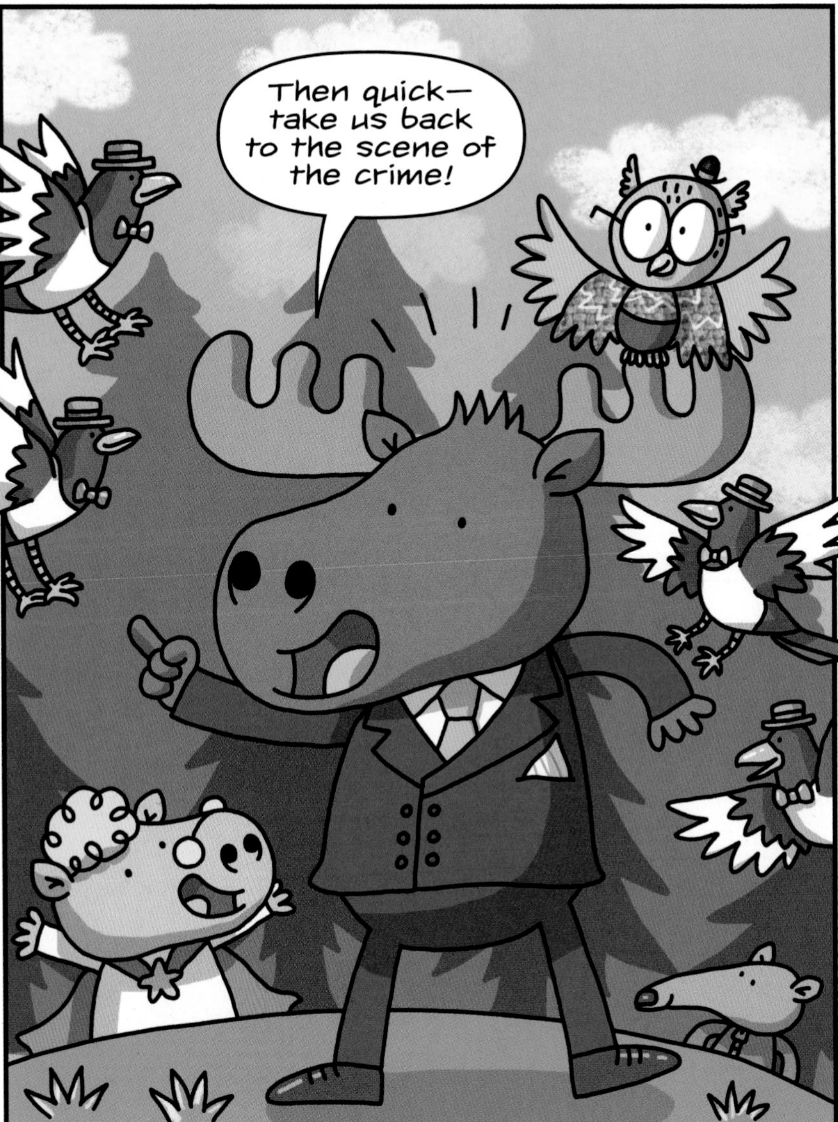
Then quick—
take us back
to the scene of
the crime!

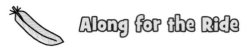

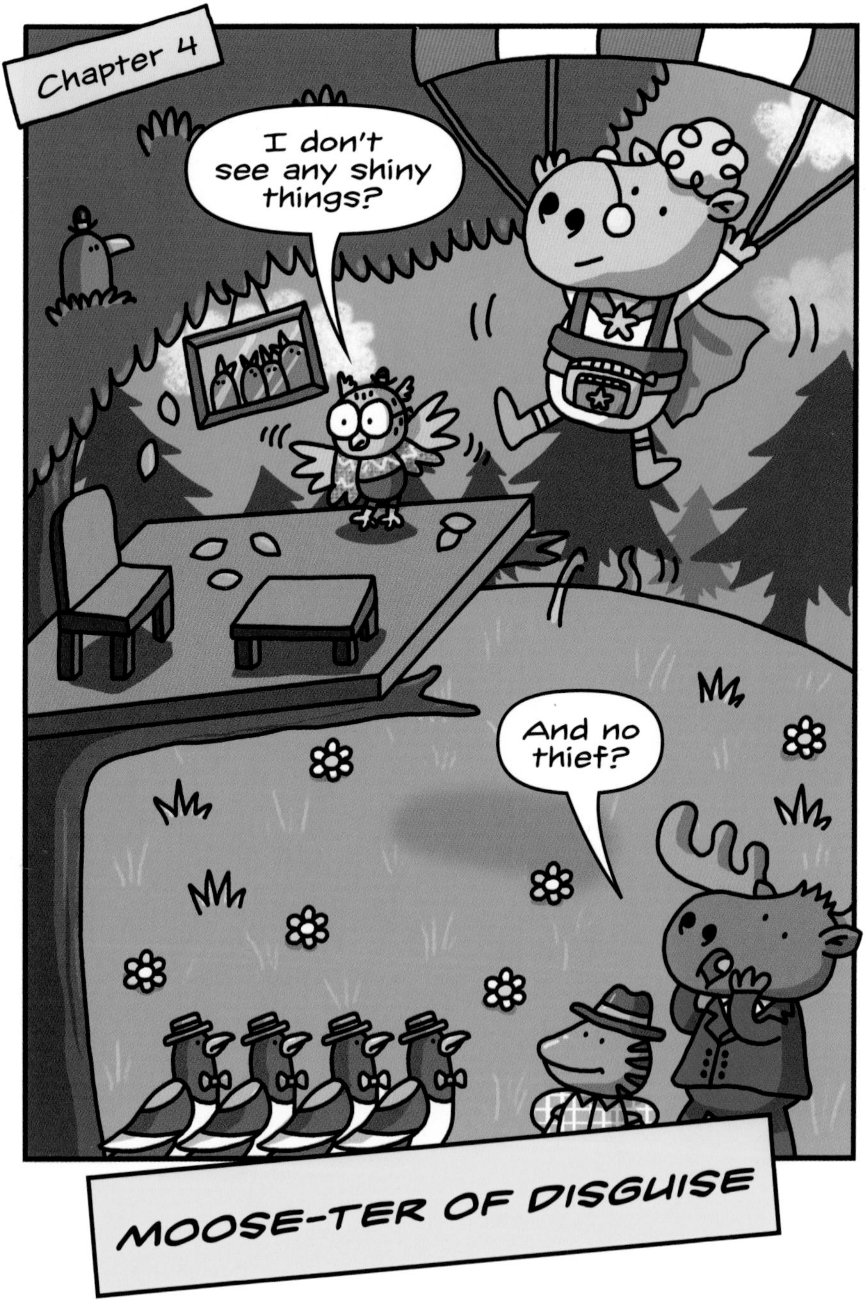
Chapter 4
I don't see any shiny things?
And no thief?
MOOSE-TER OF DISGUISE

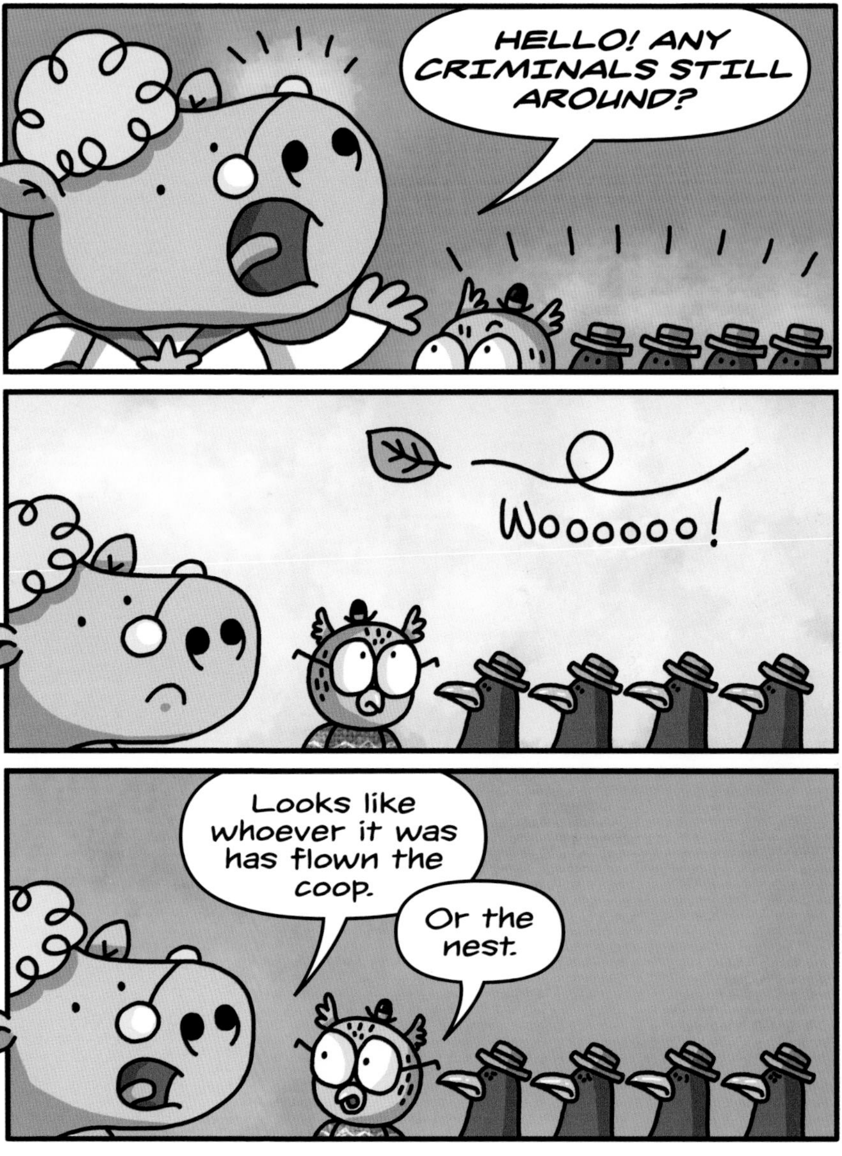
HELLO! ANY CRIMINALS STILL AROUND?
Wooooooo!
Looks like whoever it was has flown the coop.
Or the nest.

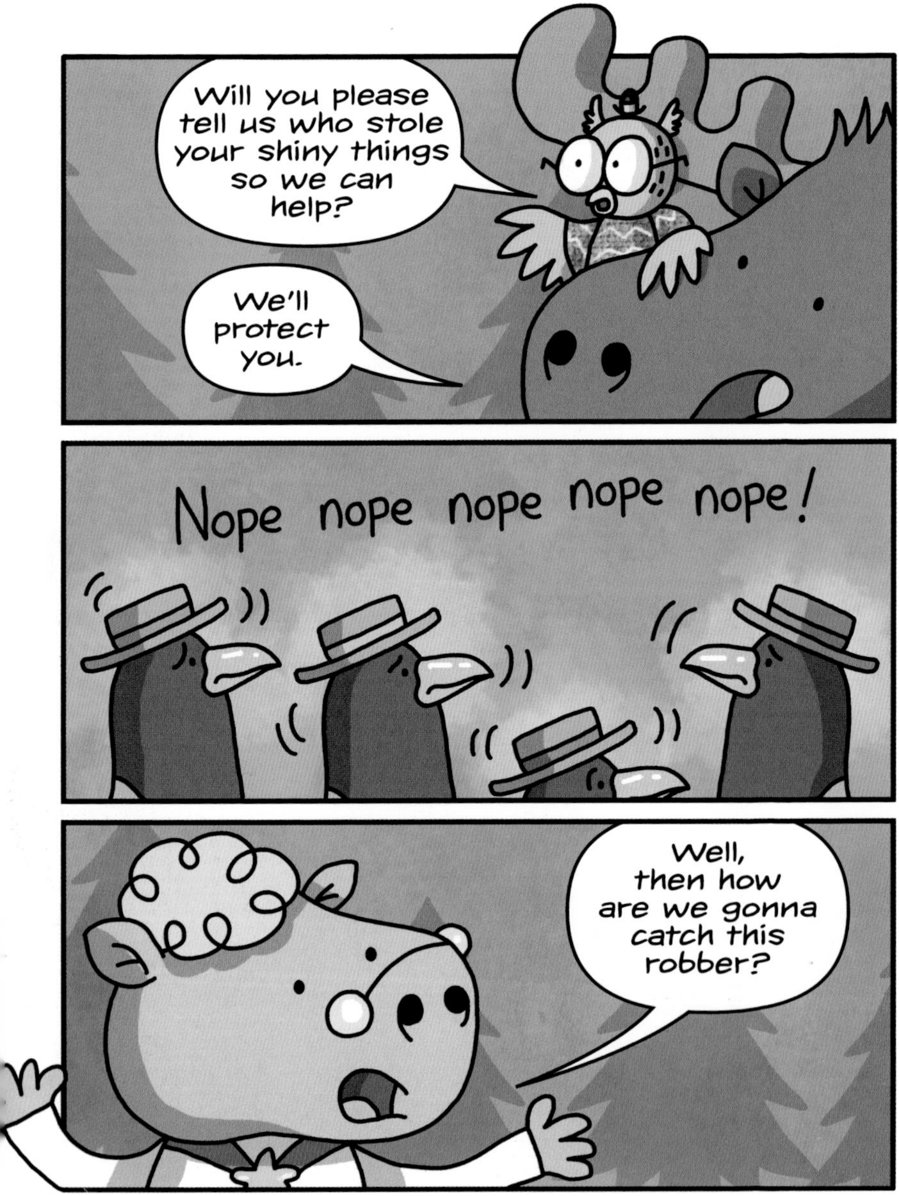
Will you please tell us who stole your shiny things so we can help?
We'll protect you.
Nope nope nope nope nope!
Well, then how are we gonna catch this robber?

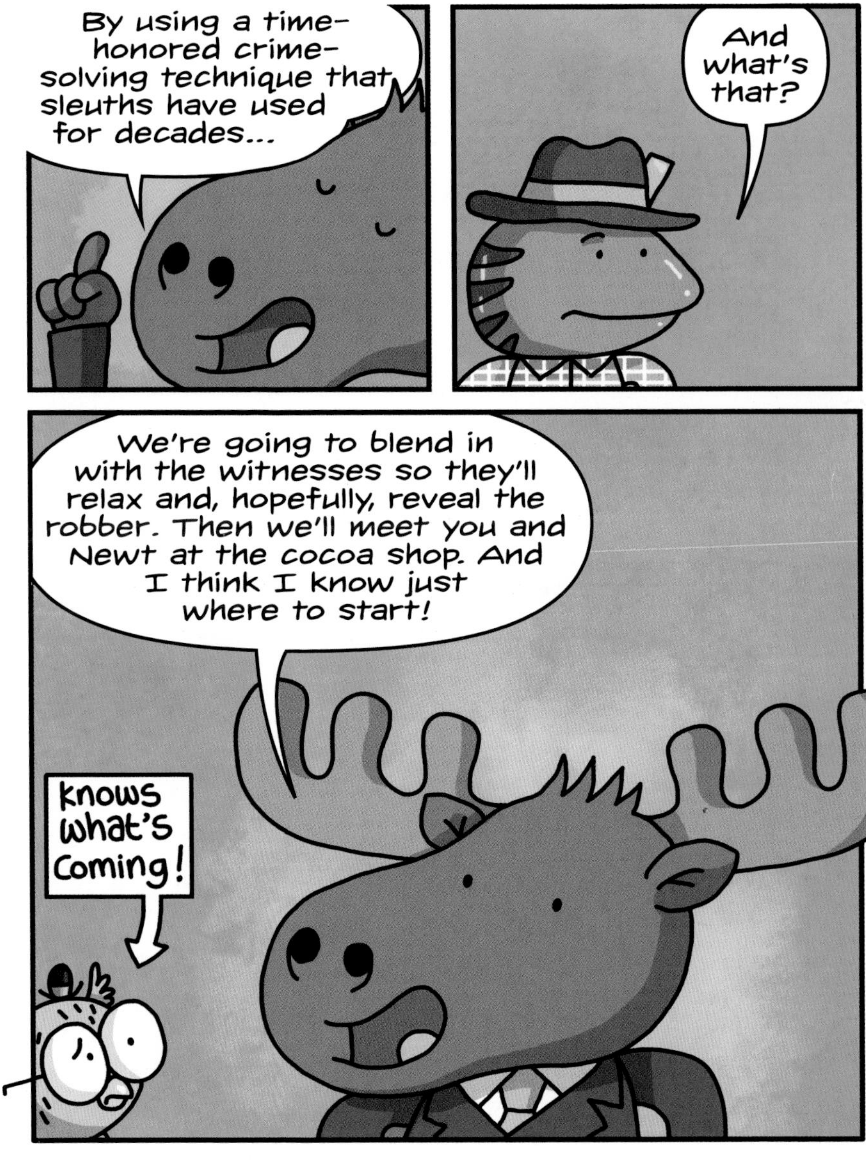
By using a time-honored crime-solving technique that sleuths have used for decades...
And what's that?
We're going to blend in with the witnesses so they'll relax and, hopefully, reveal the robber. Then we'll meet you and Newt at the cocoa shop. And I think I know just where to start!
knows what's coming!

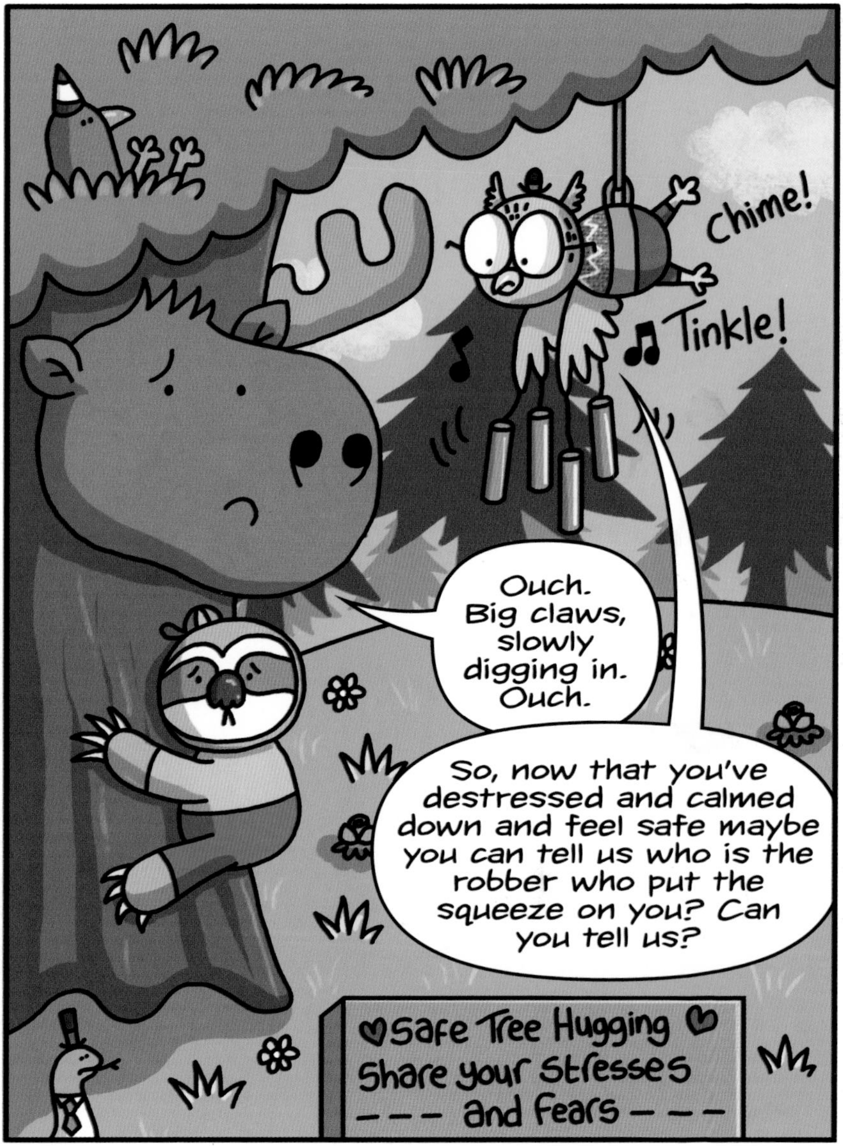
Chime!
Tinkle!
Ouch. Big claws, slowly digging in. Ouch.
So, now that you've destressed and calmed down and feel safe maybe you can tell us who is the robber who put the squeeze on you? Can you tell us?
Safe Tree Hugging
Share your Stresses and Fears

Moose-ter of Disguise

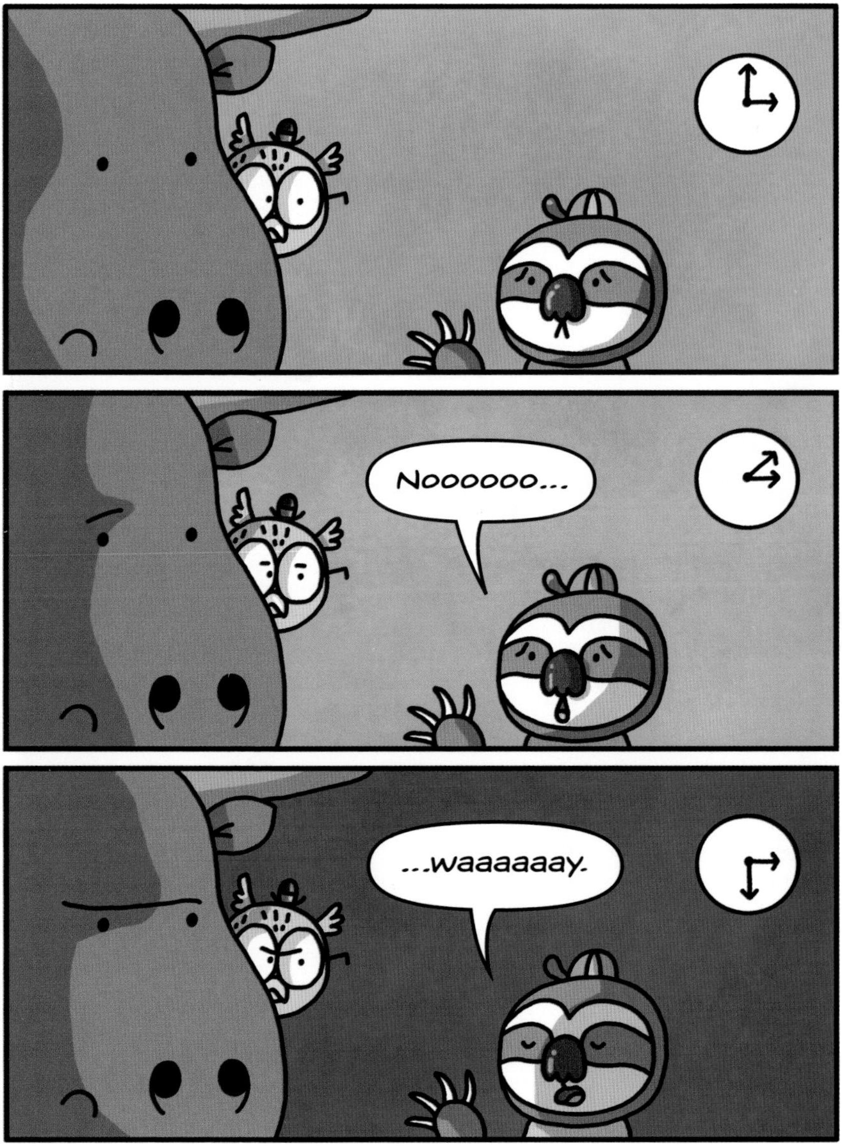

Noooooo...
...waaaaaay.

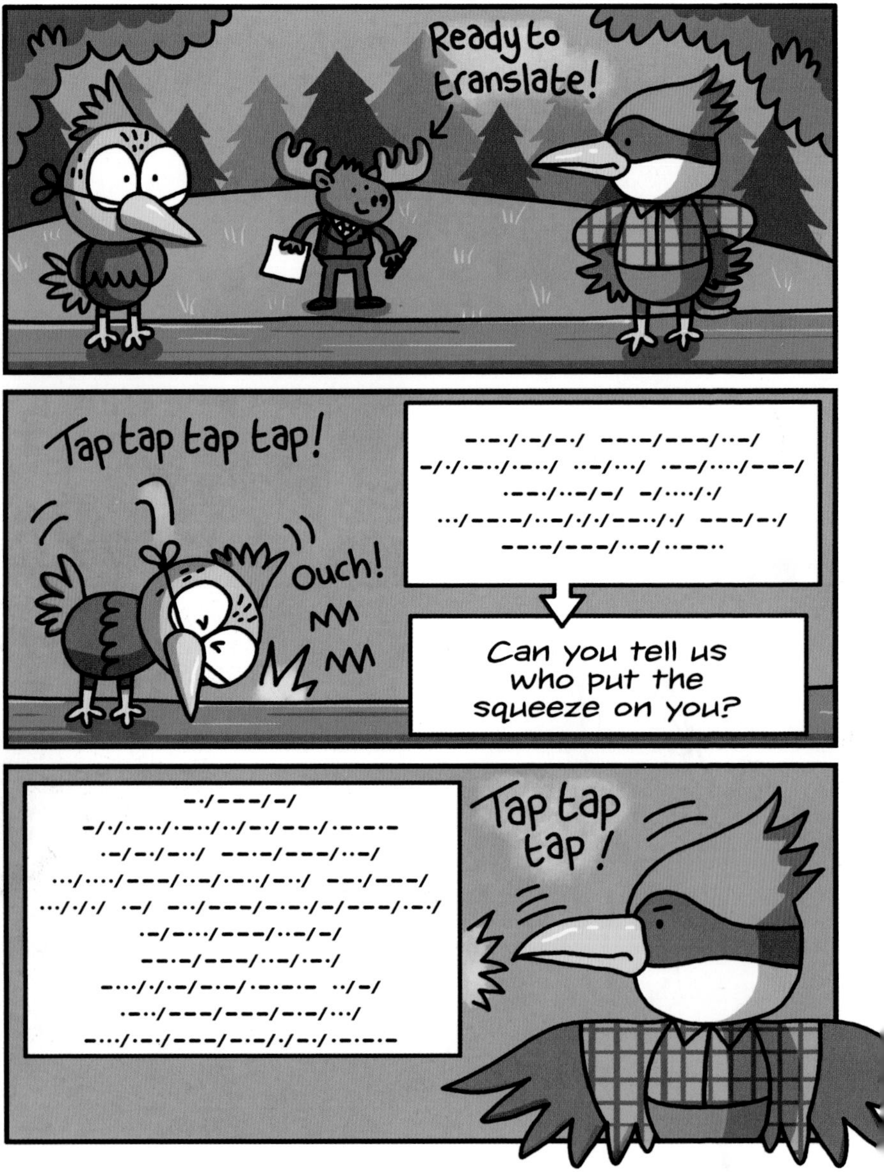
Ready to translate!
Tap tap tap tap!
Ouch!
–·–·/·–/–·/ ––·–/–––/··–/
–/·/·–··/·–··/ ··–/···/ ·––/····/–––/
·––·/··–/–/ –/····/·/
···/––·–/··–/·/·/––··/·/ –––/–·/
––·–/–––/··–/··––··
Can you tell us who put the squeeze on you?
–·/–––/–/
–/·/·–··/·–··/··/–·/––·/·–·–·–
·–/–·/–··/ ––·–/–––/··–/
···/····/–––/··–/·–··/–··/ ––·/–––/
···/·/·/ ·–/ –··/–––/–·–·/–/–––/·–·/
·–/–···/–––/··–/–/
––·–/–––/··–/·–·/
–···/·/·–/–·–/·–·–·– ··/–/
·–··/–––/–––/–·–/···/
–···/·–·/–––/–·–/·/–·/·–·–·–
Tap tap tap!

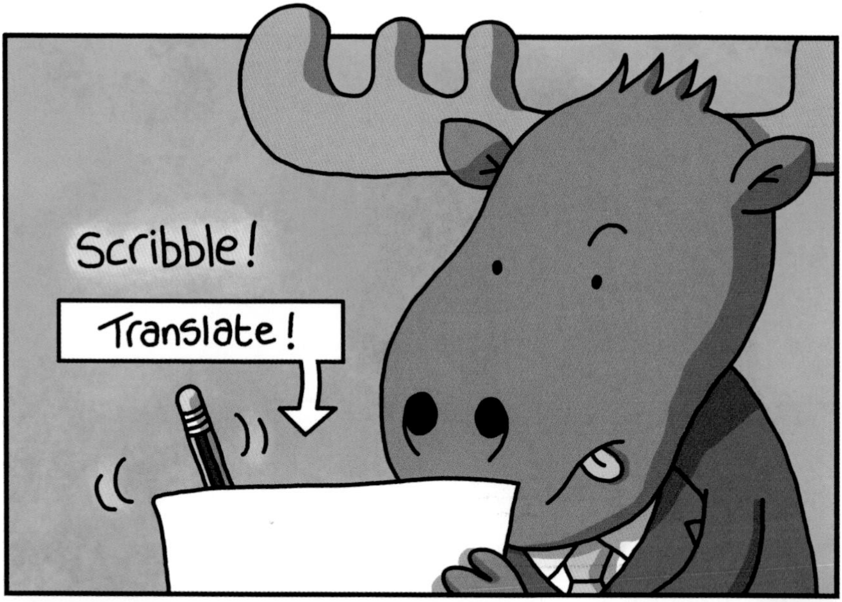
Scribble!
Translate!

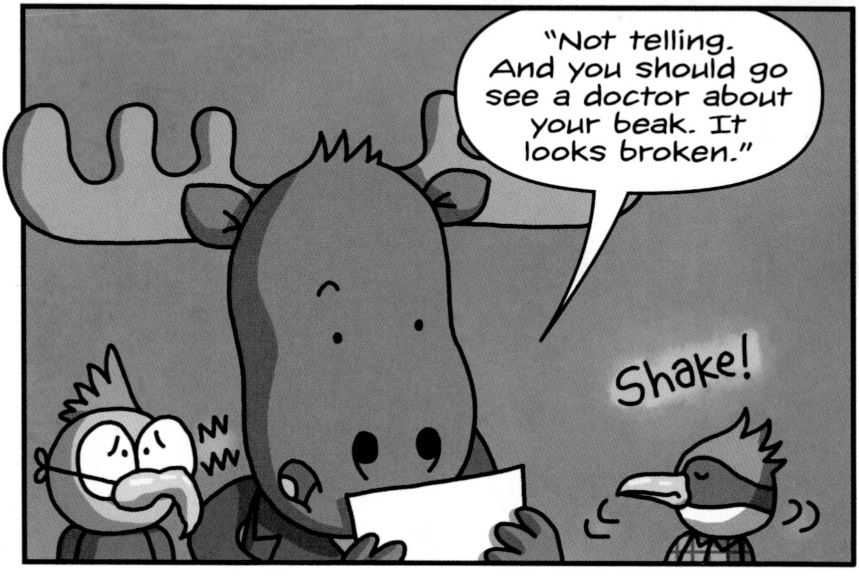
"Not telling. And you should go see a doctor about your beak. It looks broken."
Shake!

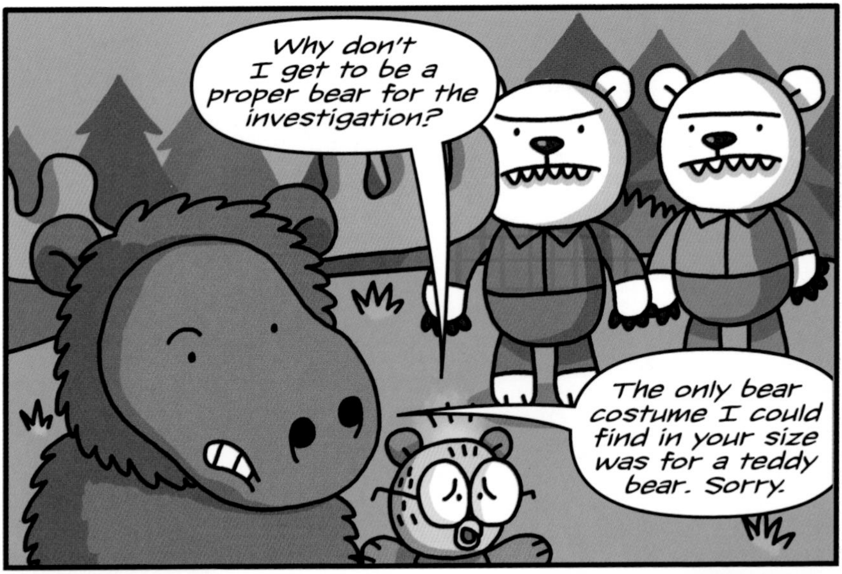
Why don't I get to be a proper bear for the investigation?
The only bear costume I could find in your size was for a teddy bear. Sorry.

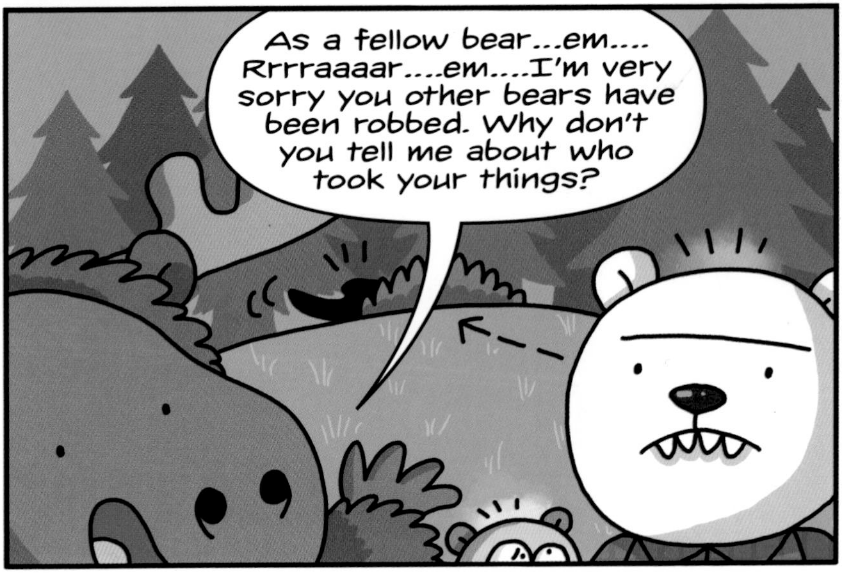
As a fellow bear....em.... Rrrraaaar....em....I'm very sorry you other bears have been robbed. Why don't you tell me about who took your things?

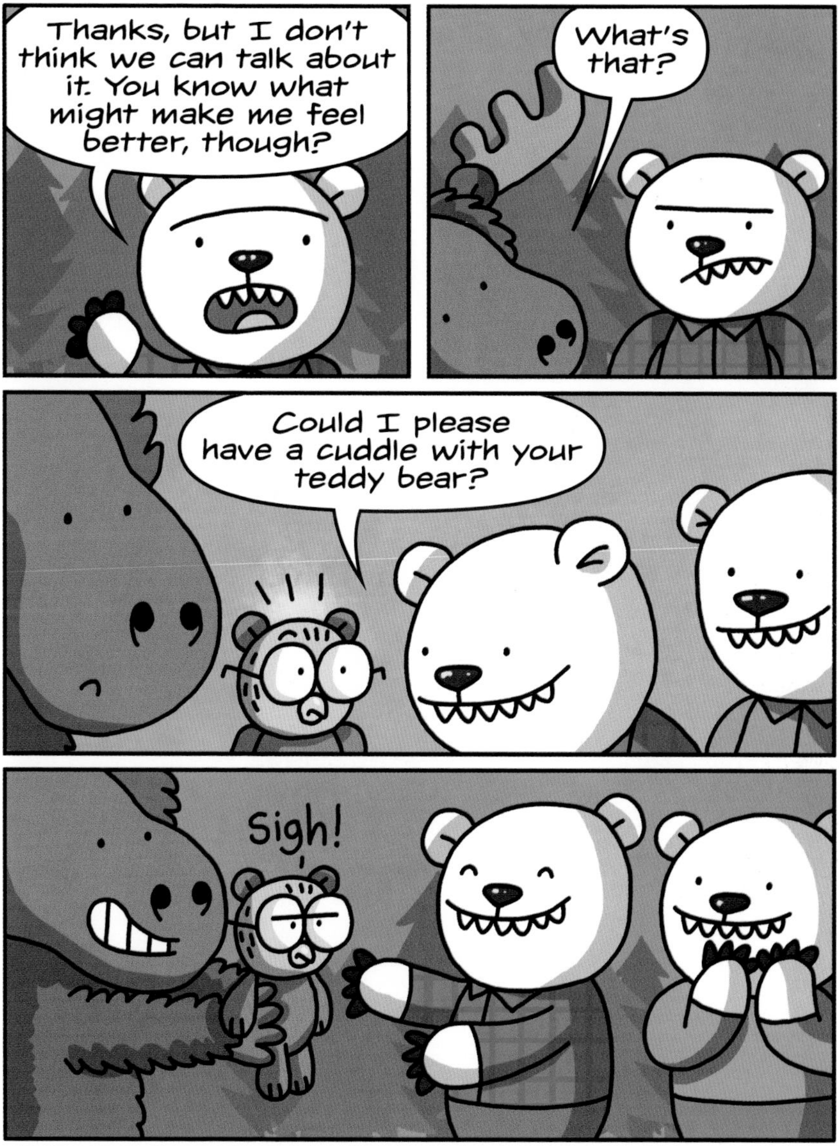
Thanks, but I don't think we can talk about it. You know what might make me feel better, though?
What's that?
Could I please have a cuddle with your teddy bear?
Sigh!

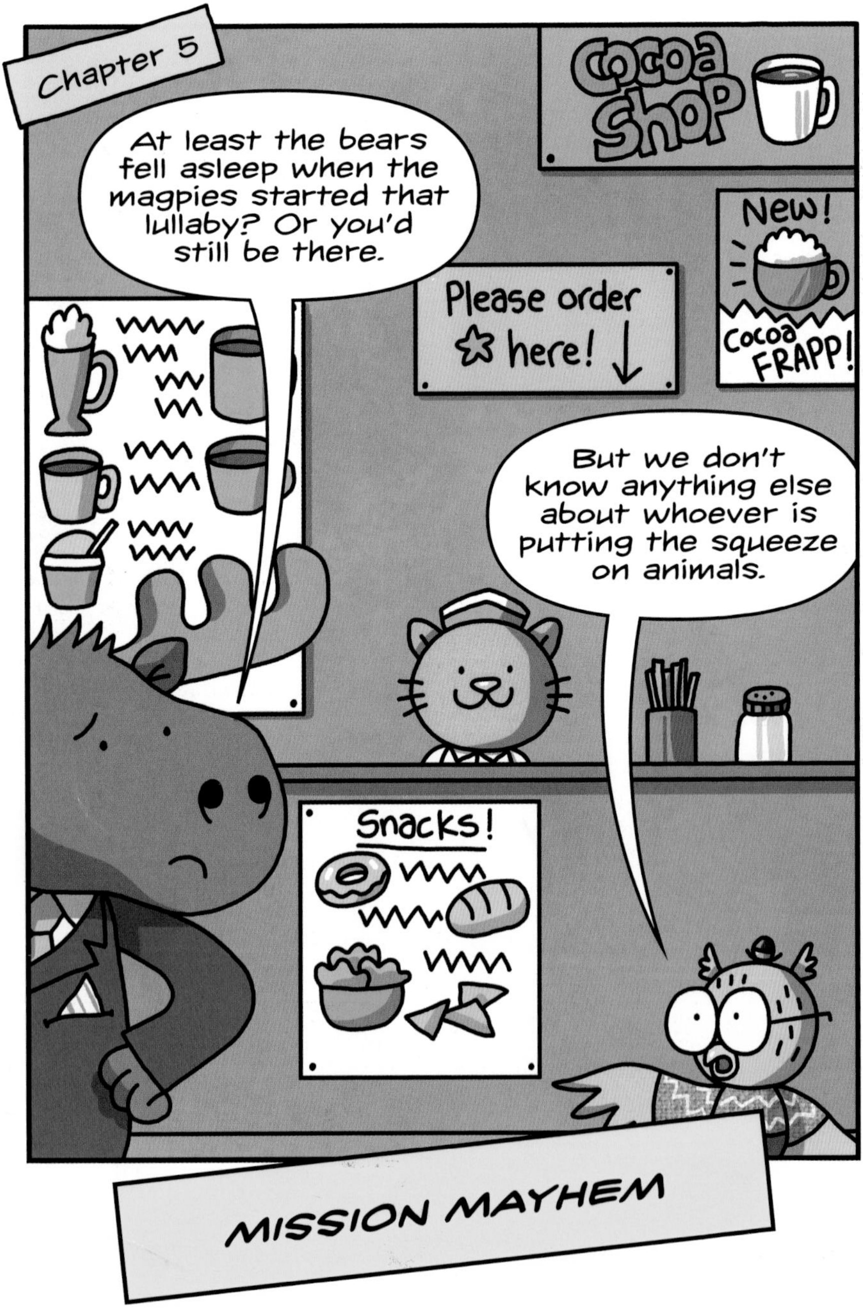
Chapter 5
Cocoa Shop
At least the bears fell asleep when the magpies started that lullaby? Or you'd still be there.
New!
Please order here!
Cocoa FRAPP!
But we don't know anything else about whoever is putting the squeeze on animals.
Snacks!

MISSION MAYHEM

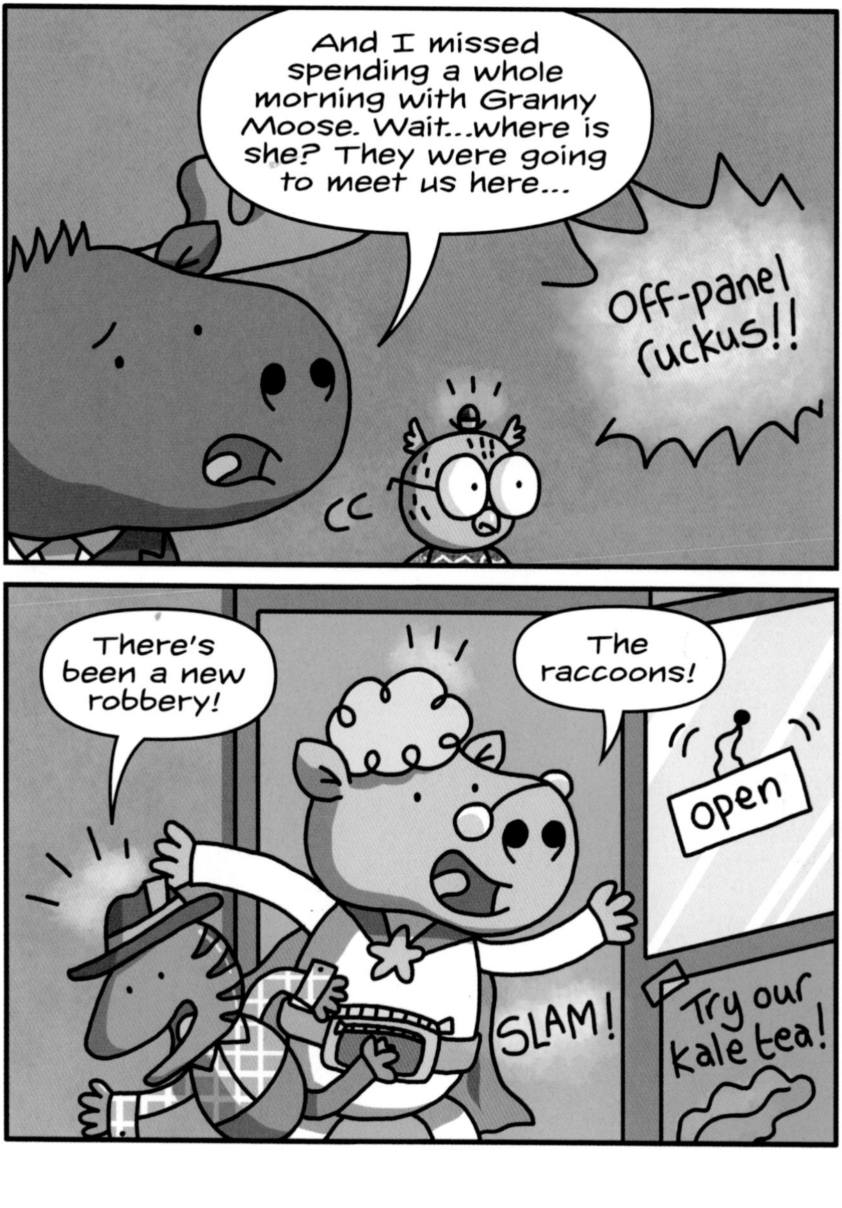
And I missed spending a whole morning with Granny Moose. Wait...where is she? They were going to meet us here...
Off-panel ruckus!!
There's been a new robbery!
The raccoons!
open
SLAM!
Try our kale tea!

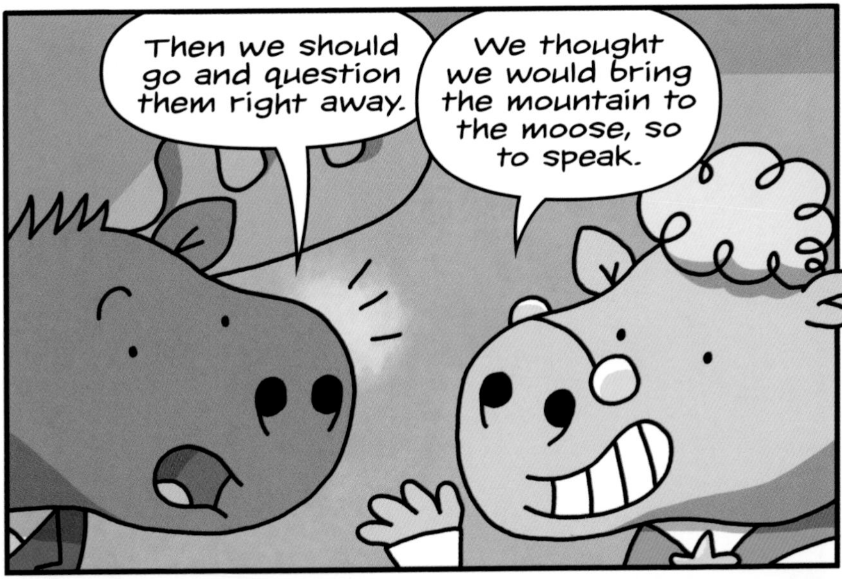
Then we should go and question them right away.
We thought we would bring the mountain to the moose, so to speak.

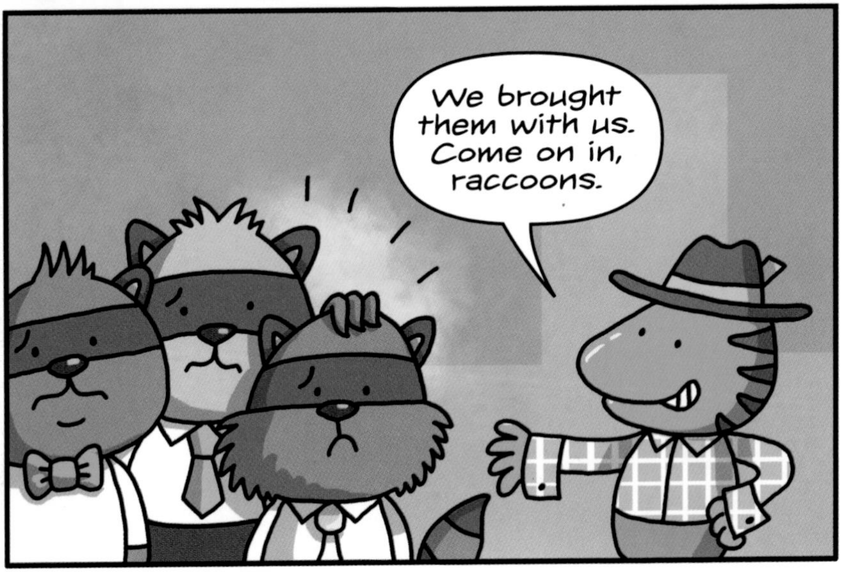
We brought them with us. Come on in, raccoons.

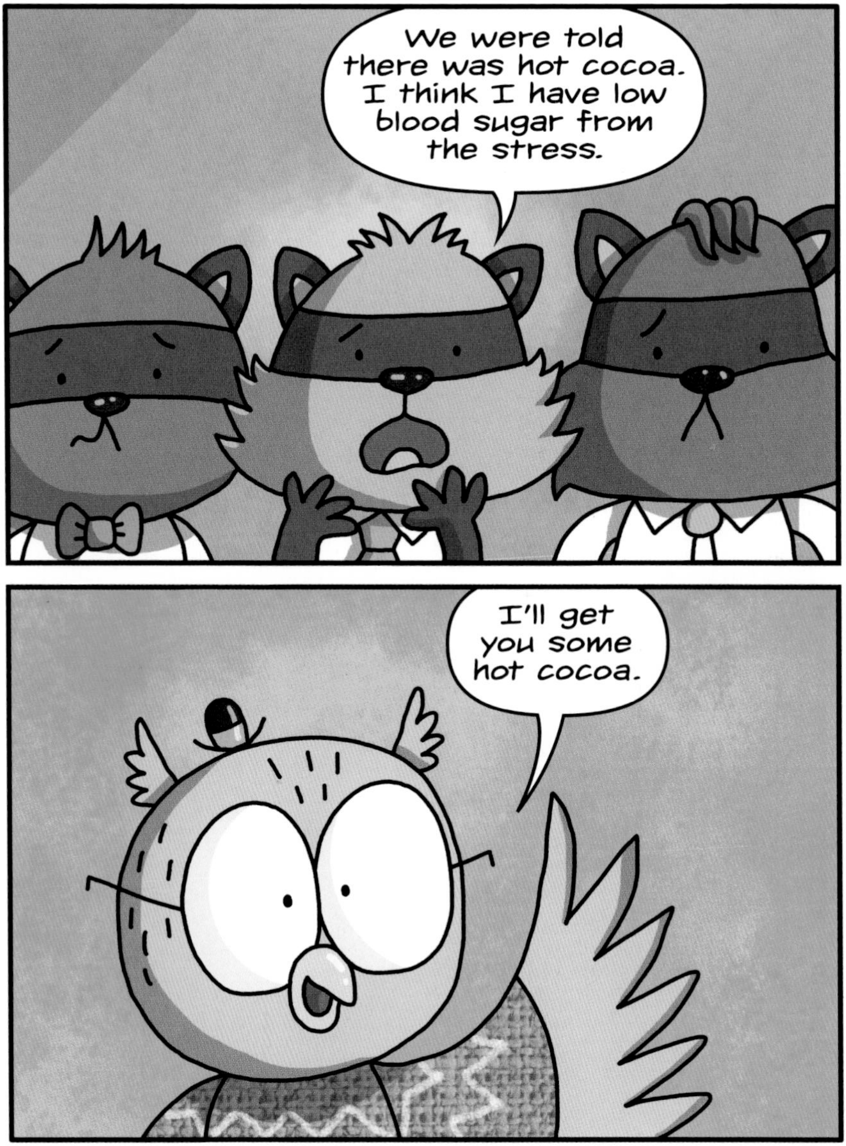
We were told there was hot cocoa. I think I have low blood sugar from the stress.
I'll get you some hot cocoa.

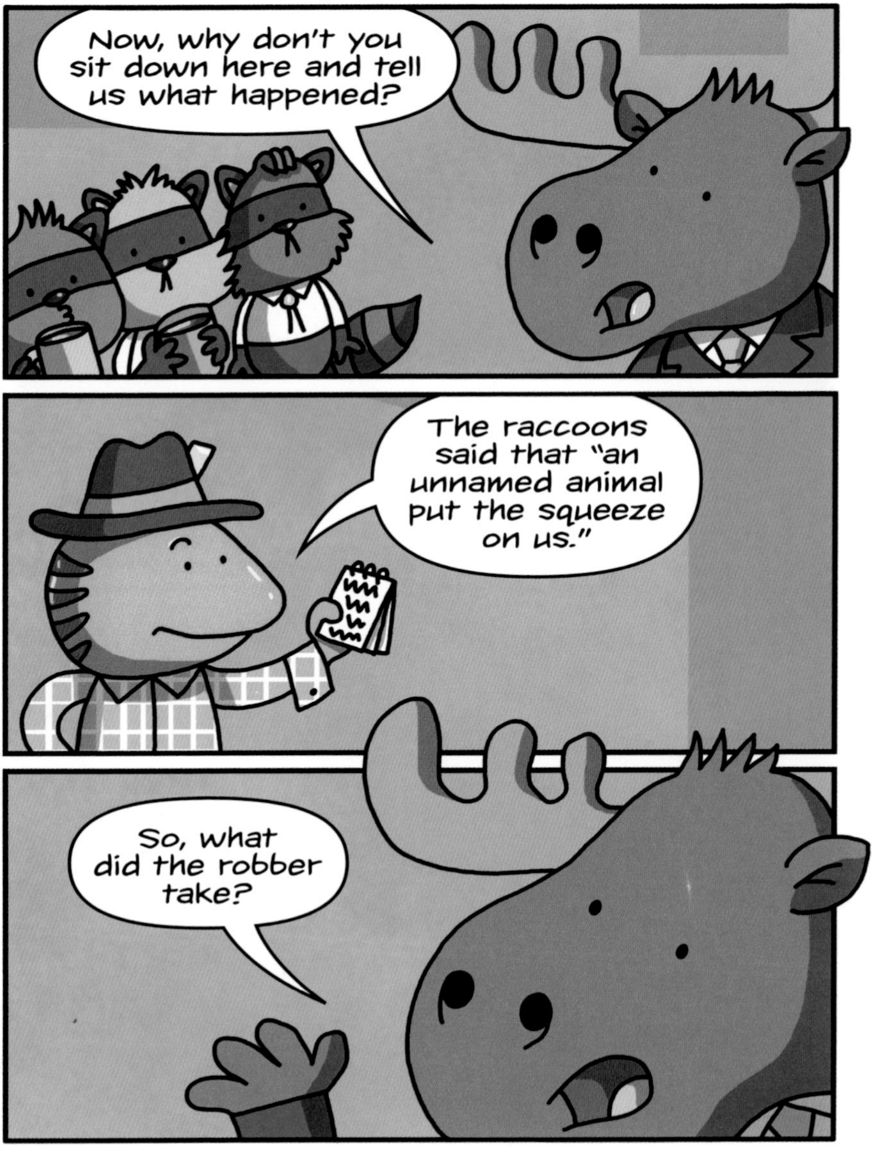
Now, why don't you sit down here and tell us what happened?
The raccoons said that "an unnamed animal put the squeeze on us."
So, what did the robber take?

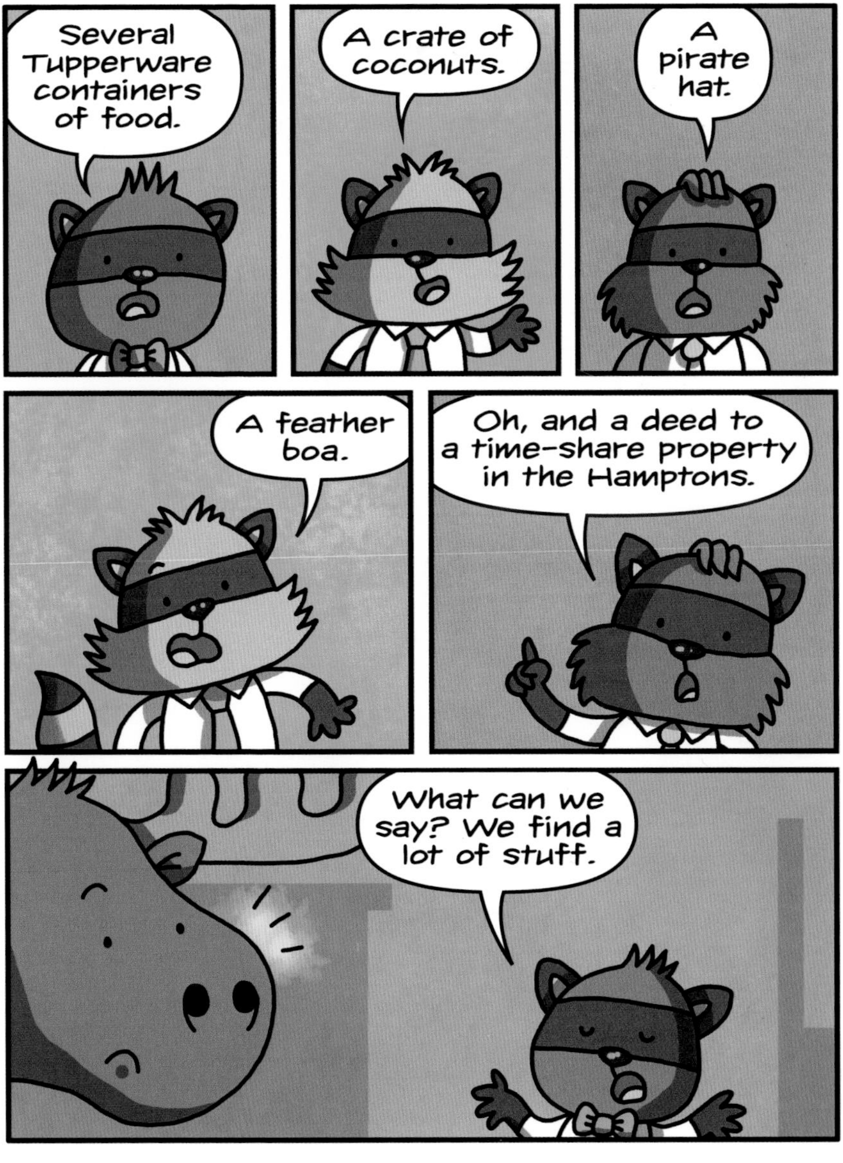
Several Tupperware containers of food.
A crate of coconuts.
A pirate hat.
A feather boa.
Oh, and a deed to a time-share property in the Hamptons.
What can we say? We find a lot of stuff.

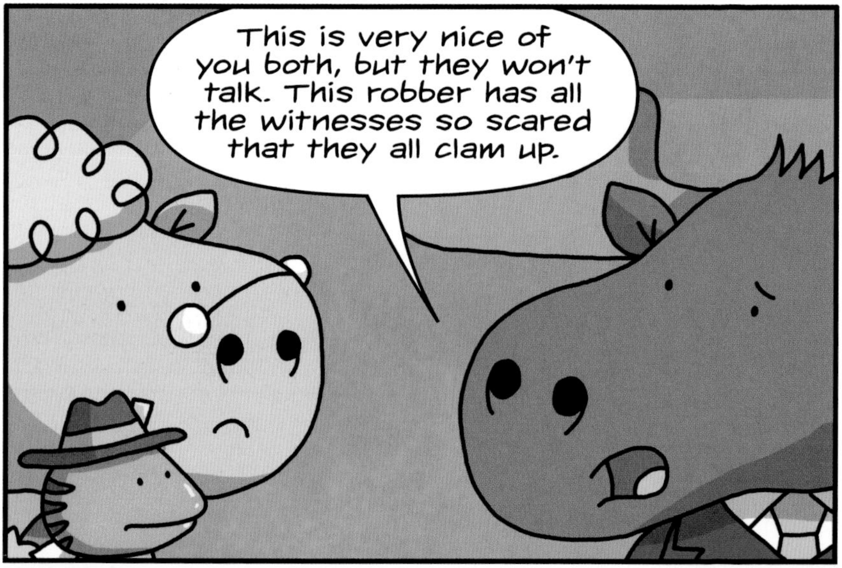
This is very nice of you both, but they won't talk. This robber has all the witnesses so scared that they all clam up.

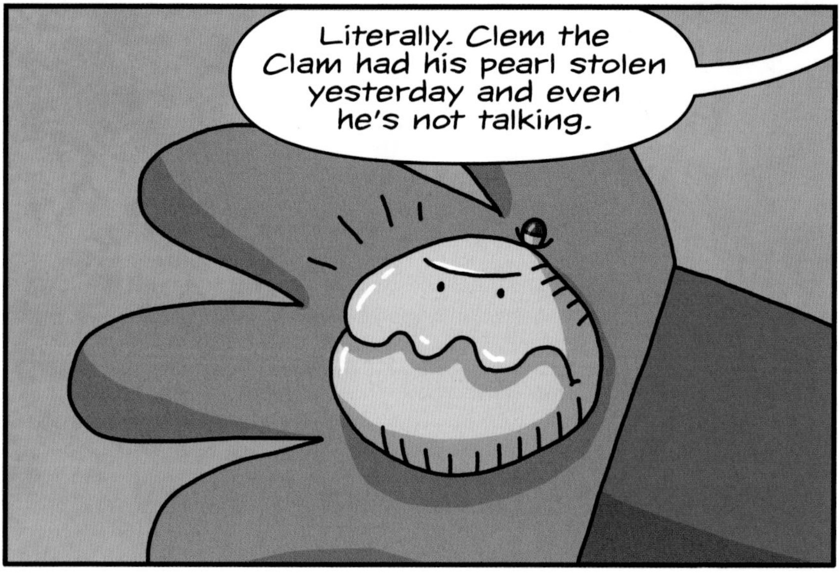
Literally. Clem the Clam had his pearl stolen yesterday and even he's not talking.

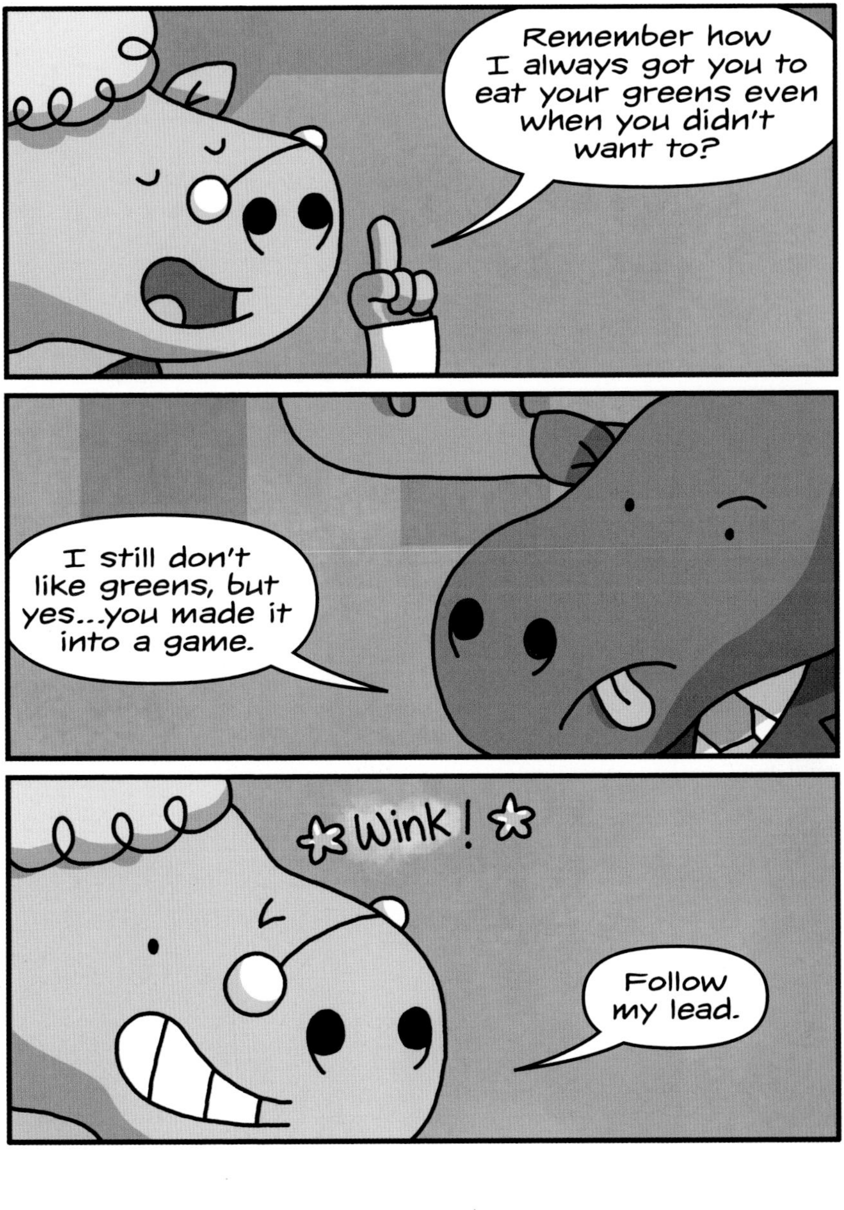
Remember how I always got you to eat your greens even when you didn't want to?
I still don't like greens, but yes...you made it into a game.
Wink!
Follow my lead.

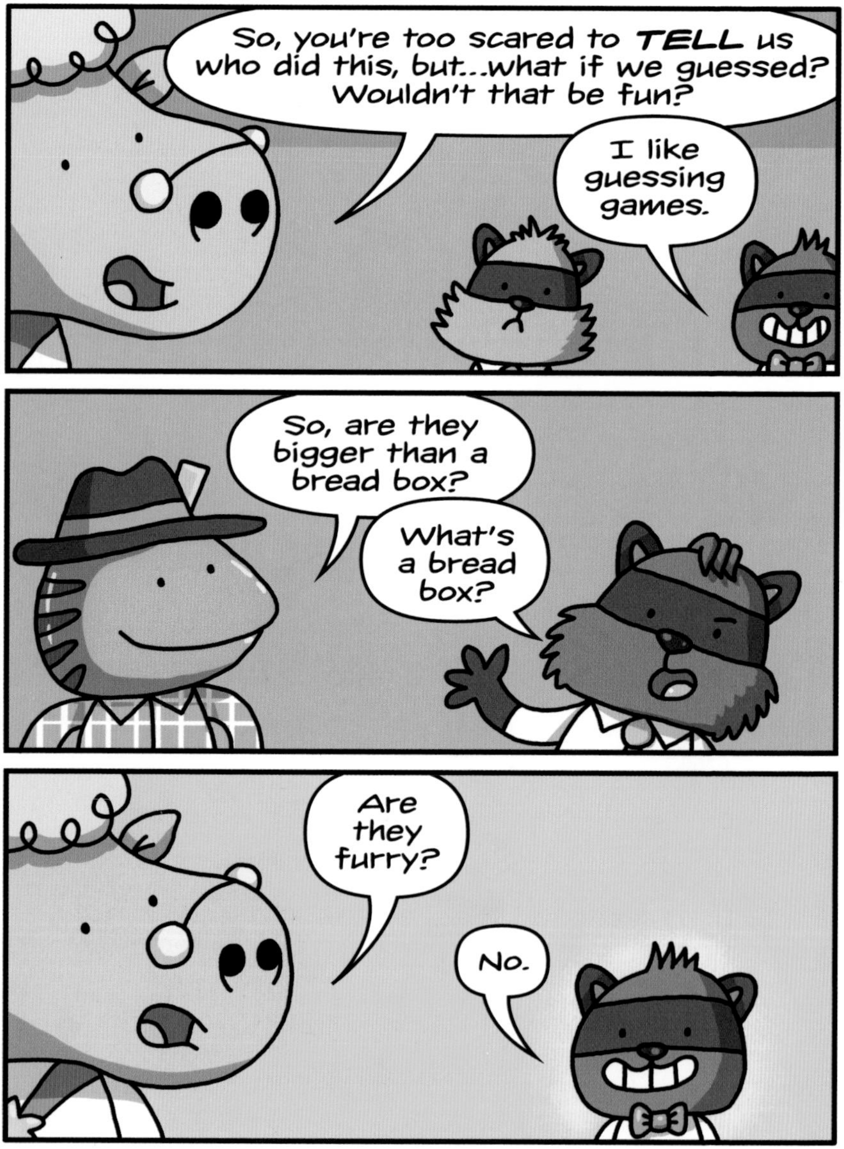
So, you're too scared to TELL us who did this, but...what if we guessed? Wouldn't that be fun?
I like guessing games.
So, are they bigger than a bread box?
What's a bread box?
Are they furry?
No.

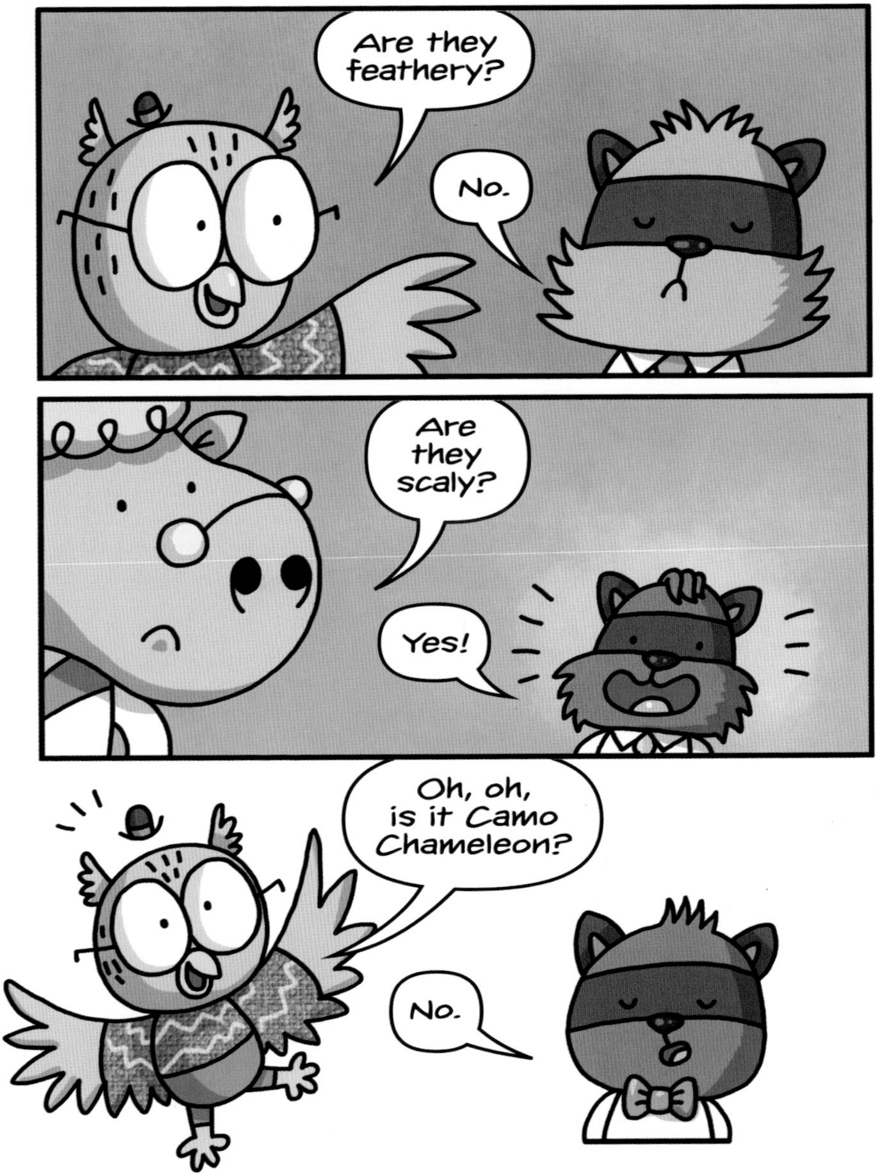
Are they feathery?
No.
Are they scaly?
Yes!
Oh, oh, is it Camo Chameleon?
No.

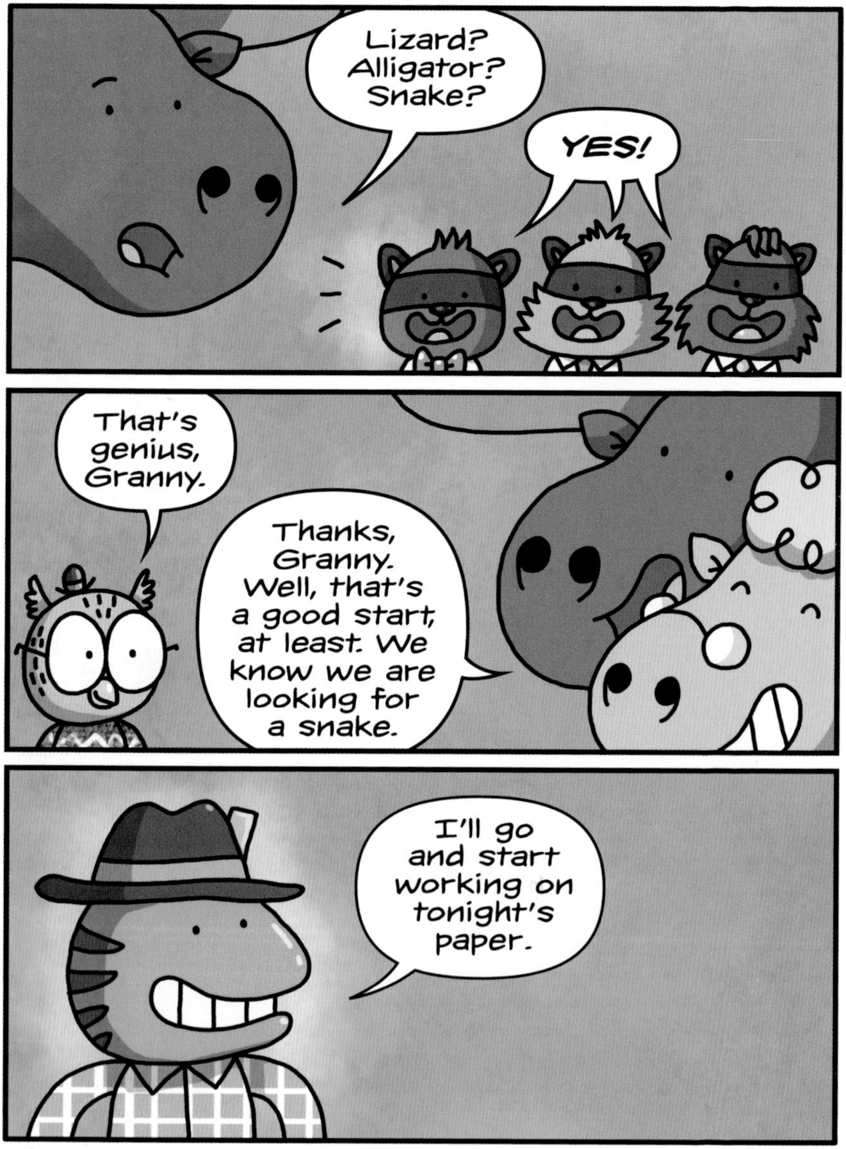
Lizard? Alligator? Snake?
YES!
That's genius, Granny.
Thanks, Granny. Well, that's a good start, at least. We know we are looking for a snake.
I'll go and start working on tonight's paper.

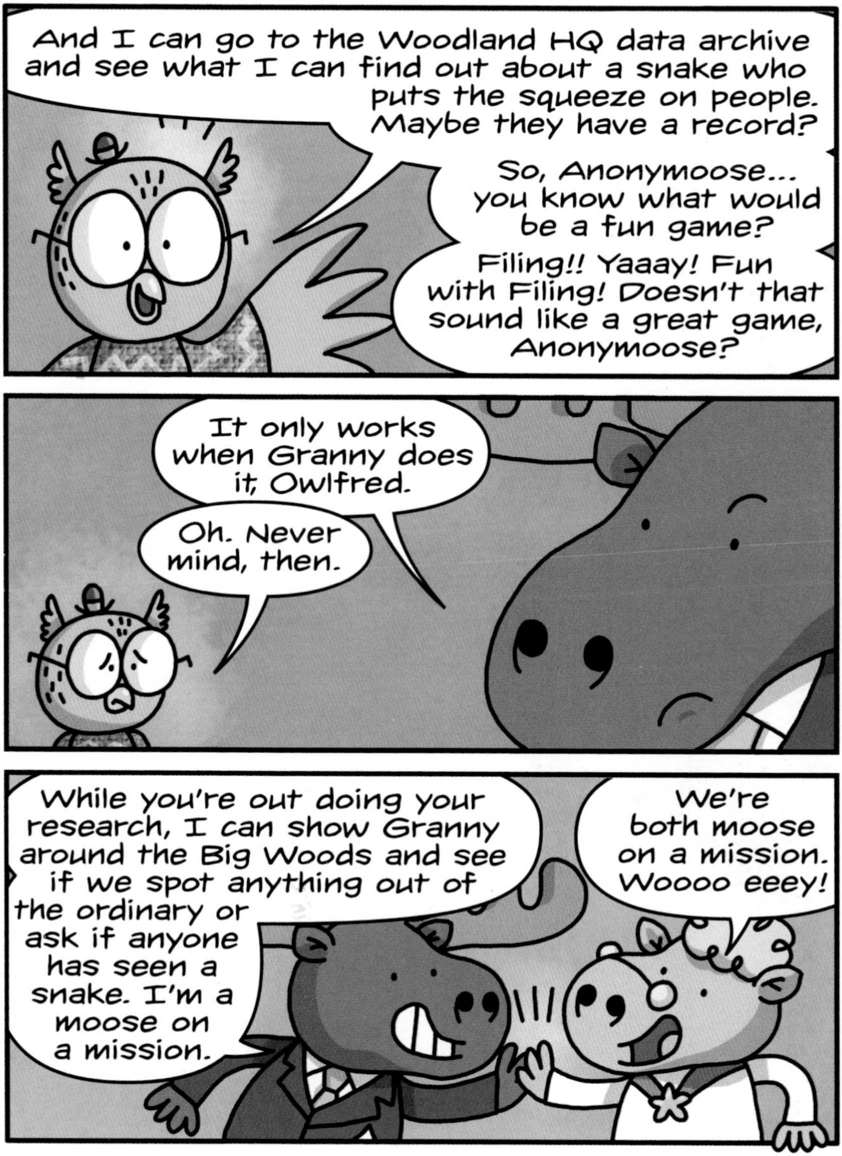
And I can go to the Woodland HQ data archive and see what I can find out about a snake who puts the squeeze on people. Maybe they have a record?
So, Anonymoose... you know what would be a fun game?
Filing!! Yaaay! Fun with Filing! Doesn't that sound like a great game, Anonymoose?
It only works when Granny does it, Owlfred.
Oh. Never mind, then.
While you're out doing your research, I can show Granny around the Big Woods and see if we spot anything out of the ordinary or ask if anyone has seen a snake. I'm a moose on a mission.
We're both moose on a mission. Woooo eeey!

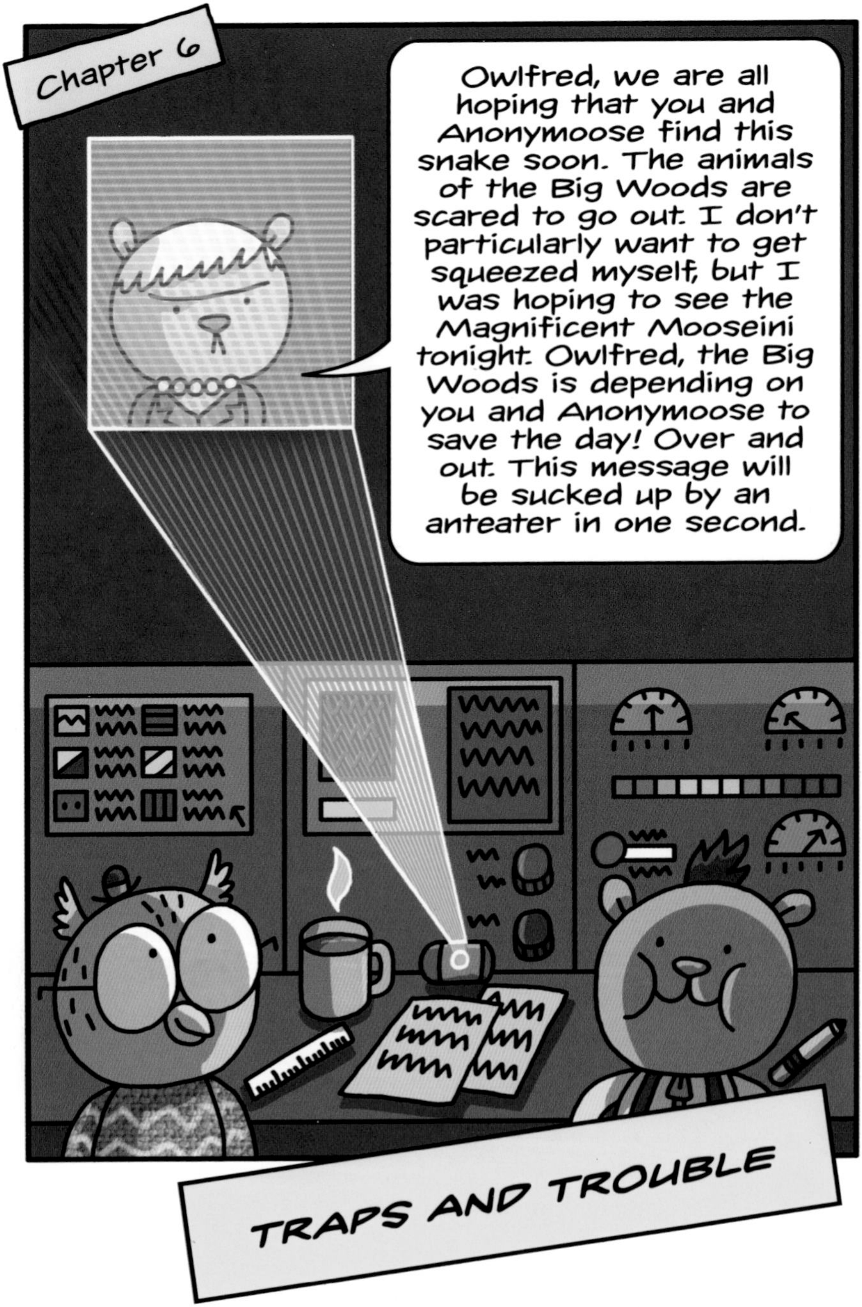
Chapter 6
Owlfred, we are all hoping that you and Anonymoose find this snake soon. The animals of the Big Woods are scared to go out. I don't particularly want to get squeezed myself, but I was hoping to see the Magnificent Mooseini tonight. Owlfred, the Big Woods is depending on you and Anonymoose to save the day! Over and out. This message will be sucked up by an anteater in one second.
TRAPS AND TROUBLE

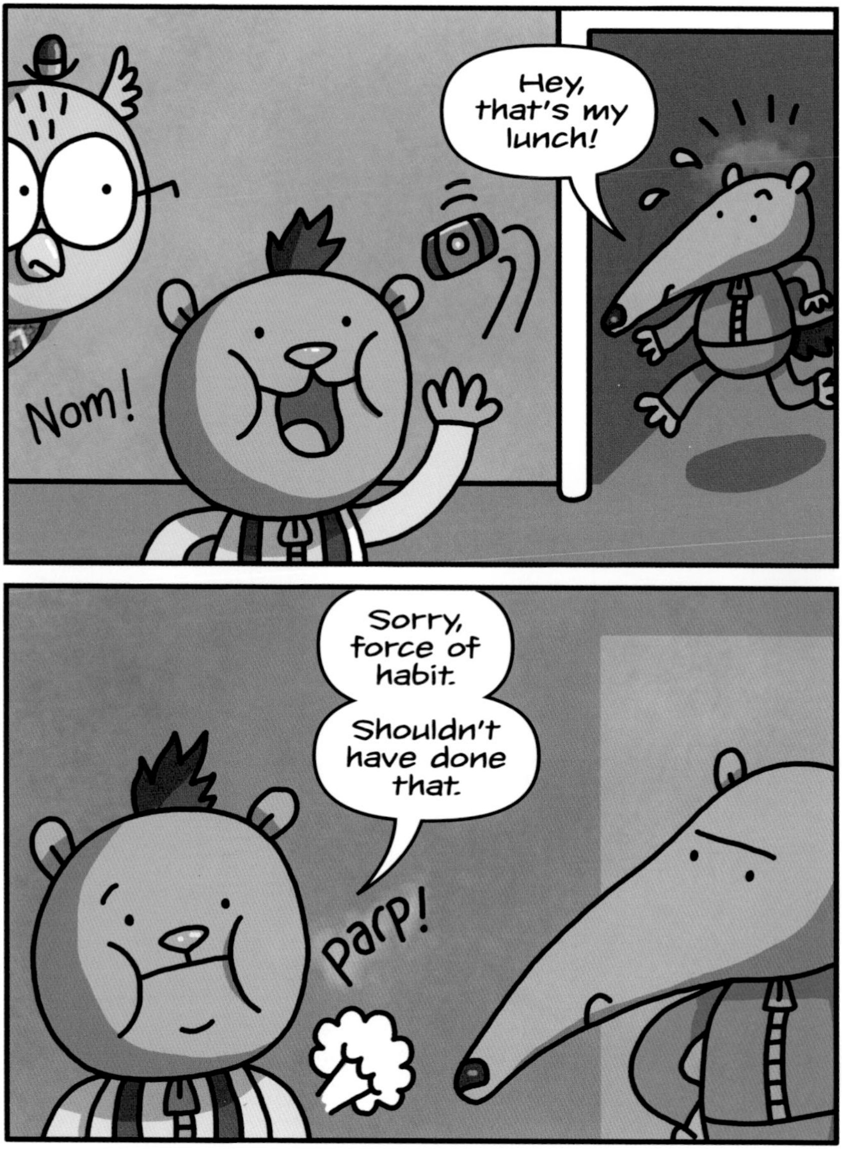
Nom!
Hey, that's my lunch!
Sorry, force of habit.
Shouldn't have done that.
parp!

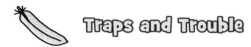

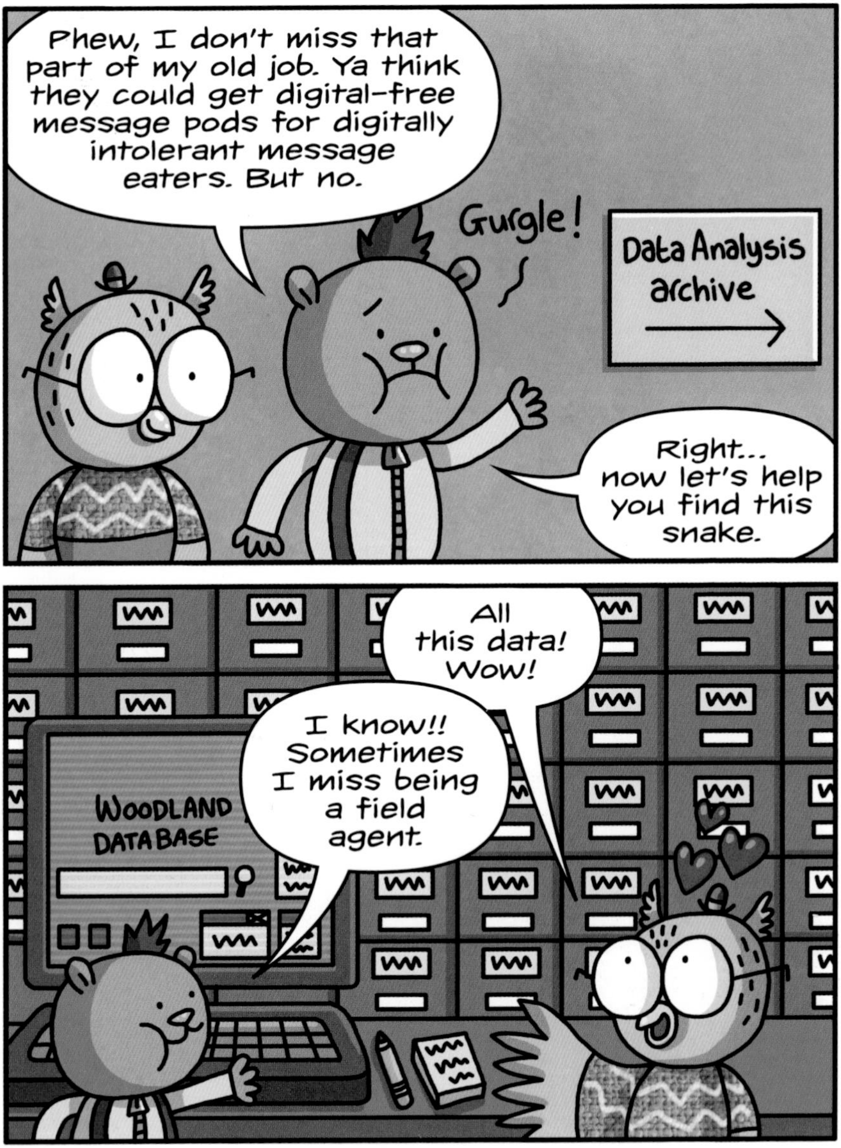
Phew, I don't miss that part of my old job. Ya think they could get digital-free message pods for digitally intolerant message eaters. But no.
Gurgle!
Data Analysis archive
Right... now let's help you find this snake.
All this data! Wow!
I know!! Sometimes I miss being a field agent.
WOODLAND DATABASE

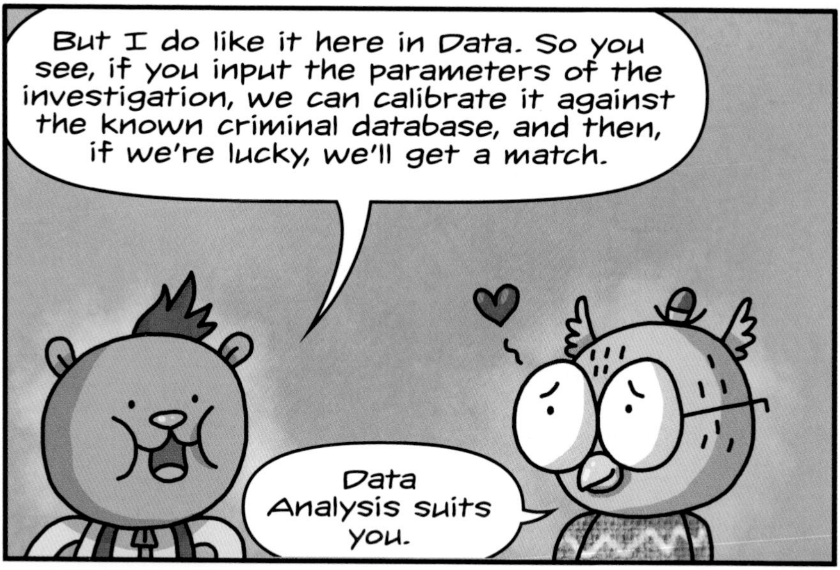
But I do like it here in Data. So you see, if you input the parameters of the investigation, we can calibrate it against the known criminal database, and then, if we're lucky, we'll get a match.
Data Analysis suits you.

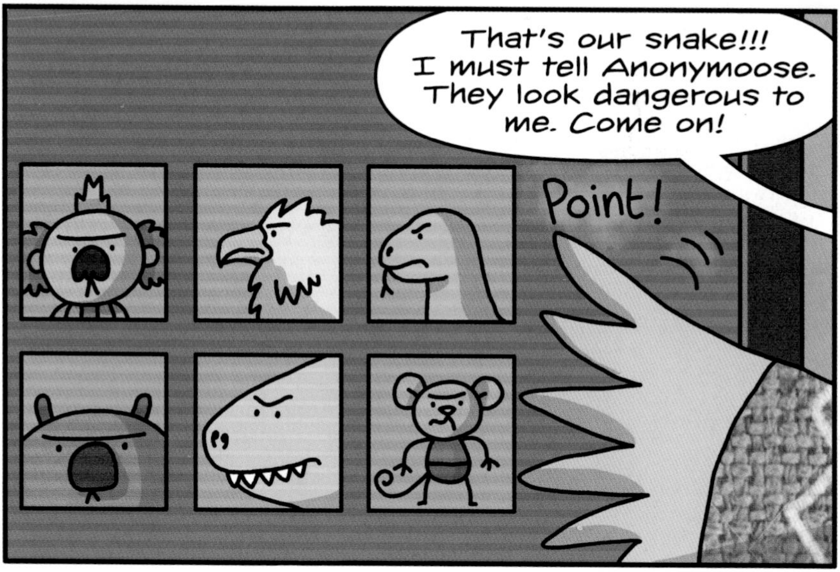
That's our snake!!! I must tell Anonymoose. They look dangerous to me. Come on!
Point!

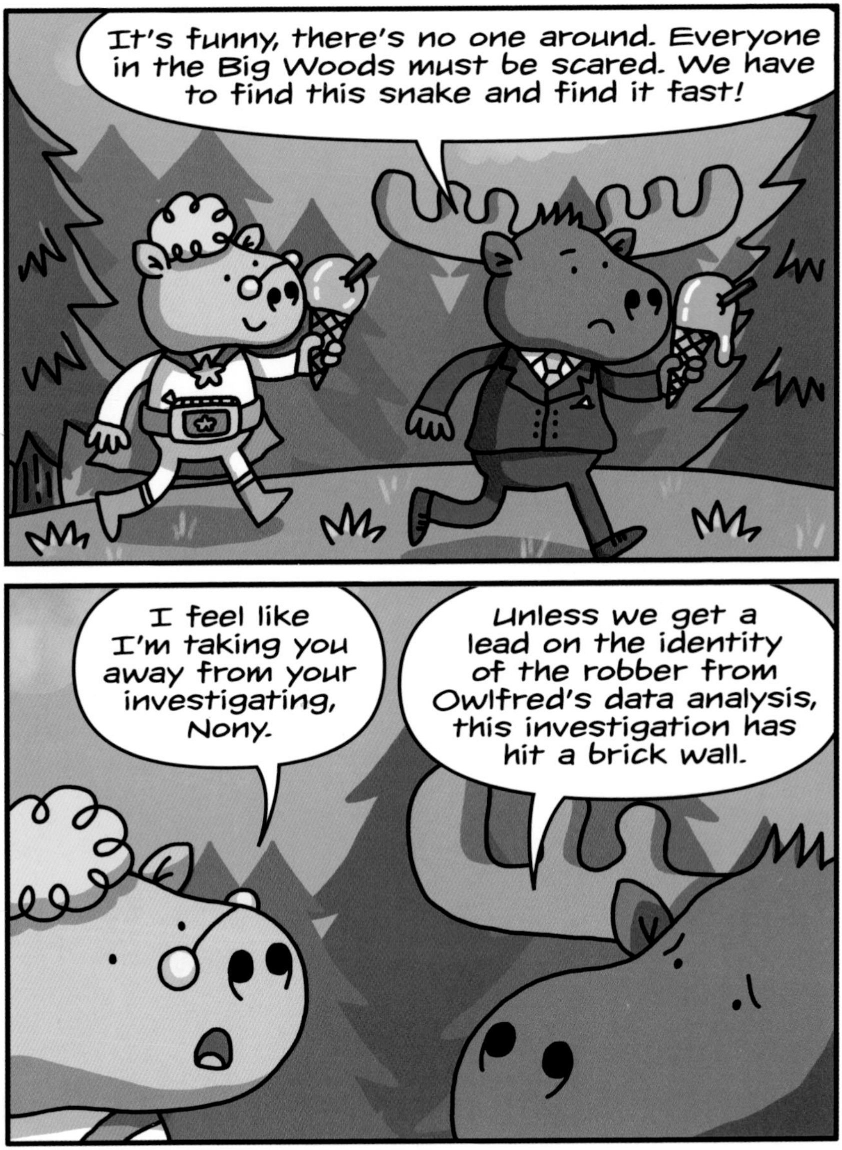
It's funny, there's no one around. Everyone in the Big Woods must be scared. We have to find this snake and find it fast!
I feel like I'm taking you away from your investigating, Nony.
Unless we get a lead on the identity of the robber from Owlfred's data analysis, this investigation has hit a brick wall.

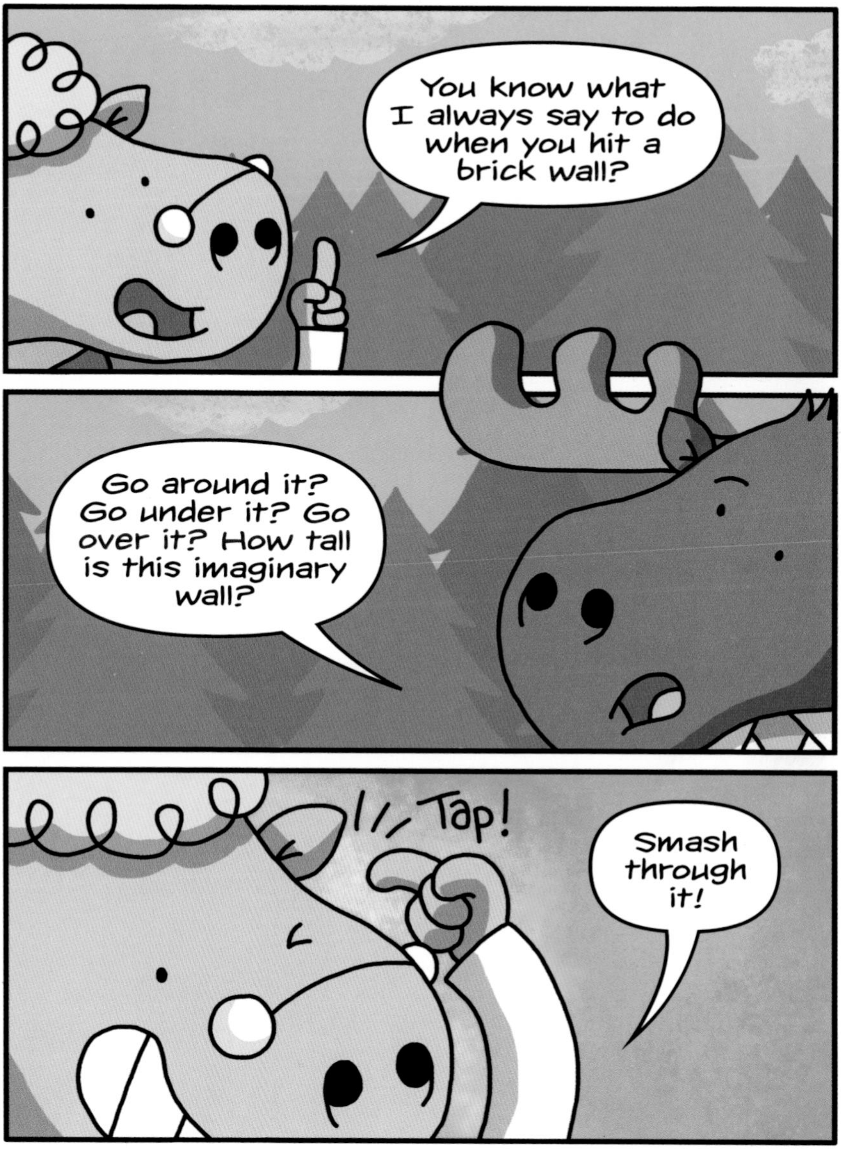
You know what I always say to do when you hit a brick wall?
Go around it? Go under it? Go over it? How tall is this imaginary wall?
Tap!
Smash through it!

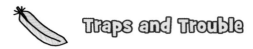

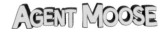

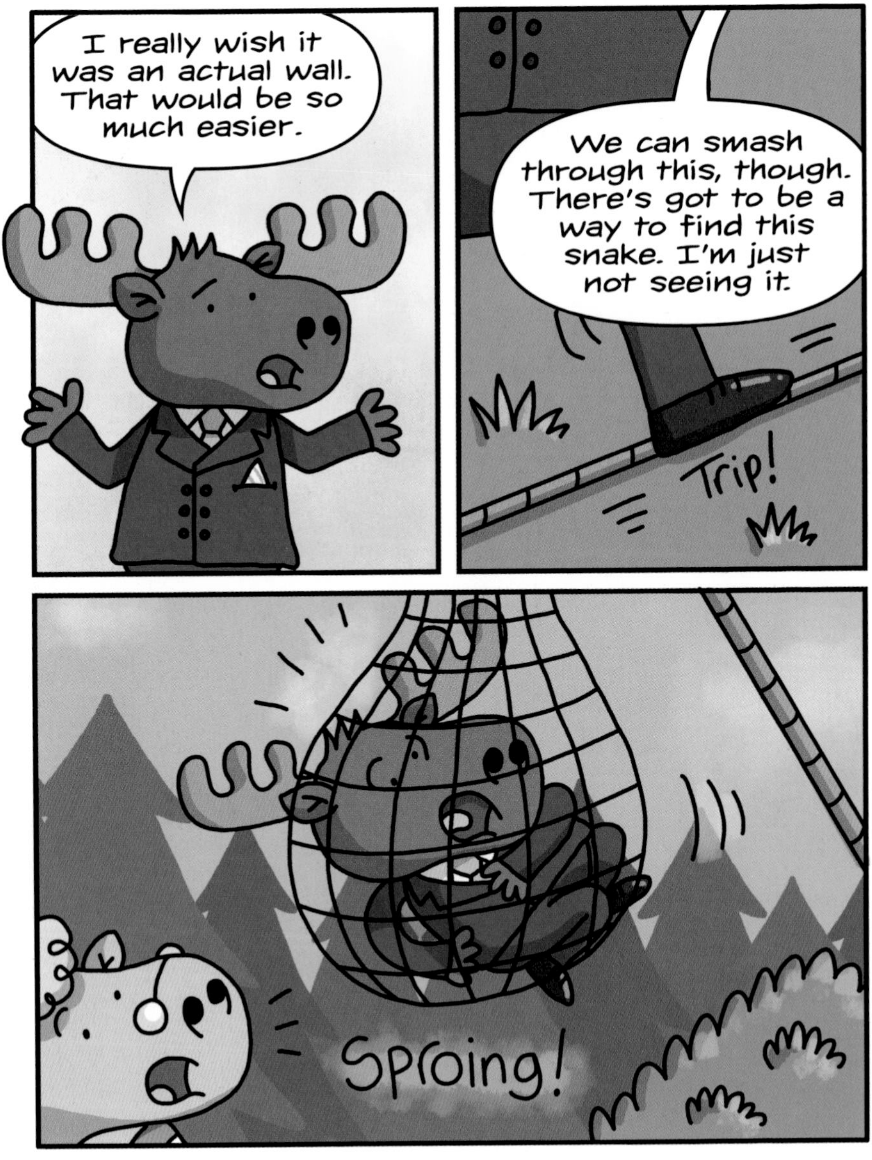
I really wish it was an actual wall. That would be so much easier.
We can smash through this, though. There's got to be a way to find this snake. I'm just not seeing it.
Trip!
Sproing!

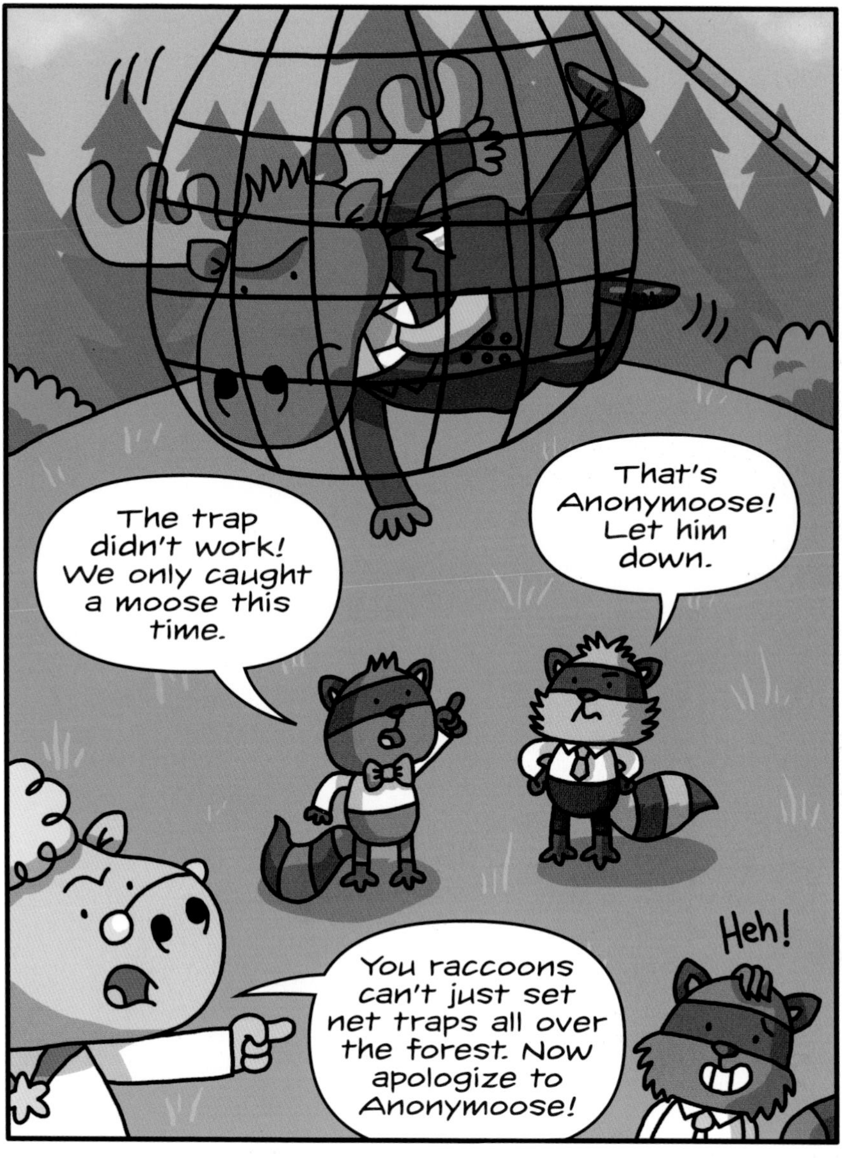
The trap didn't work! We only caught a moose this time.
That's Anonymoose! Let him down.
You raccoons can't just set net traps all over the forest. Now apologize to Anonymoose!
Heh!

AGENT MOOSE

Sorry, Anonymoose!

Are you okay?

Never better.

Thank you, raccoons. You just gave me an idea. I've been looking at this all wrong. We're trying to find the robber, when we should be making the robber come to us. We have to set a trap that they fall into!

Now you're talking.

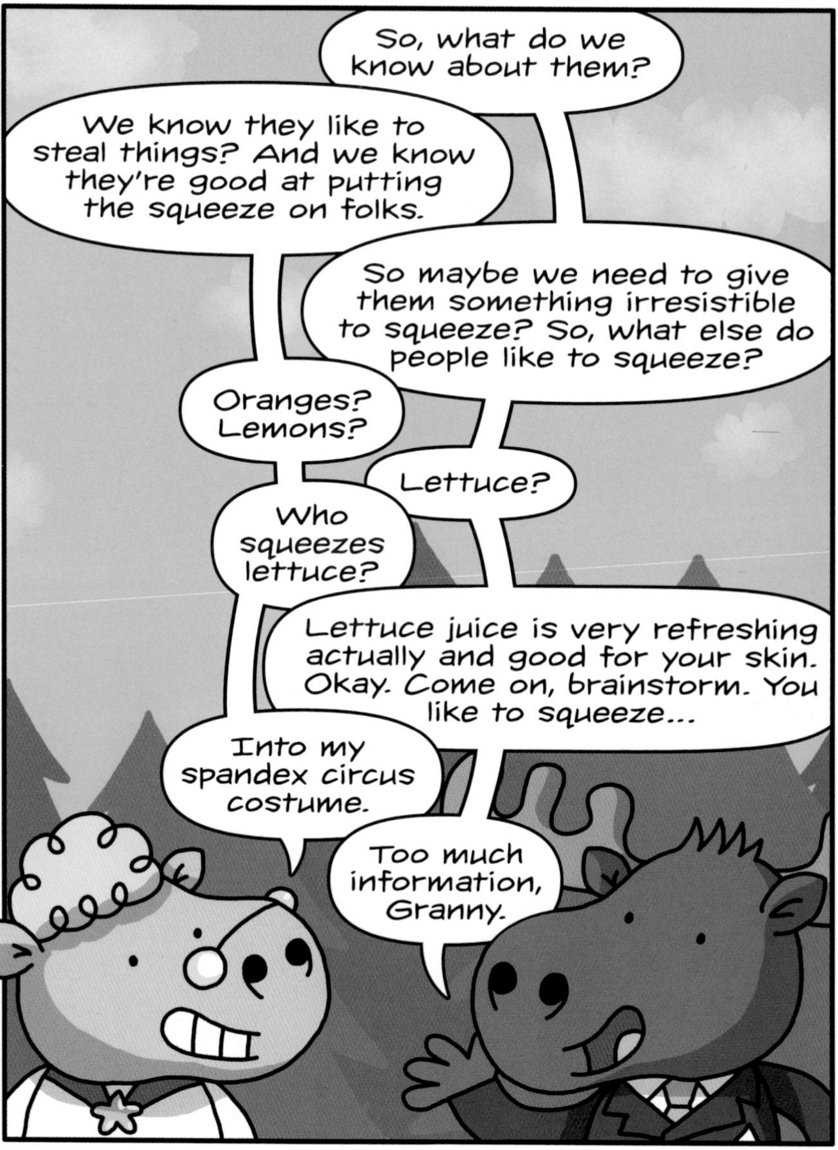
So, what do we know about them?
We know they like to steal things? And we know they're good at putting the squeeze on folks.
So maybe we need to give them something irresistible to squeeze? So, what else do people like to squeeze?
Oranges? Lemons?
Lettuce?
Who squeezes lettuce?
Lettuce juice is very refreshing actually and good for your skin. Okay. Come on, brainstorm. You like to squeeze...
Into my spandex circus costume.
Too much information, Granny.

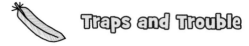

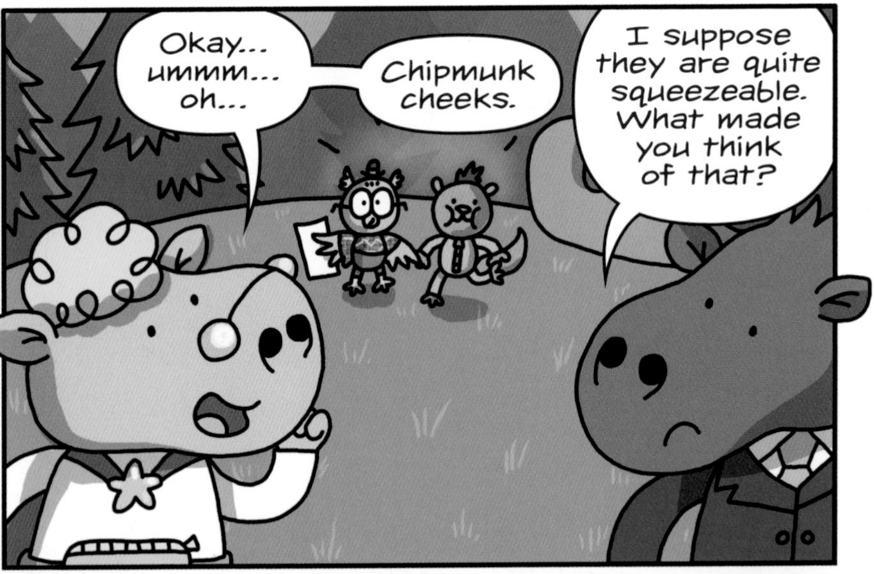
Okay... ummm... oh...
Chipmunk cheeks.
I suppose they are quite squeezeable. What made you think of that?

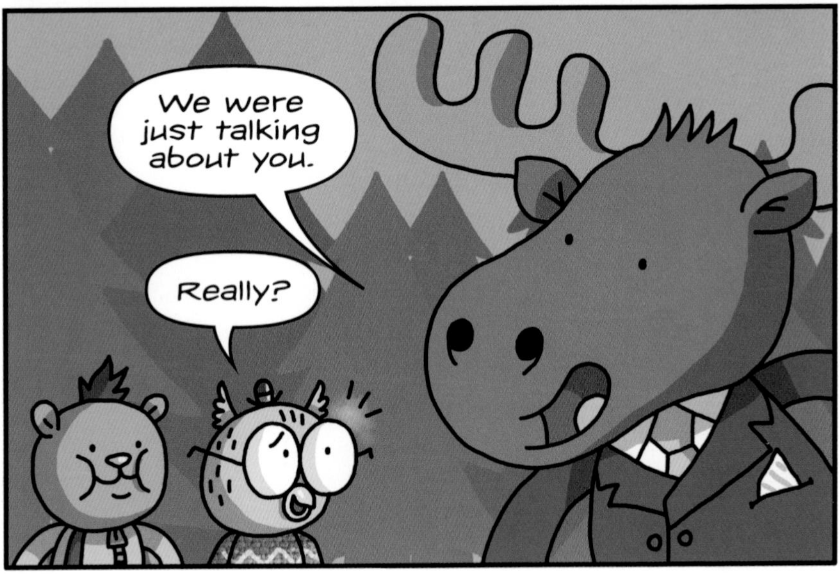
We were just talking about you.
Really?

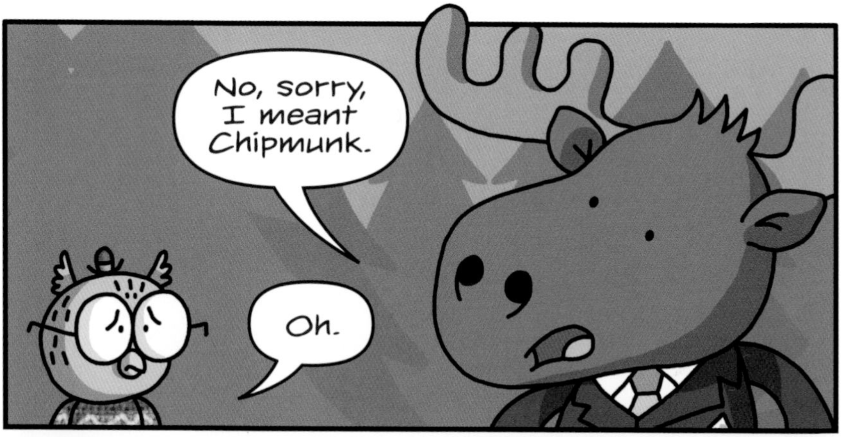
No, sorry, I meant Chipmunk.
Oh.

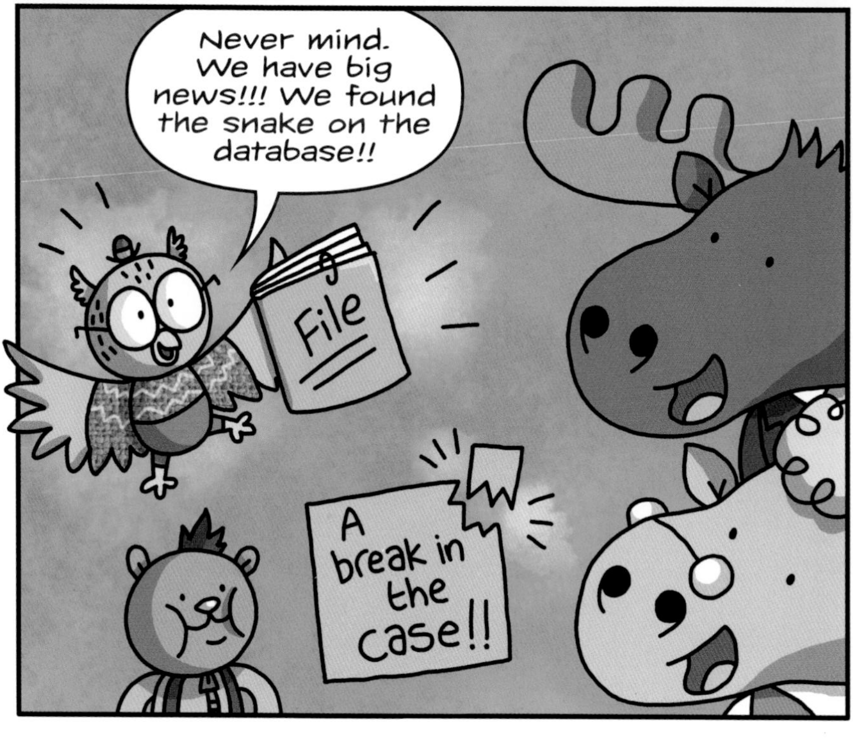
Never mind. We have big news!!! We found the snake on the database!!
File
A break in the case!!

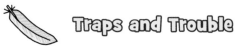

Name:

Anna-CON-da

Description:

Colorful 15-ft snake with lots of muscle

Whereabouts:

Recently released from Woodland Prison. Whereabouts unknown

Hobbies:

Accordion playing. Making fresh-squeezed orange juice

Criminal Convictions:

Robbery, intimidation of forest animals

MO (Most Obvious way of doing crimes):

Putting the squeeze on folks and forcing them to give away their possessions

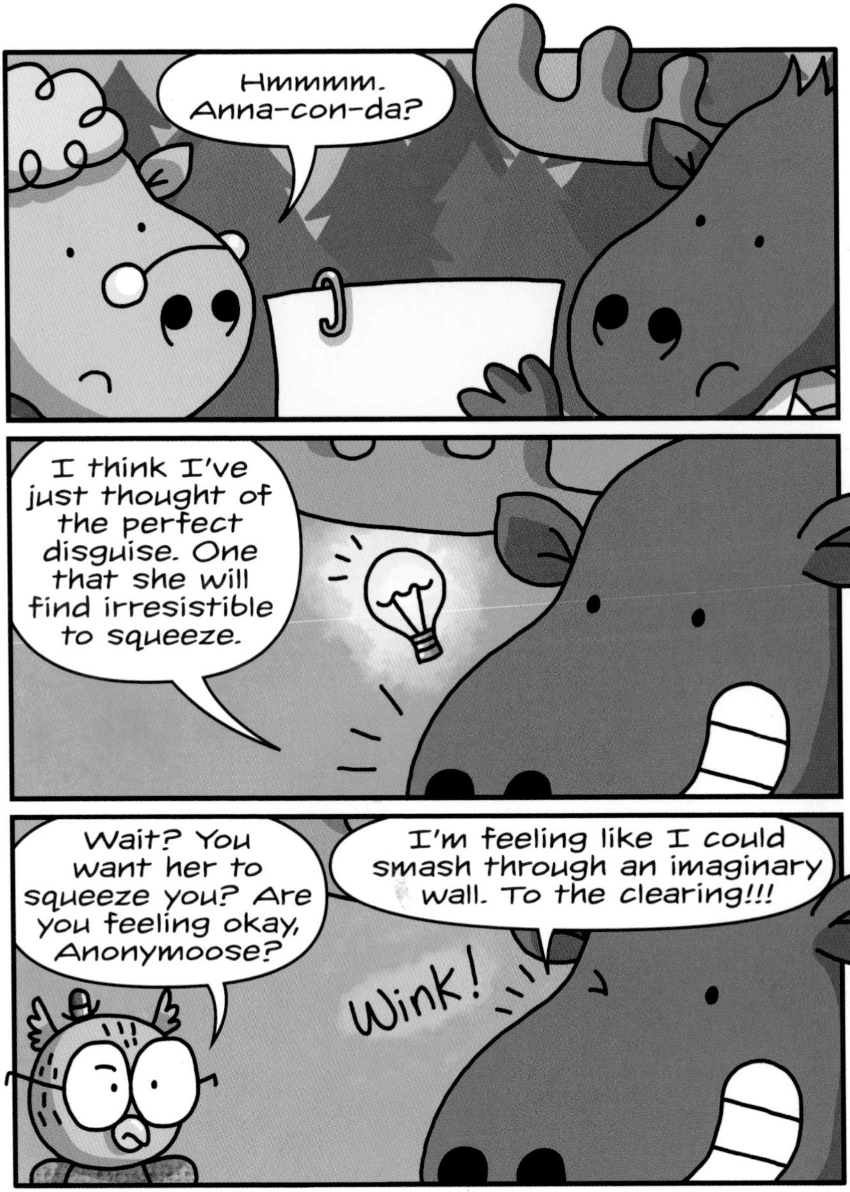
Hmmmm. Anna-con-da?
I think I've just thought of the perfect disguise. One that she will find irresistible to squeeze.
Wait? You want her to squeeze you? Are you feeling okay, Anonymoose?
I'm feeling like I could smash through an imaginary wall. To the clearing!!!
Wink!

Chapter 7

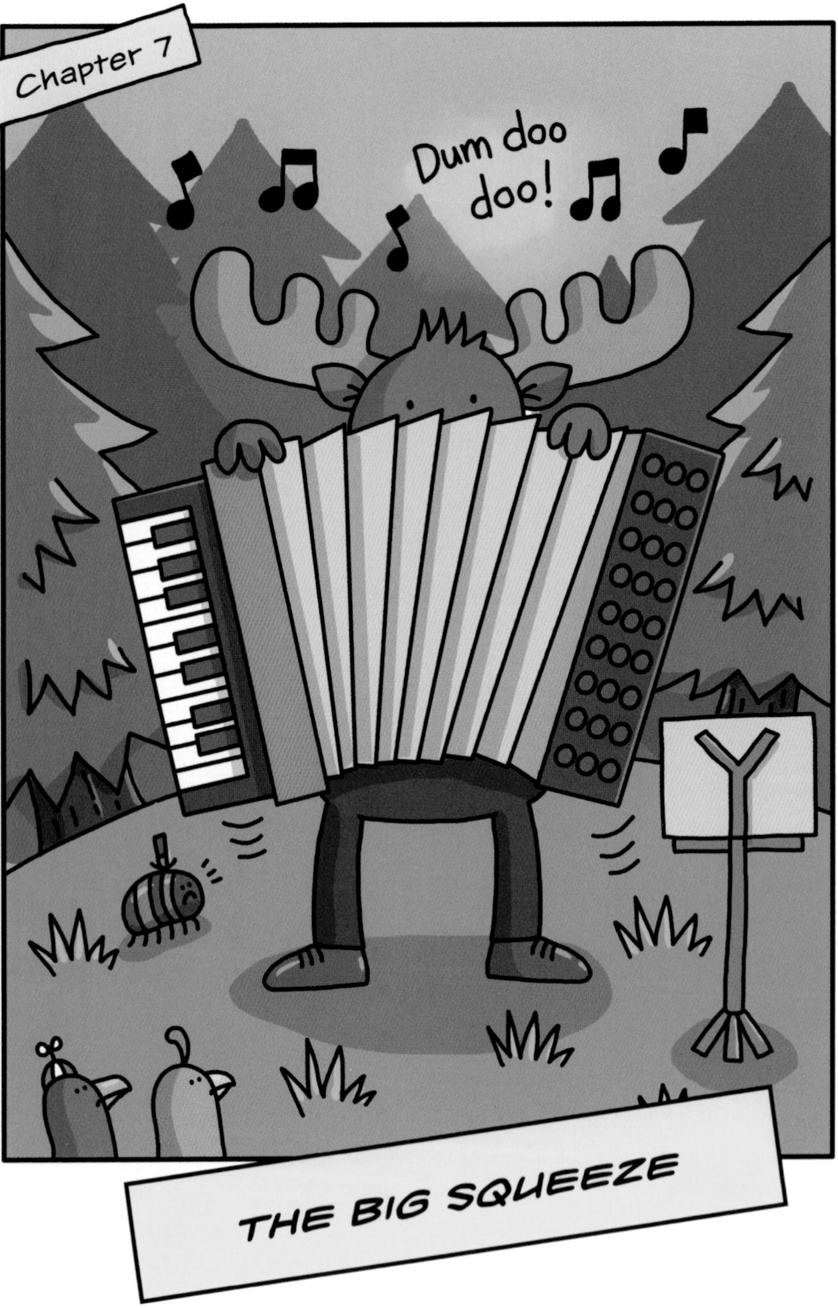
Dum doo doo!

THE BIG SQUEEZE

The Big Squeeze

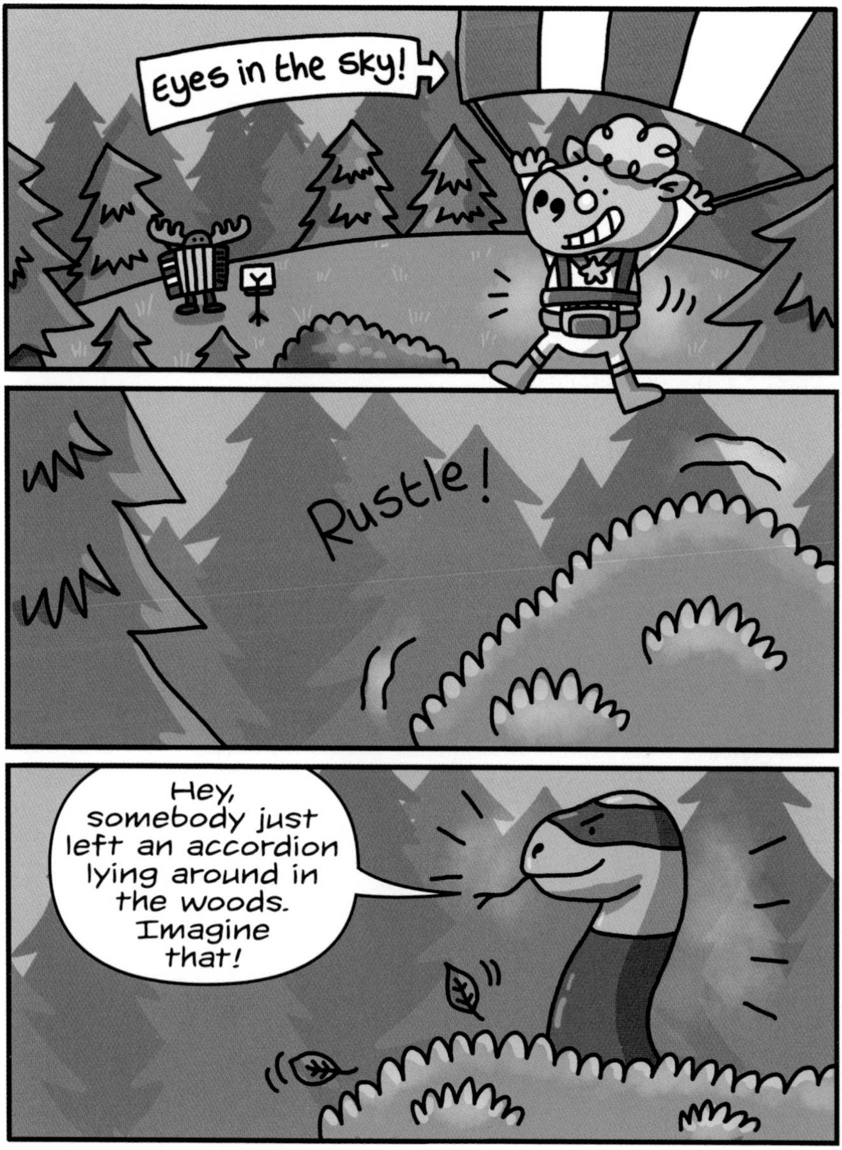

Eyes in the sky!
Rustle!
Hey, somebody just left an accordion lying around in the woods. Imagine that!

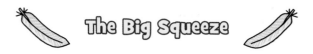

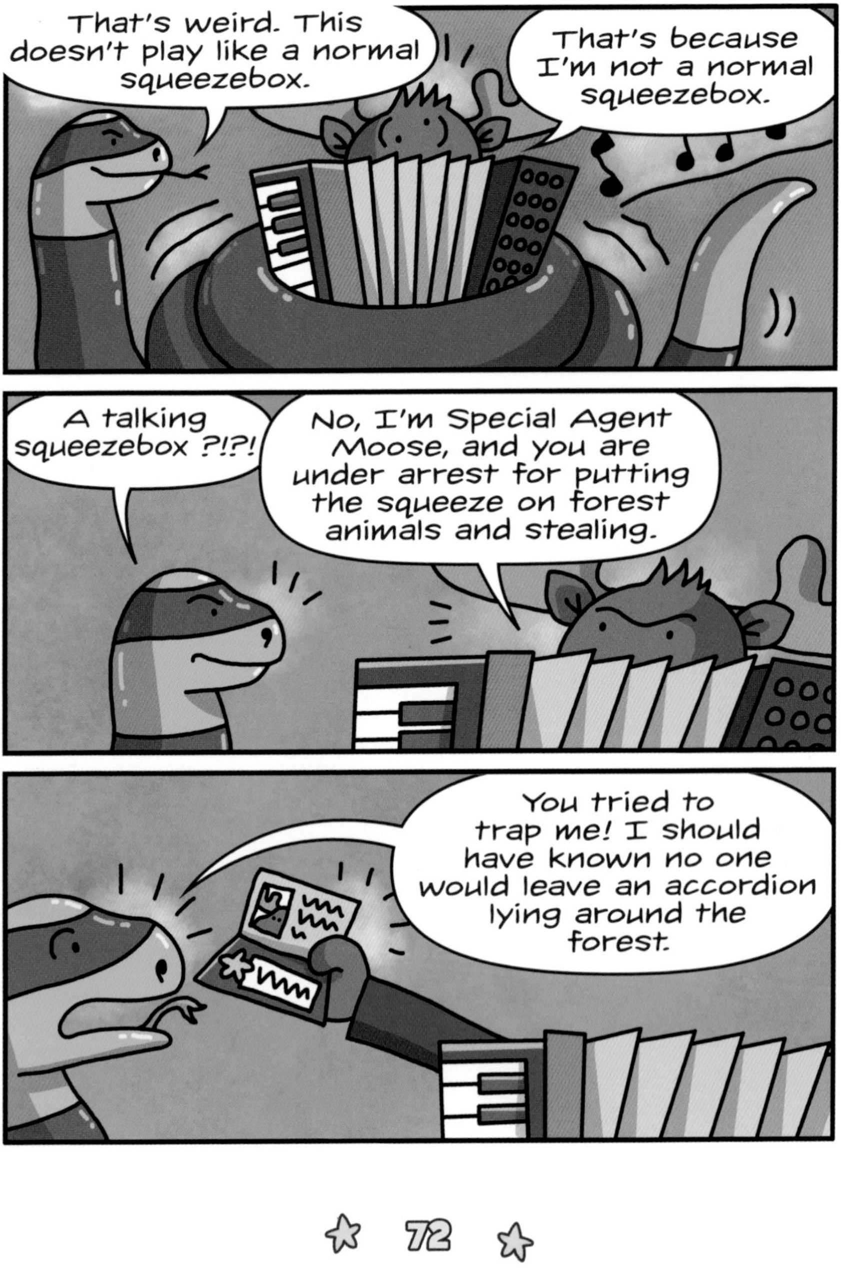
That's weird. This doesn't play like a normal squeezebox.
That's because I'm not a normal squeezebox.
A talking squeezebox ?!?!
No, I'm Special Agent Moose, and you are under arrest for putting the squeeze on forest animals and stealing.
You tried to trap me! I should have known no one would leave an accordion lying around the forest.

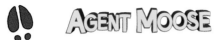

The Big Squeeze

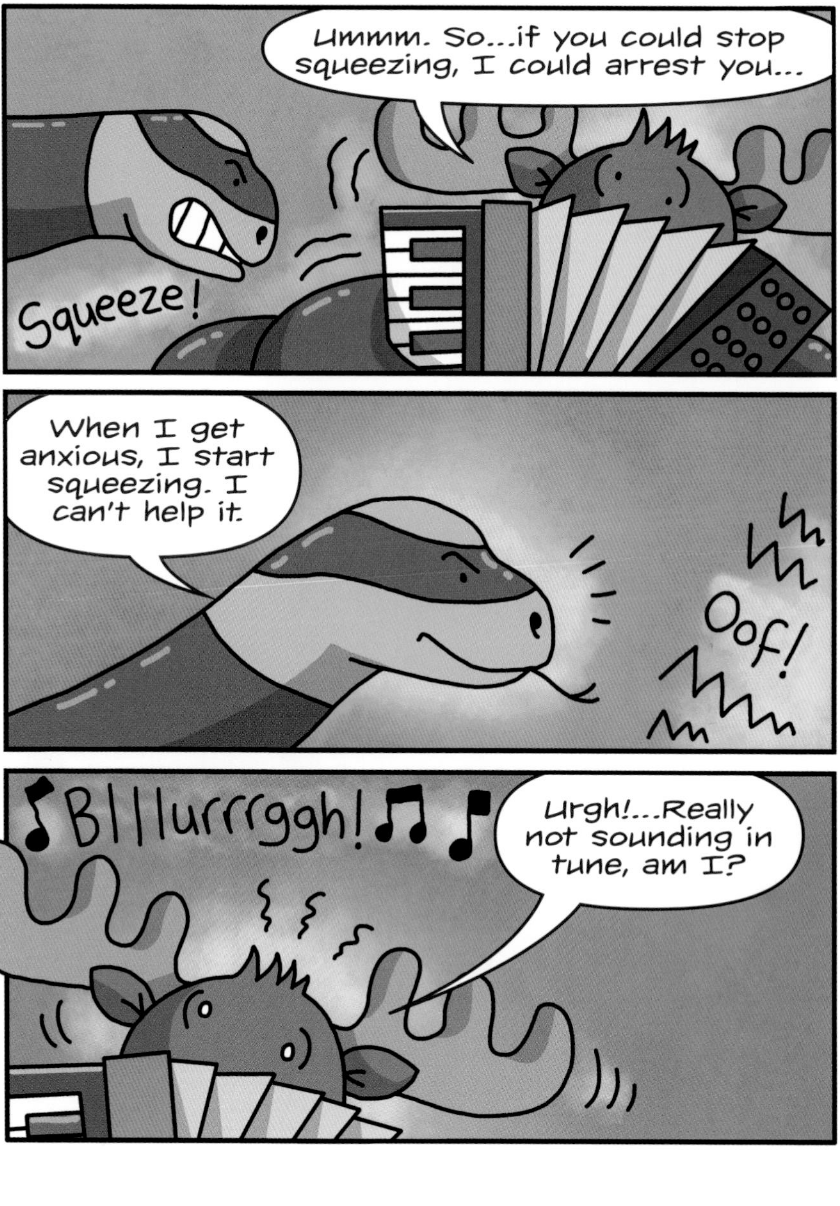
Ummm. So...if you could stop squeezing, I could arrest you...
Squeeze!
When I get anxious, I start squeezing. I can't help it.
Oof!
Blllurrrggh!
Urgh!...Really not sounding in tune, am I?

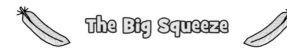

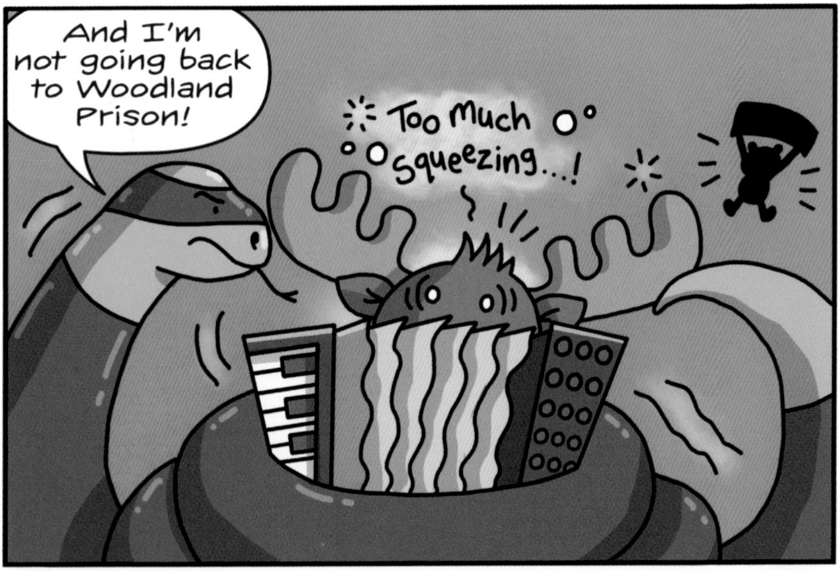
And I'm not going back to Woodland Prison!
Too much squeezing...!

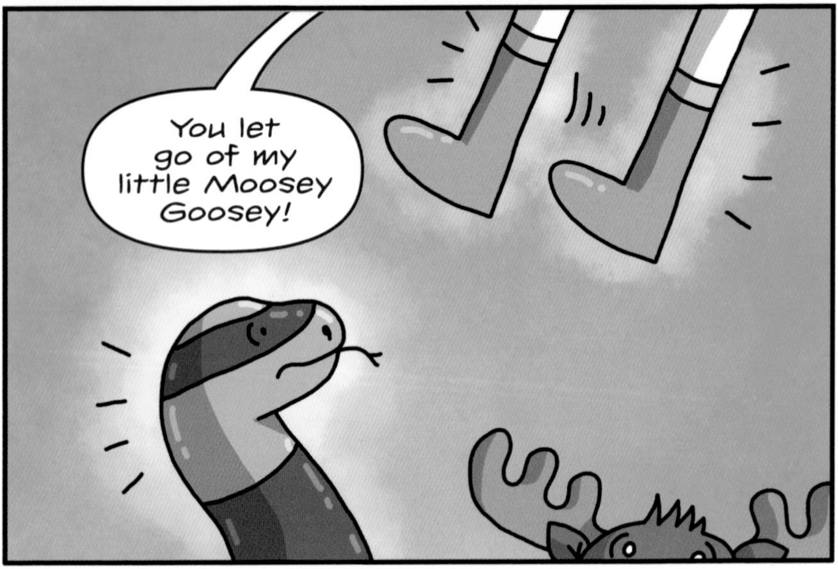
You let go of my little Moosey Goosey!

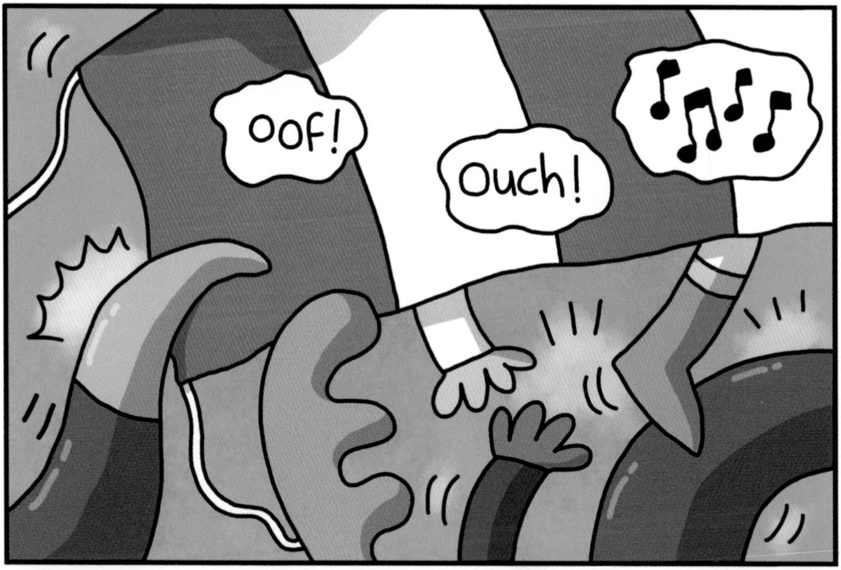
OOF!
Ouch!

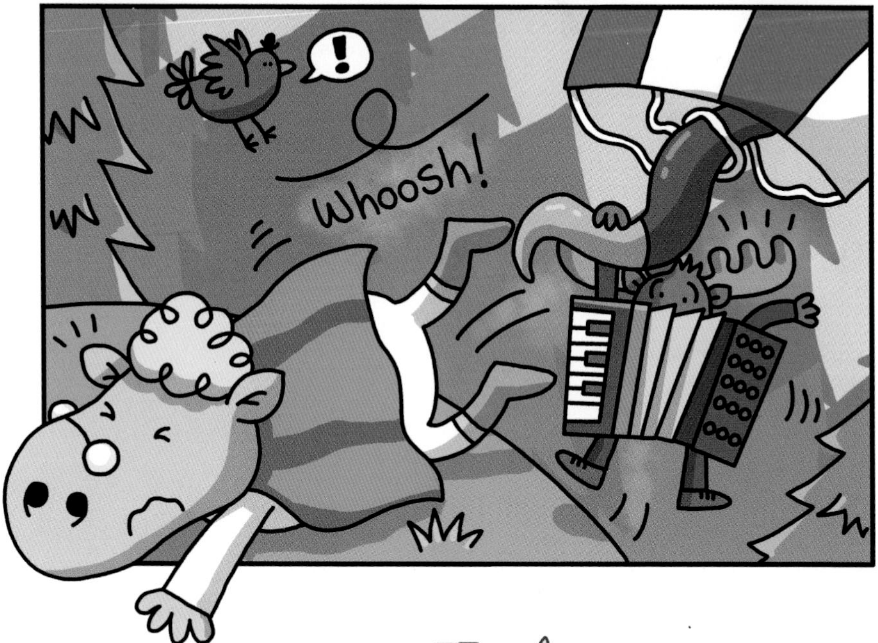
!
Whoosh!

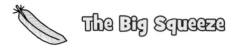

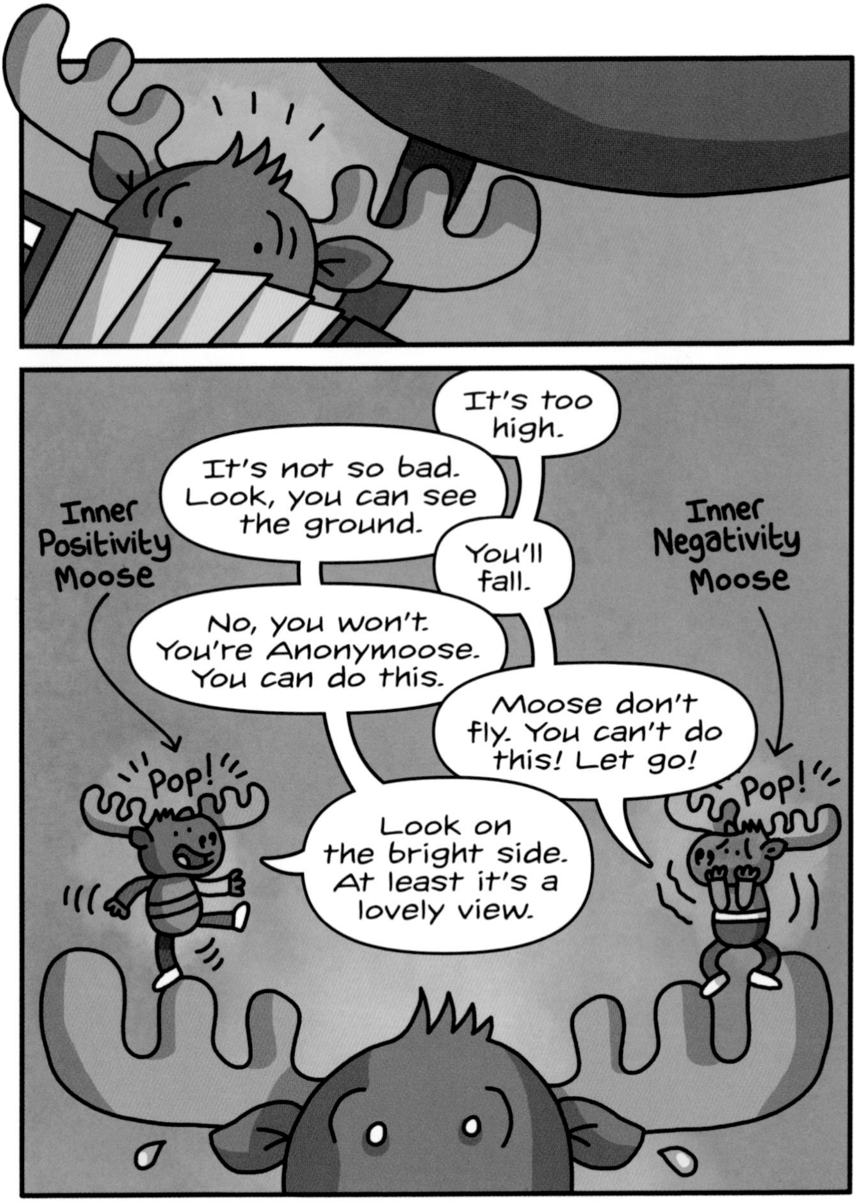
It's too high.
It's not so bad. Look, you can see the ground.
Inner Positivity Moose
You'll fall.
Inner Negativity Moose
No, you won't. You're Anonymoose. You can do this.
Moose don't fly. You can't do this! Let go!
Pop!
Pop!
Look on the bright side. At least it's a lovely view.

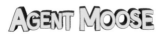

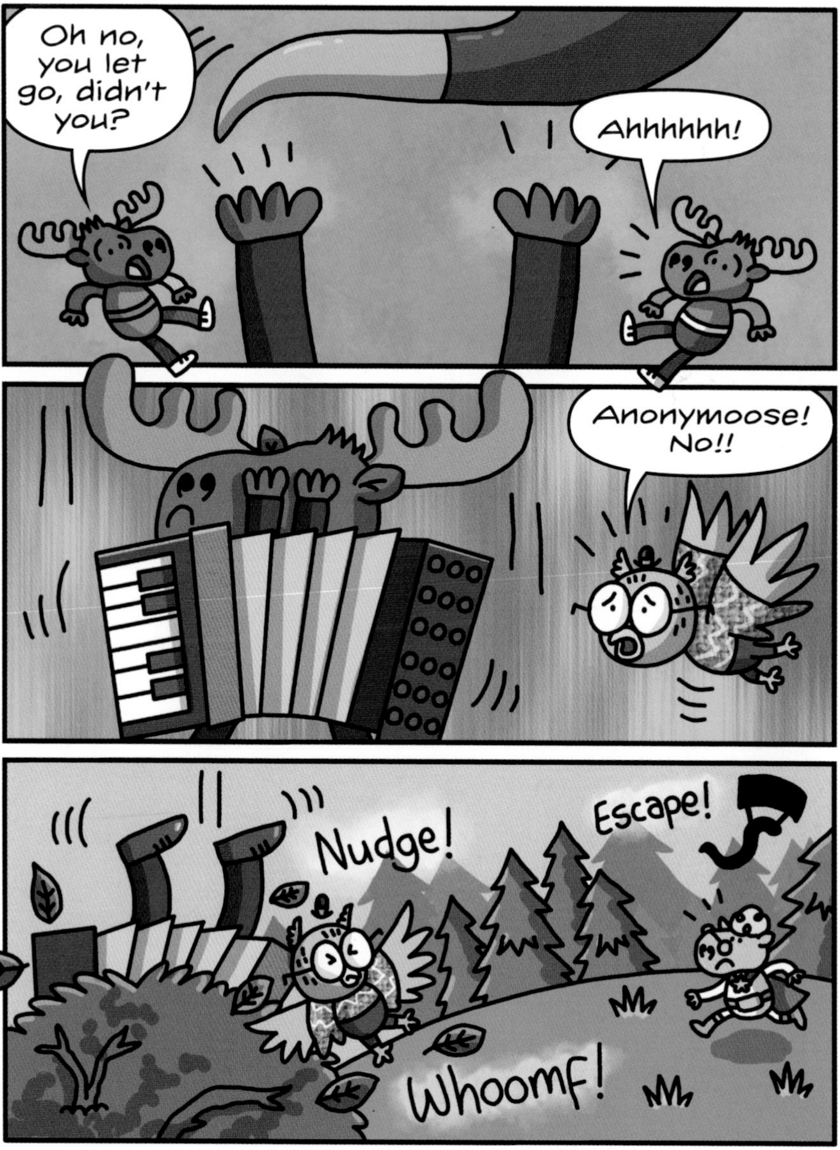
Oh no, you let go, didn't you?
Ahhhhhh!
Anonymoose! No!!
Nudge!
Escape!
Whoomf!

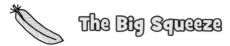

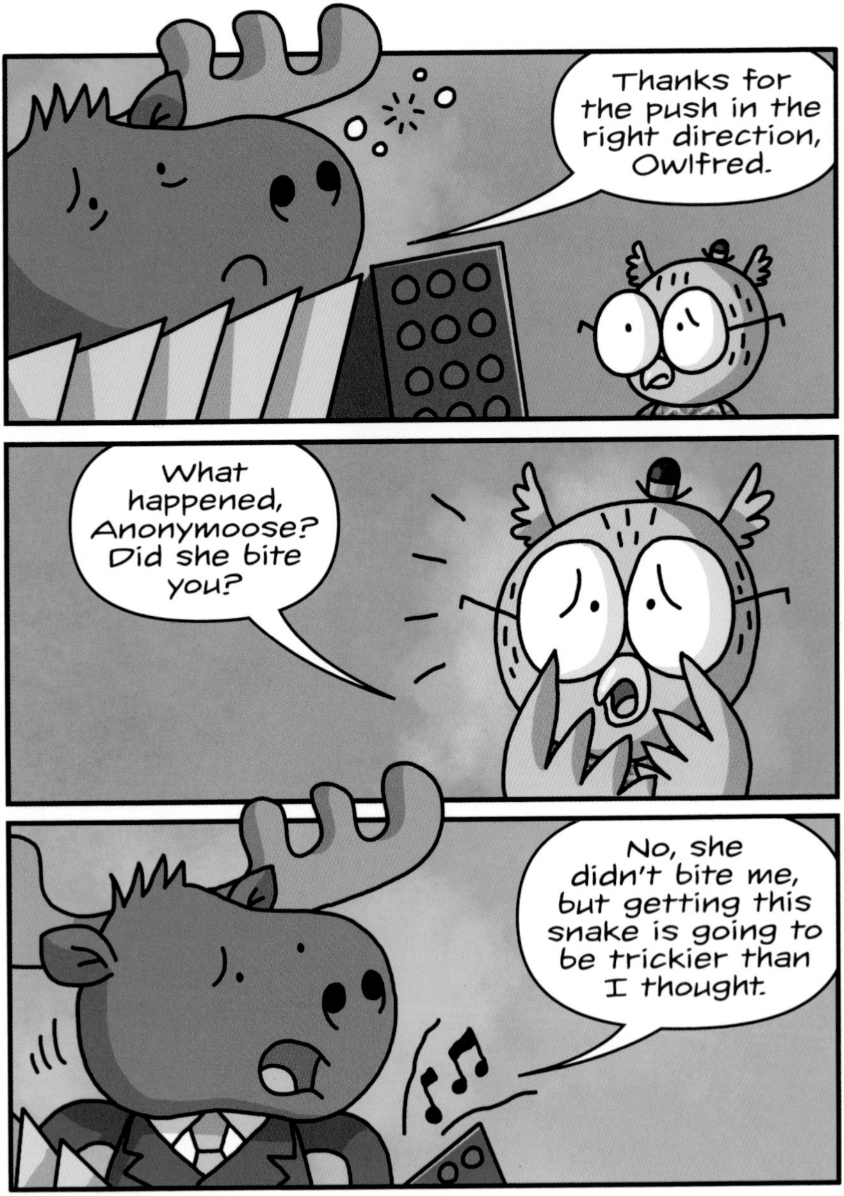
Thanks for the push in the right direction, Owlfred.
What happened, Anonymoose? Did she bite you?
No, she didn't bite me, but getting this snake is going to be trickier than I thought.

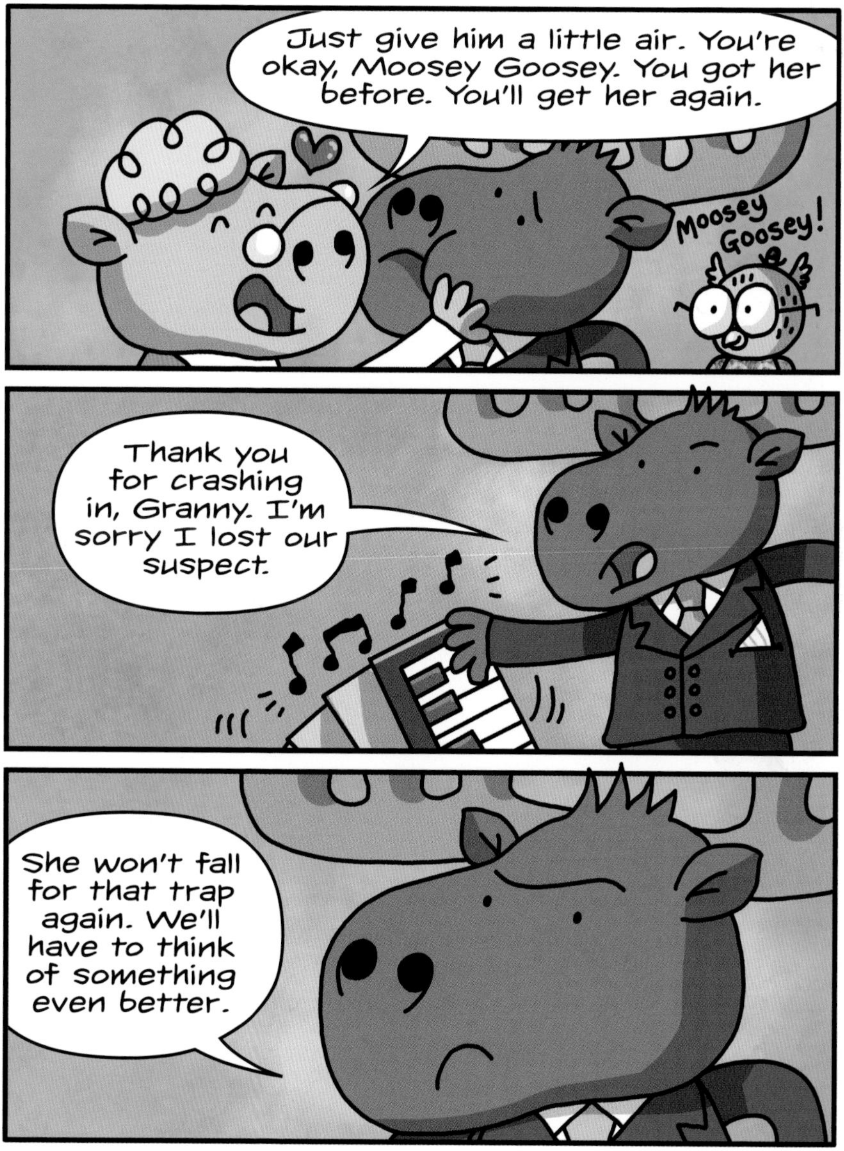
Just give him a little air. You're okay, Moosey Goosey. You got her before. You'll get her again.
Moosey Goosey!
Thank you for crashing in, Granny. I'm sorry I lost our suspect.
She won't fall for that trap again. We'll have to think of something even better.

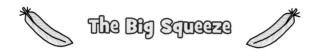

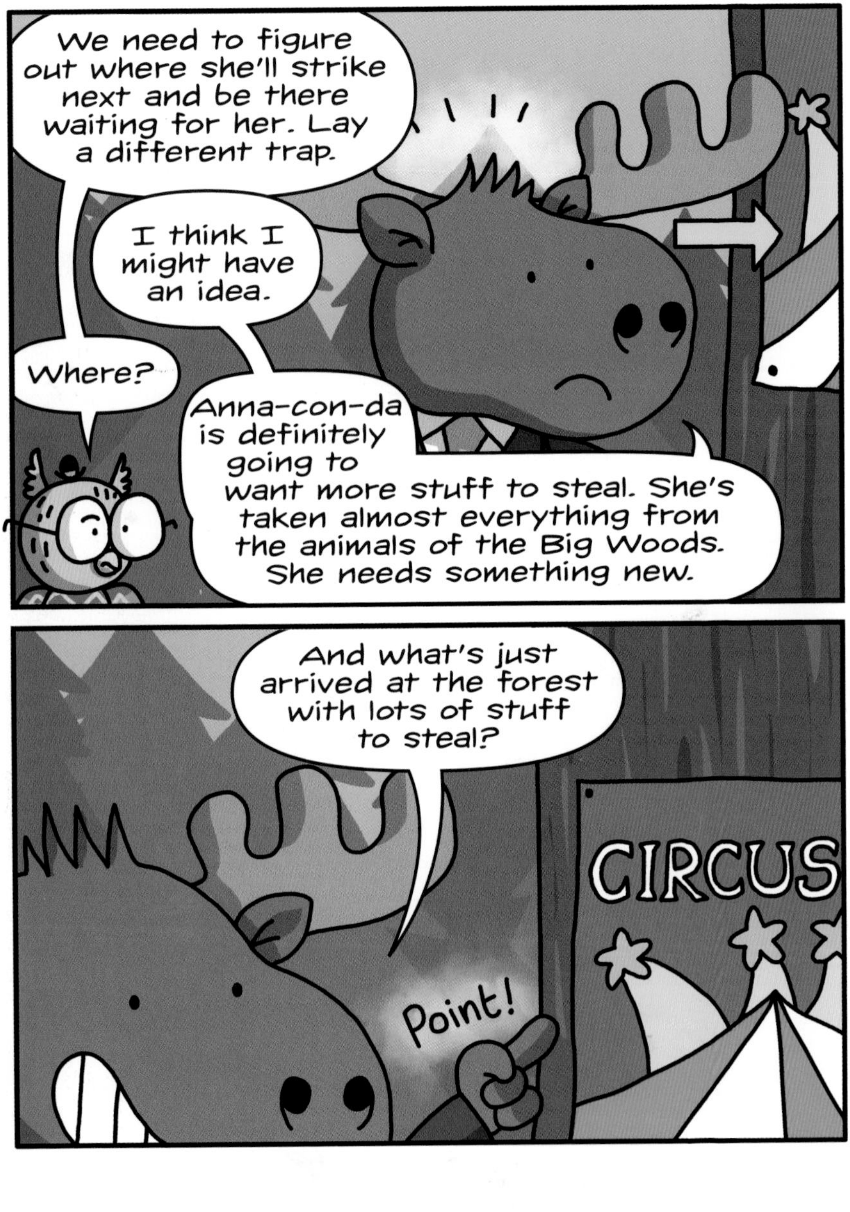
We need to figure out where she'll strike next and be there waiting for her. Lay a different trap.
I think I might have an idea.
Where?
Anna-con-da is definitely going to want more stuff to steal. She's taken almost everything from the animals of the Big Woods. She needs something new.
And what's just arrived at the forest with lots of stuff to steal?
Point!
CIRCUS

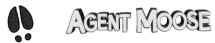

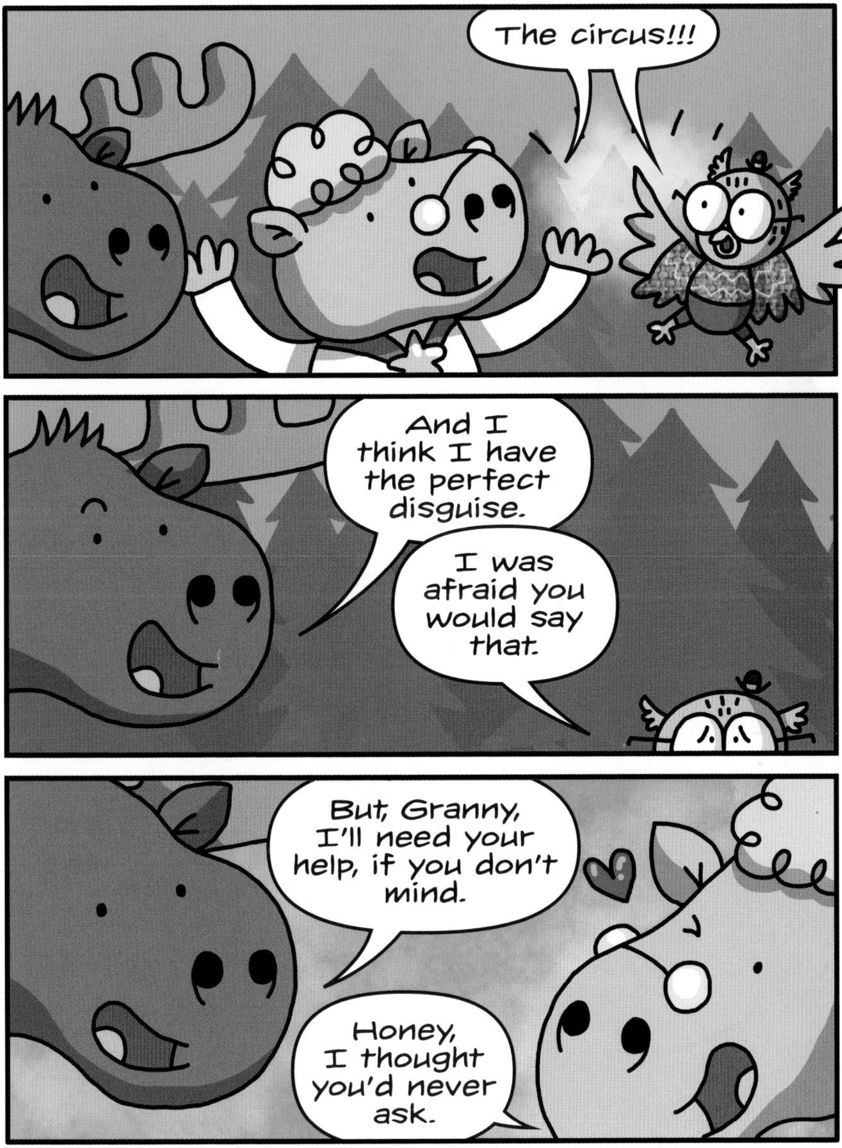
The circus!!!
And I think I have the perfect disguise.
I was afraid you would say that.
But, Granny, I'll need your help, if you don't mind.
Honey, I thought you'd never ask.

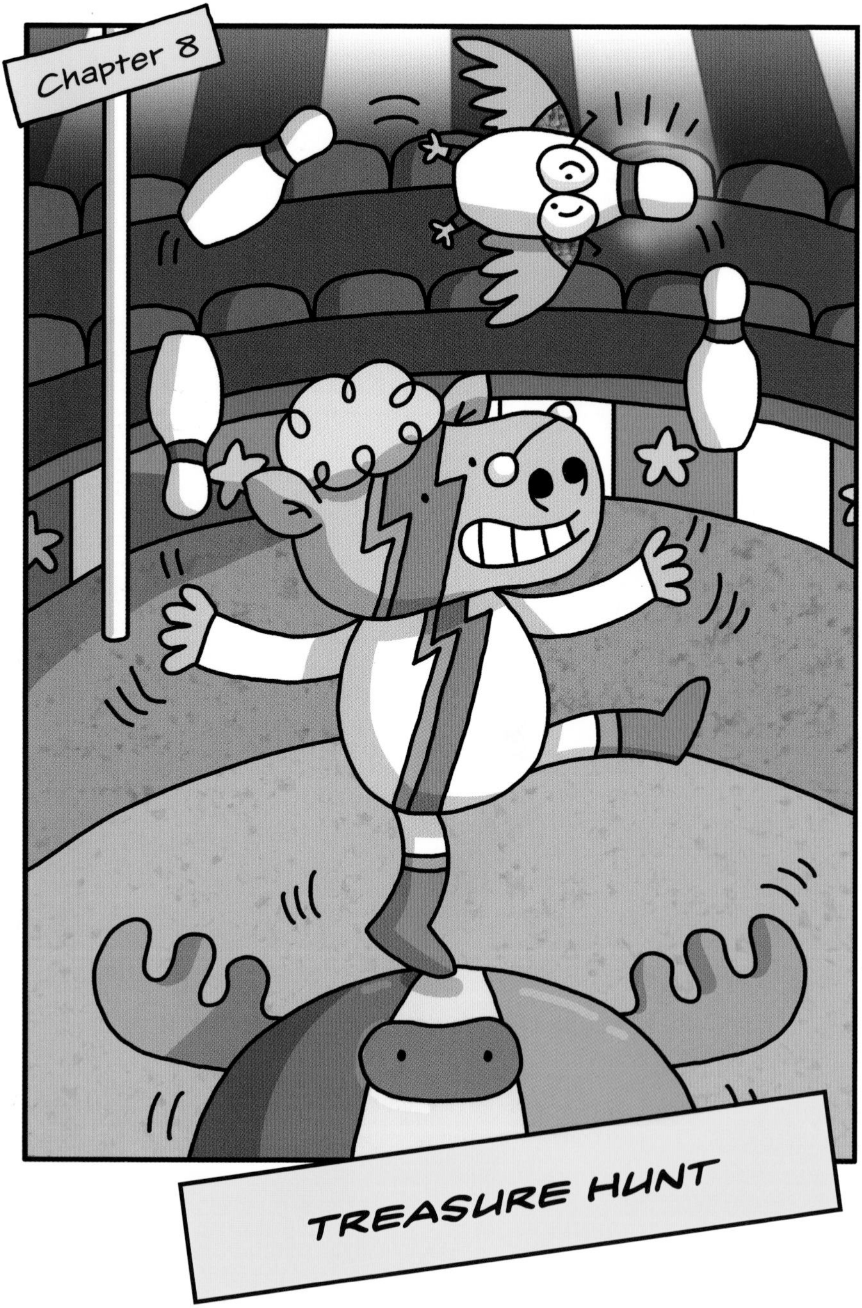
Chapter 8
TREASURE HUNT

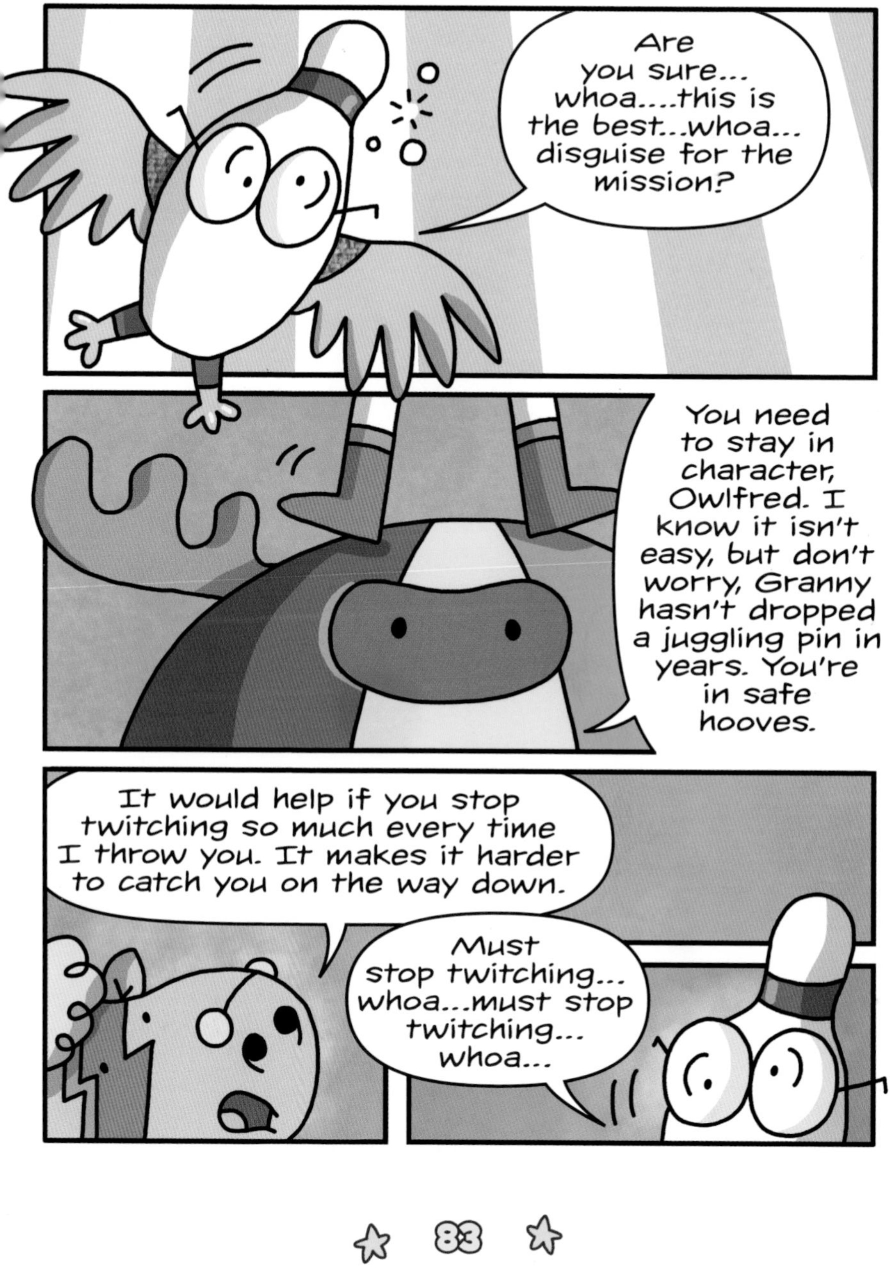
Are you sure... whoa....this is the best...whoa... disguise for the mission?
You need to stay in character, Owlfred. I know it isn't easy, but don't worry, Granny hasn't dropped a juggling pin in years. You're in safe hooves.
It would help if you stop twitching so much every time I throw you. It makes it harder to catch you on the way down.
Must stop twitching... whoa...must stop twitching... whoa...

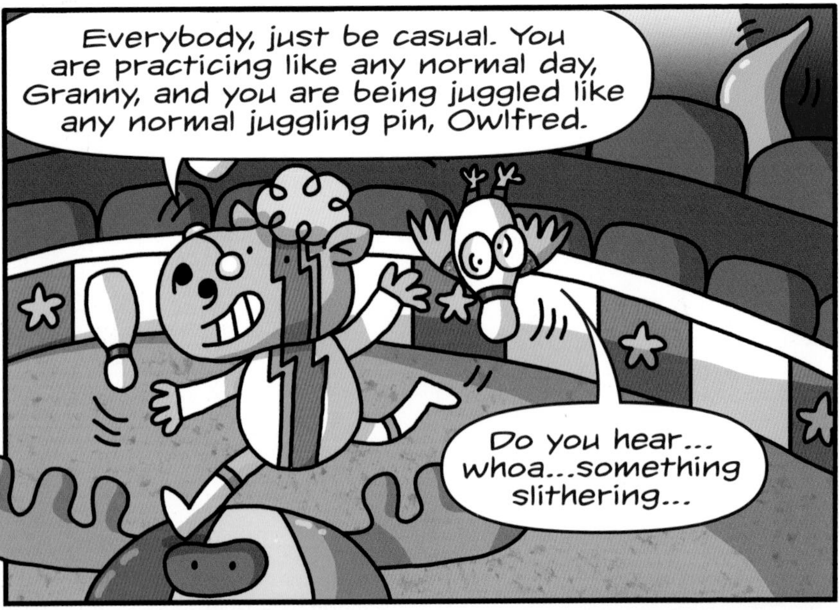
Everybody, just be casual. You are practicing like any normal day, Granny, and you are being juggled like any normal juggling pin, Owlfred.
Do you hear... whoa...something slithering...

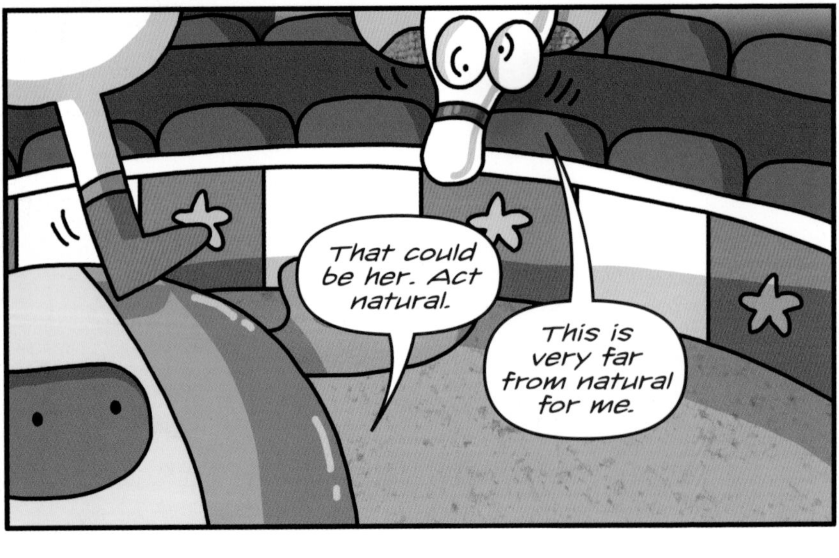
That could be her. Act natural.
This is very far from natural for me.

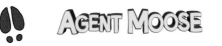

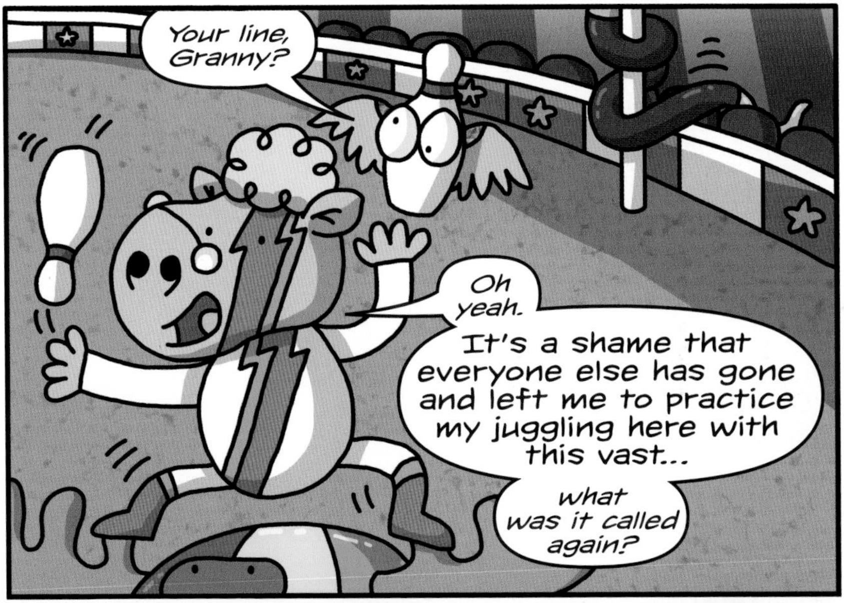
Your line, Granny?
Oh yeah.
It's a shame that everyone else has gone and left me to practice my juggling here with this vast...
what was it called again?

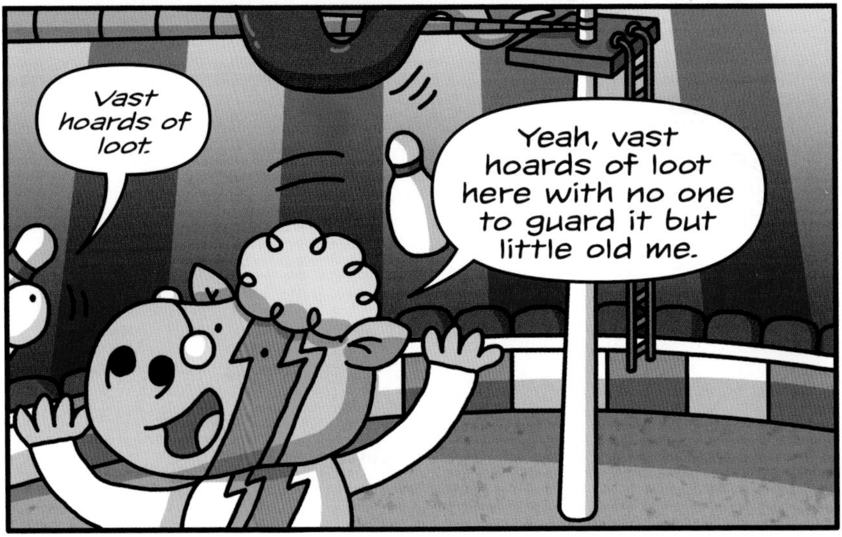
Vast hoards of loot.
Yeah, vast hoards of loot here with no one to guard it but little old me.

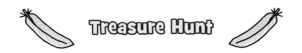

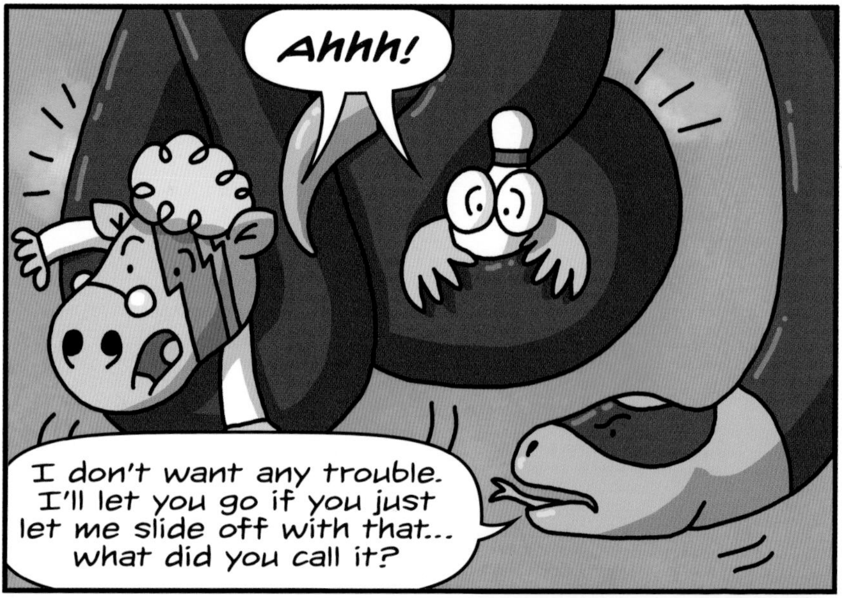
Ahhh!
I don't want any trouble. I'll let you go if you just let me slide off with that... what did you call it?

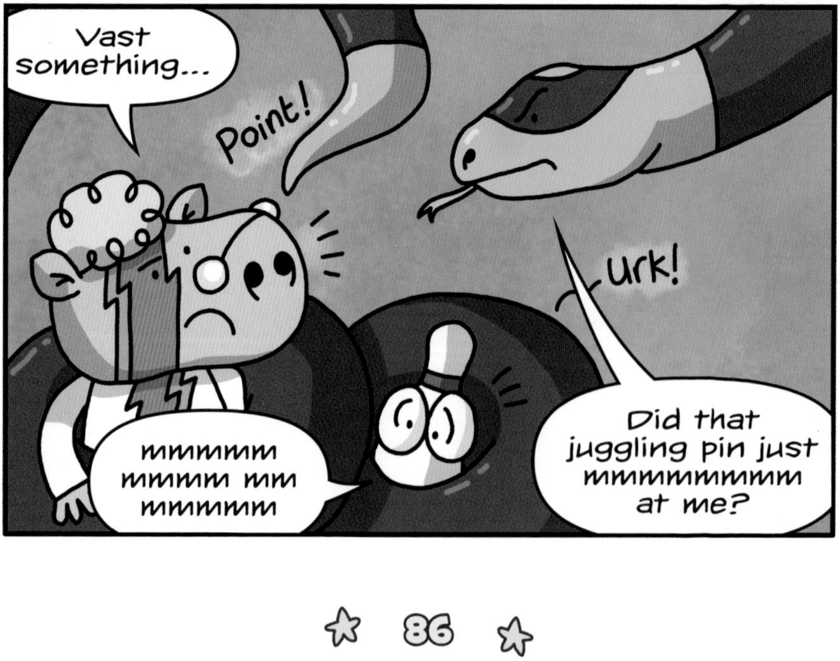
Vast something...
Point!
Urk!
mmmmm mmmm mm mmmmm
Did that juggling pin just mmmmmmmm at me?

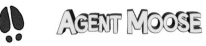

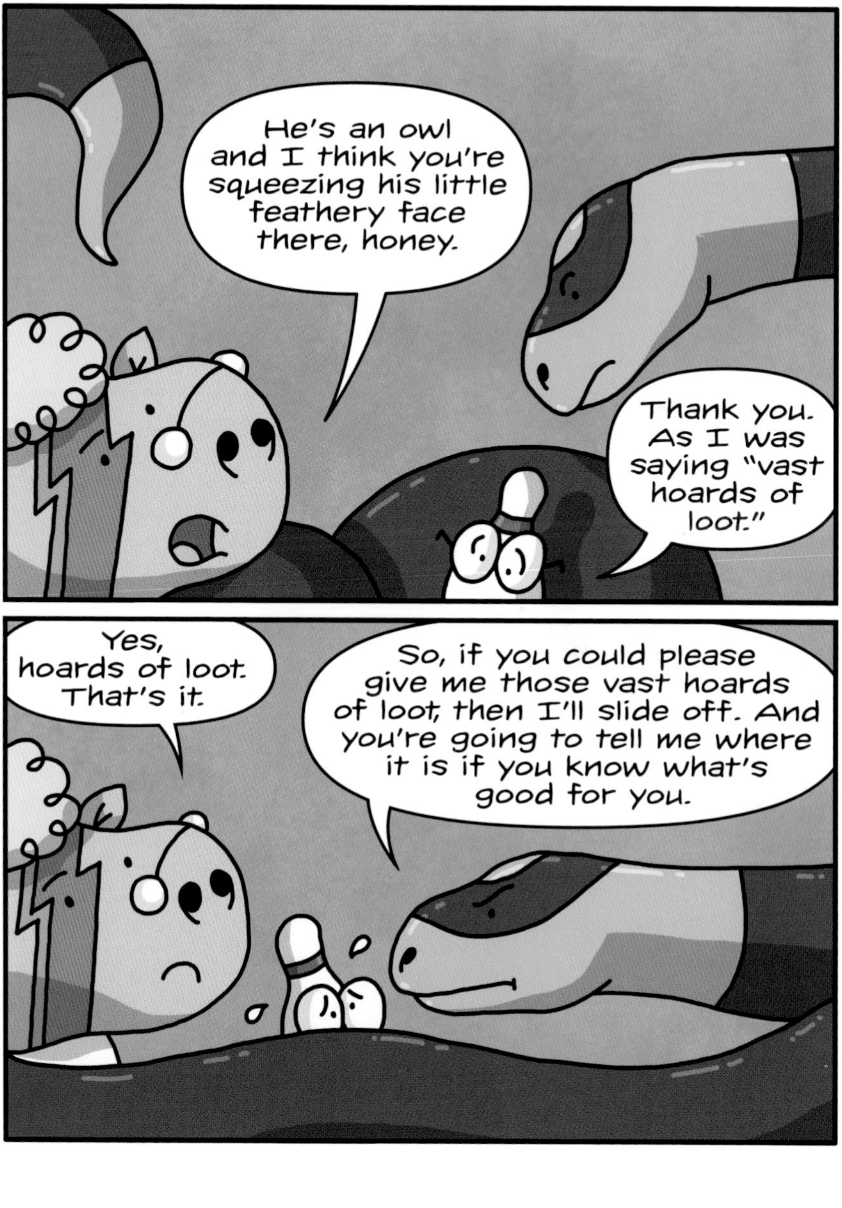
He's an owl and I think you're squeezing his little feathery face there, honey.
Thank you. As I was saying "vast hoards of loot."
Yes, hoards of loot. That's it.
So, if you could please give me those vast hoards of loot, then I'll slide off. And you're going to tell me where it is if you know what's good for you.

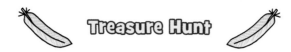

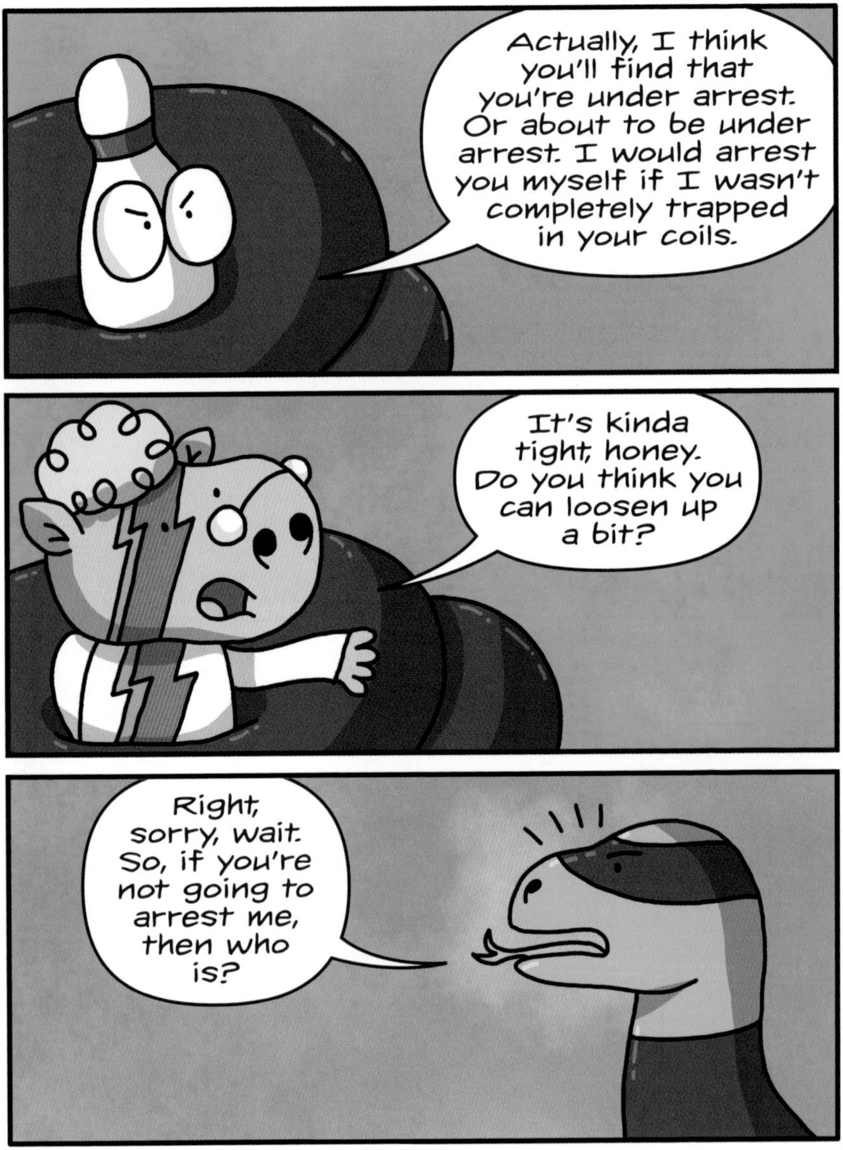
Actually, I think you'll find that you're under arrest. Or about to be under arrest. I would arrest you myself if I wasn't completely trapped in your coils.
It's kinda tight, honey. Do you think you can loosen up a bit?
Right, sorry, wait. So, if you're not going to arrest me, then who is?

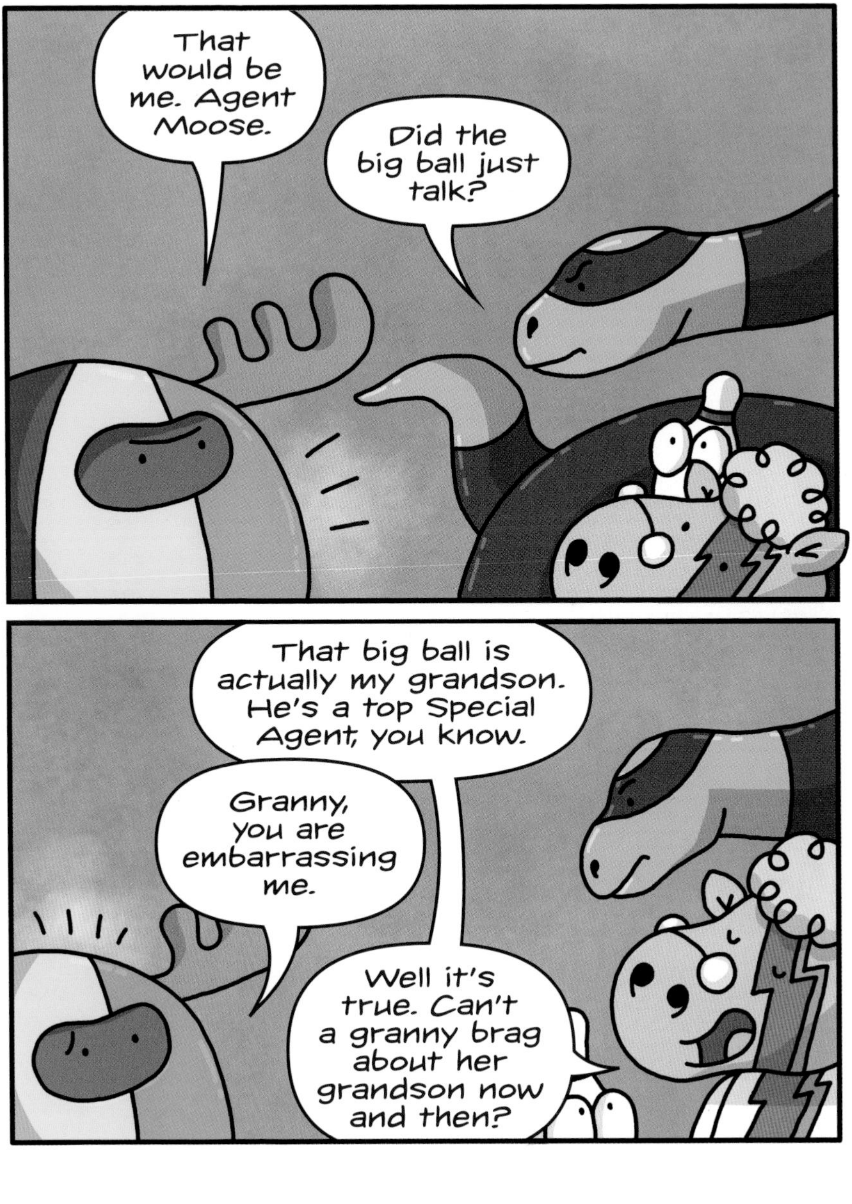
That would be me. Agent Moose.
Did the big ball just talk?
That big ball is actually my grandson. He's a top Special Agent, you know.
Granny, you are embarrassing me.
Well it's true. Can't a granny brag about her grandson now and then?

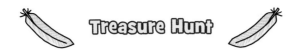

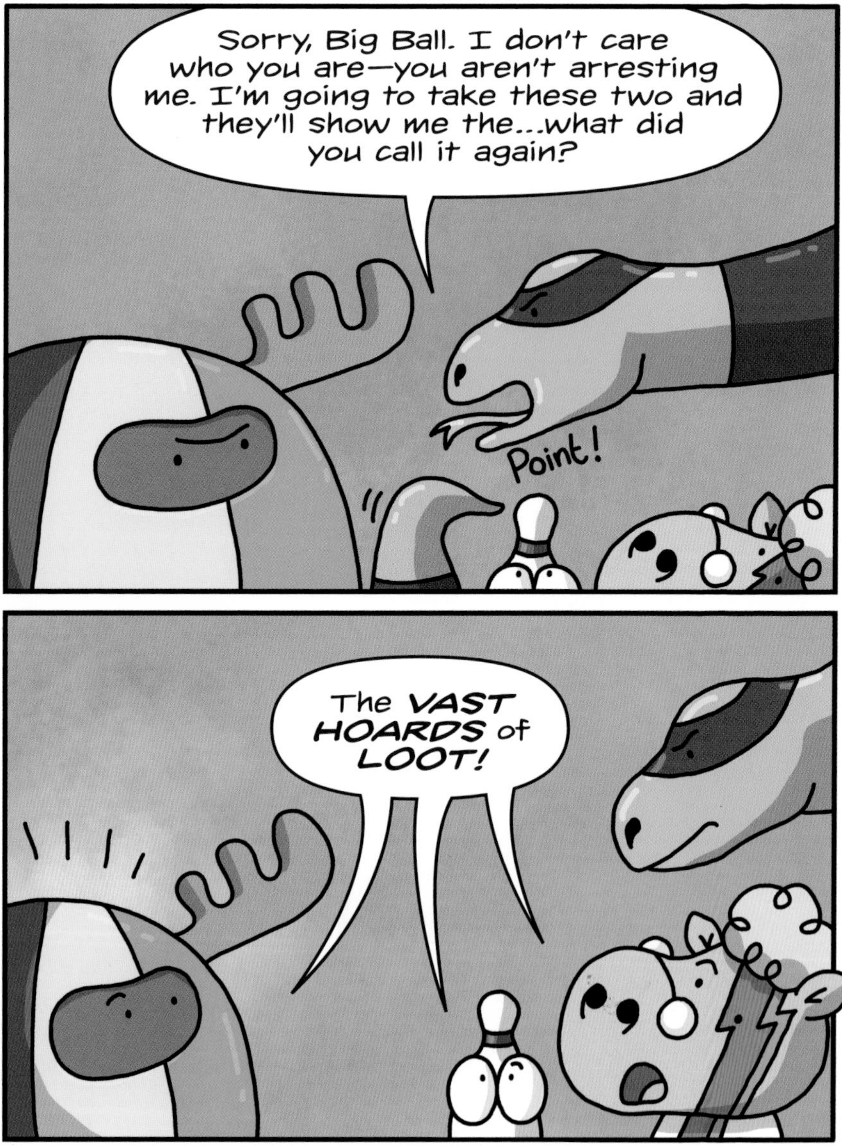
Sorry, Big Ball. I don't care who you are—you aren't arresting me. I'm going to take these two and they'll show me the...what did you call it again?
Point!
The VAST HOARDS of LOOT!

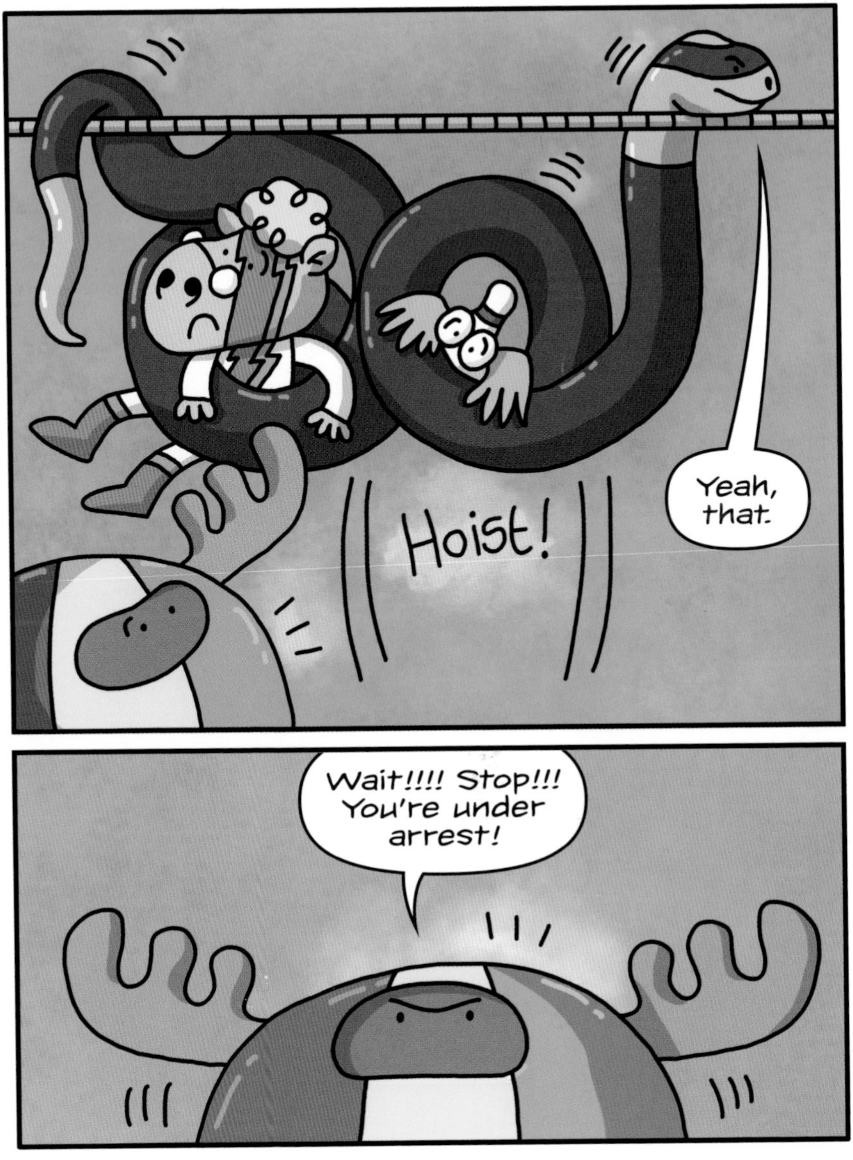
Hoist!
Yeah, that.
Wait!!!! Stop!!! You're under arrest!

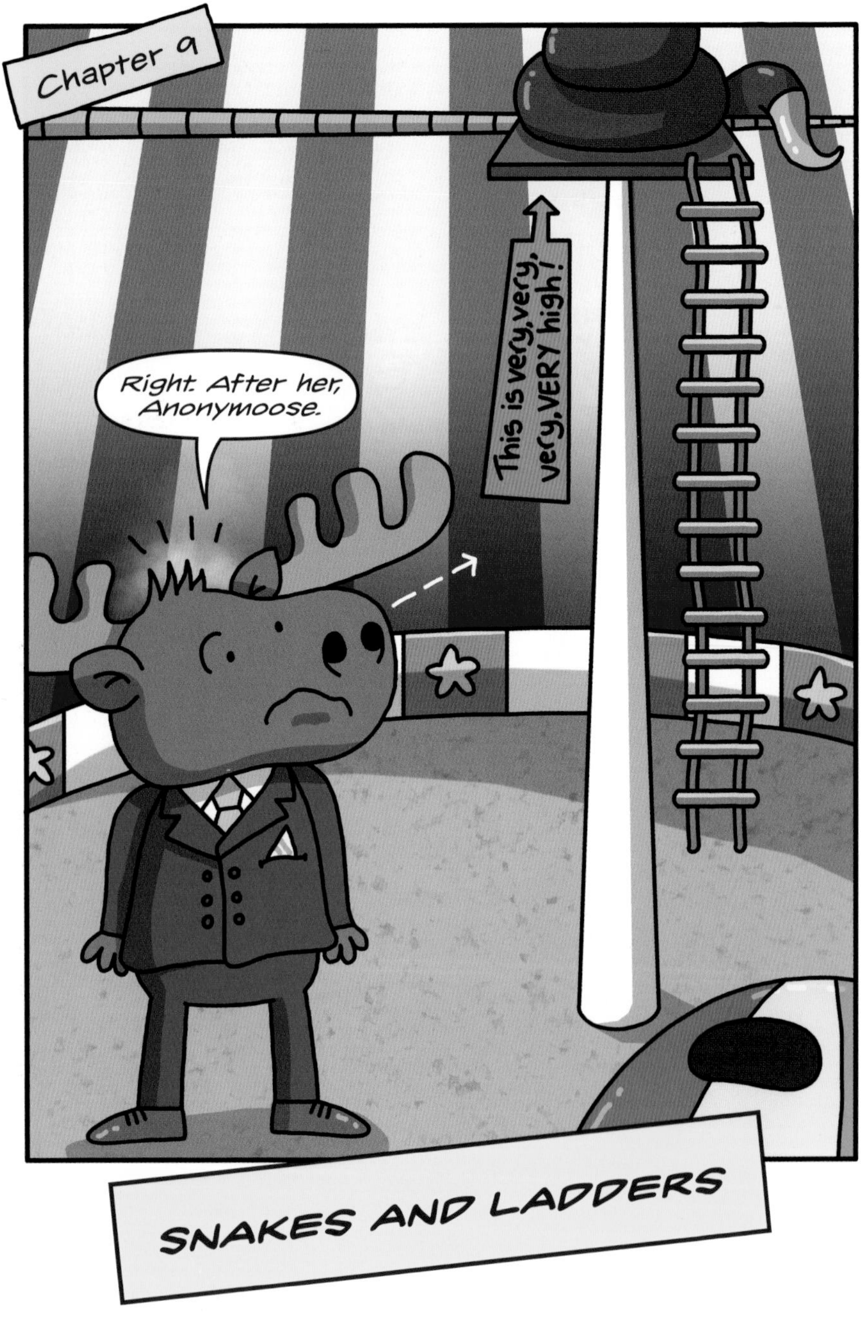
Chapter 9
This is very, very, very, VERY high!
Right. After her, Anonymoose.
SNAKES AND LADDERS

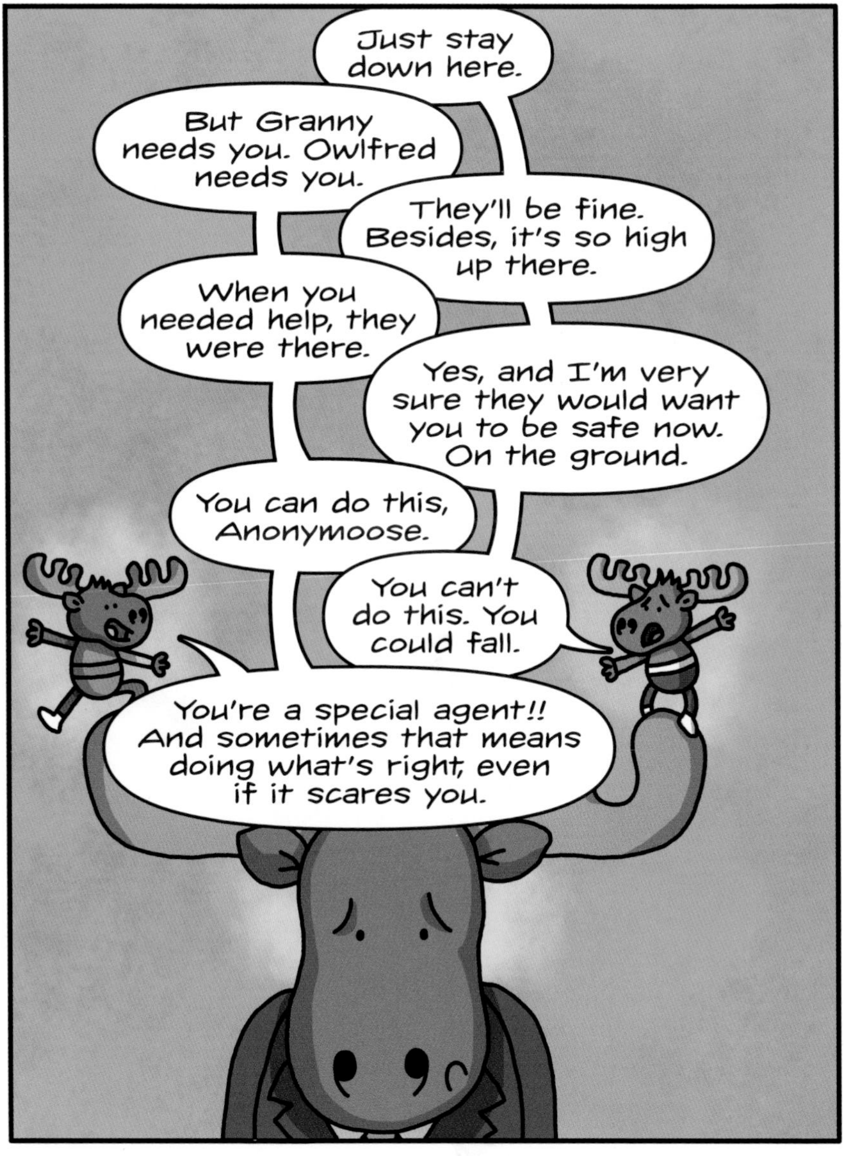
Just stay down here.
But Granny needs you. Owlfred needs you.
They'll be fine. Besides, it's so high up there.
When you needed help, they were there.
Yes, and I'm very sure they would want you to be safe now. On the ground.
You can do this, Anonymoose.
You can't do this. You could fall.
You're a special agent!! And sometimes that means doing what's right, even if it scares you.

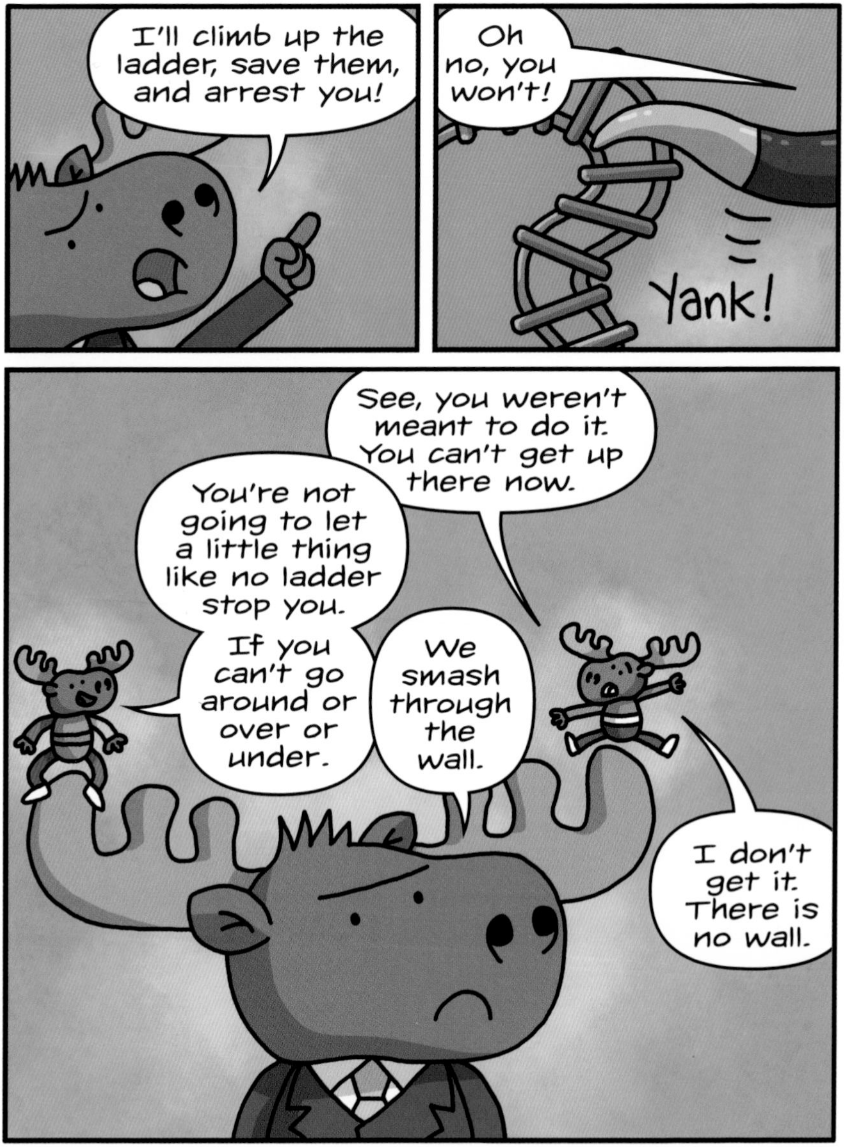
I'll climb up the ladder, save them, and arrest you!
Oh no, you won't!
Yank!
See, you weren't meant to do it. You can't get up there now.
You're not going to let a little thing like no ladder stop you.
If you can't go around or over or under.
We smash through the wall.
I don't get it. There is no wall.

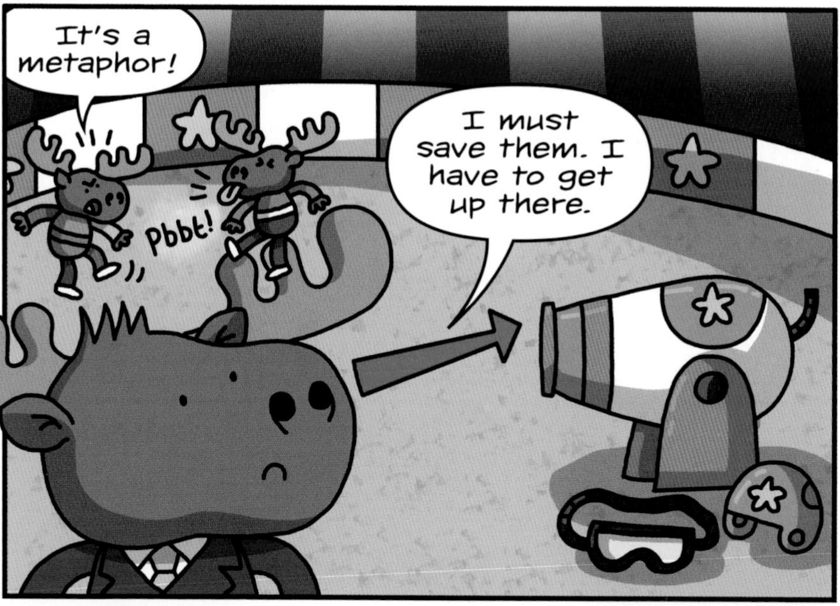
It's a metaphor!
Pbbt!
I must save them. I have to get up there.

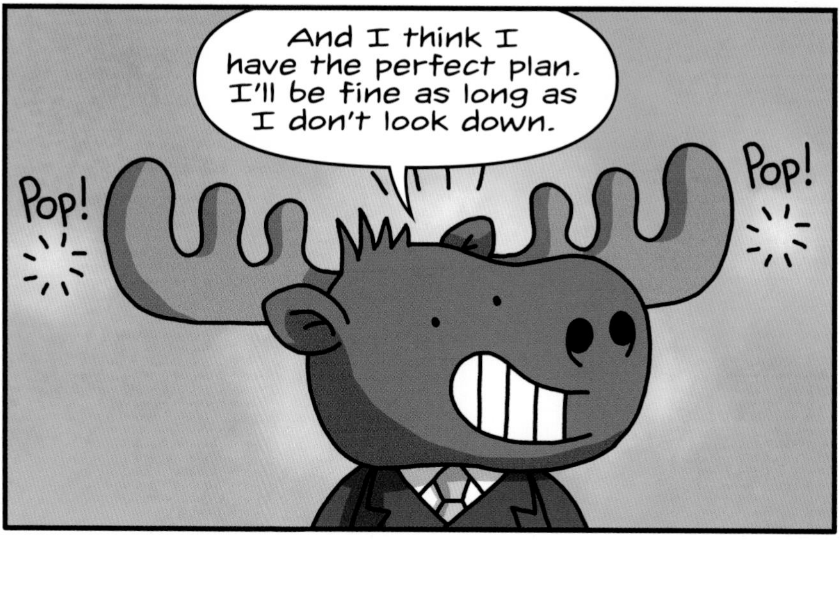
And I think I have the perfect plan. I'll be fine as long as I don't look down.
Pop!
Pop!

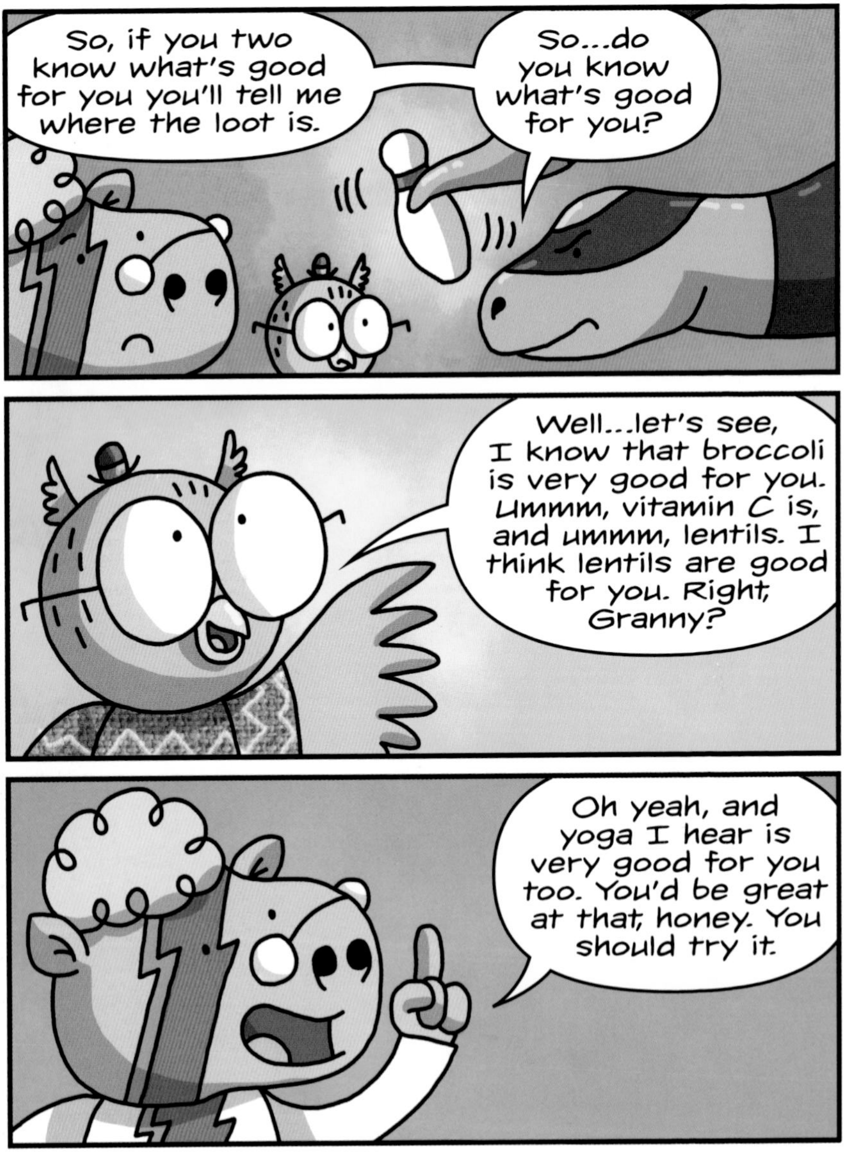
So, if you two know what's good for you you'll tell me where the loot is.
So...do you know what's good for you?
Well...let's see, I know that broccoli is very good for you. Ummm, vitamin C is, and ummm, lentils. I think lentils are good for you. Right, Granny?
Oh yeah, and yoga I hear is very good for you too. You'd be great at that, honey. You should try it.

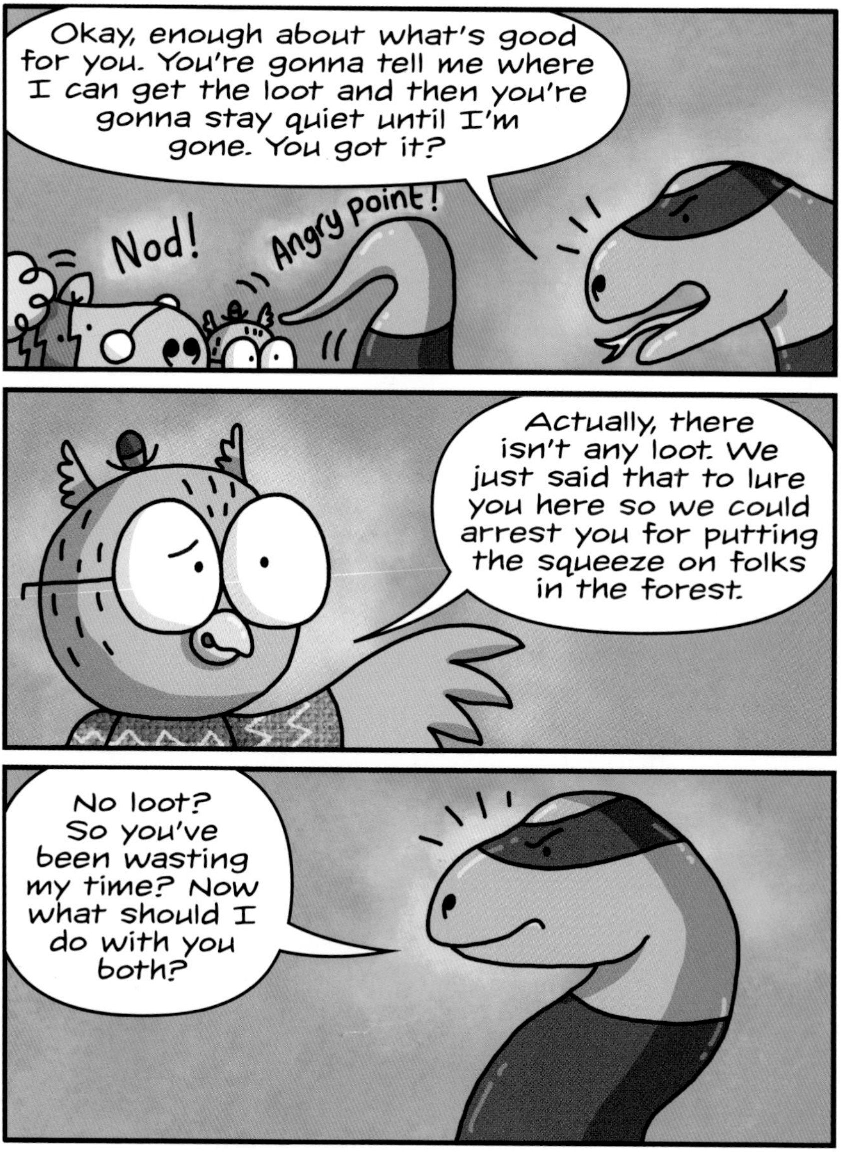
Okay, enough about what's good for you. You're gonna tell me where I can get the loot and then you're gonna stay quiet until I'm gone. You got it?
Nod!
Angry Point!
Actually, there isn't any loot. We just said that to lure you here so we could arrest you for putting the squeeze on folks in the forest.
No loot? So you've been wasting my time? Now what should I do with you both?

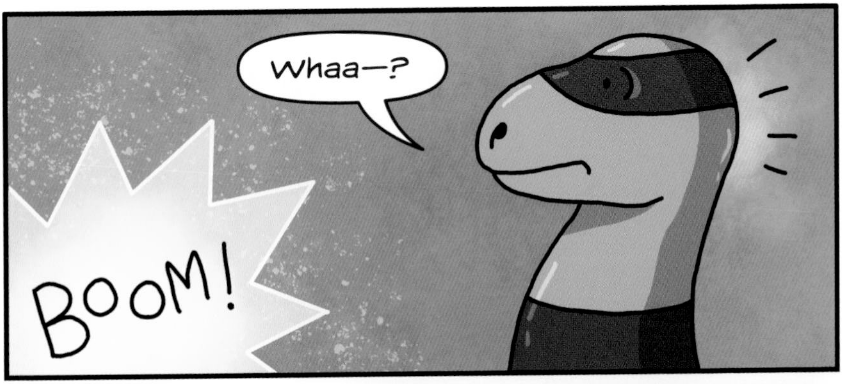
Whaa—?
BOOM!

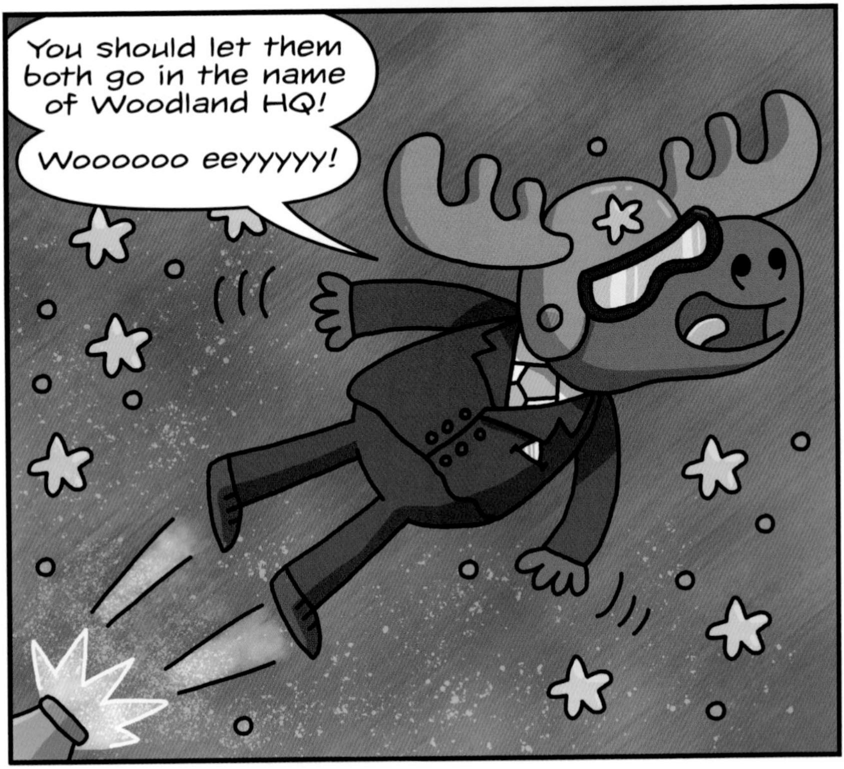
You should let them both go in the name of Woodland HQ!
Woooooo eeyyyyy!

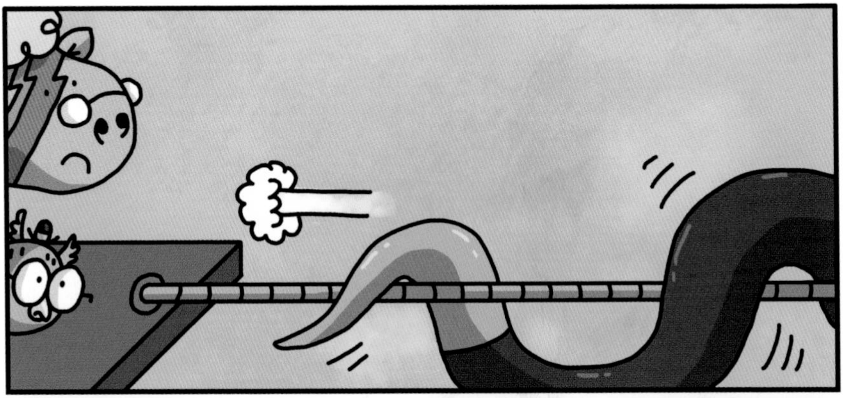

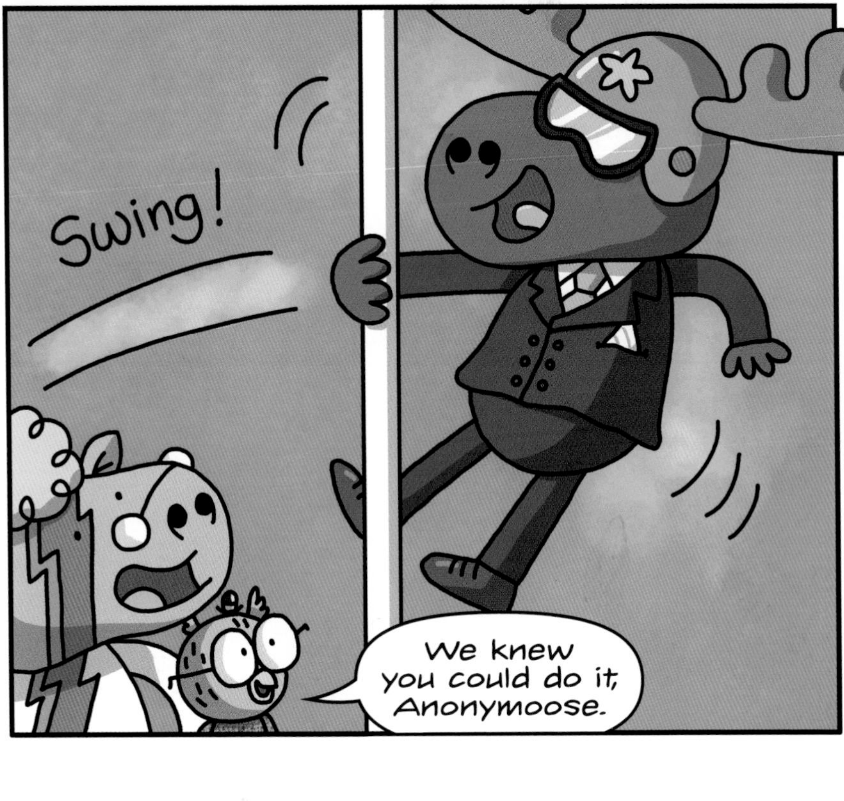
Swing!
We knew you could do it, Anonymoose.

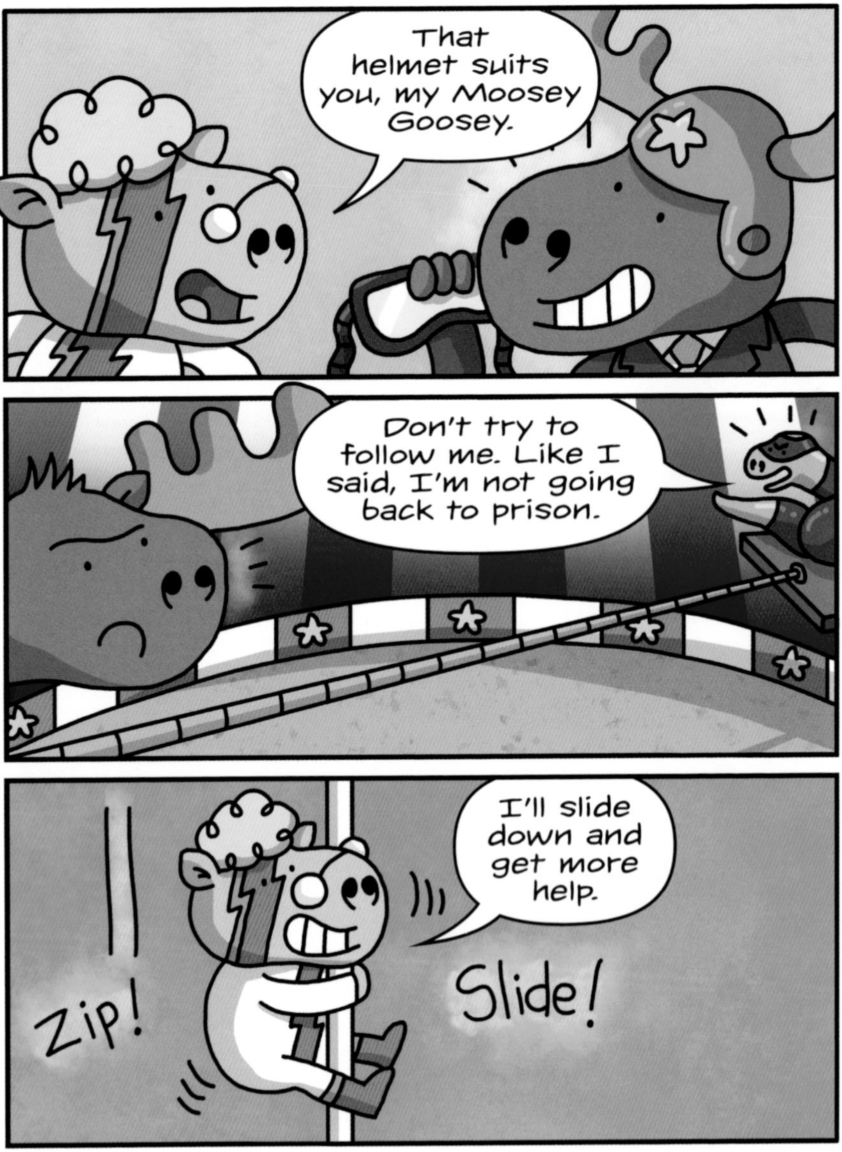
That helmet suits you, my Moosey Goosey.
Don't try to follow me. Like I said, I'm not going back to prison.
I'll slide down and get more help.
Zip!
Slide!

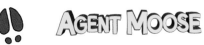

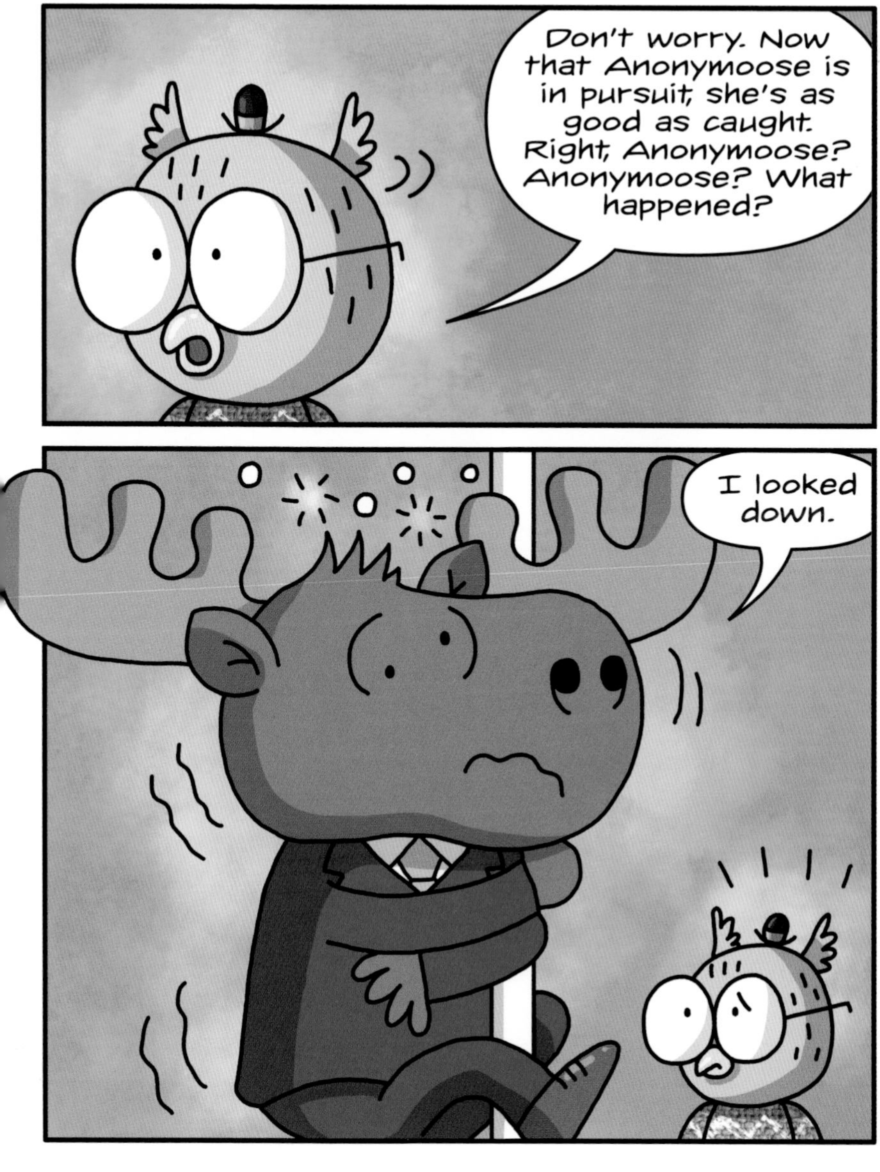
Don't worry. Now that Anonymoose is in pursuit, she's as good as caught. Right, Anonymoose? Anonymoose? What happened?
I looked down.

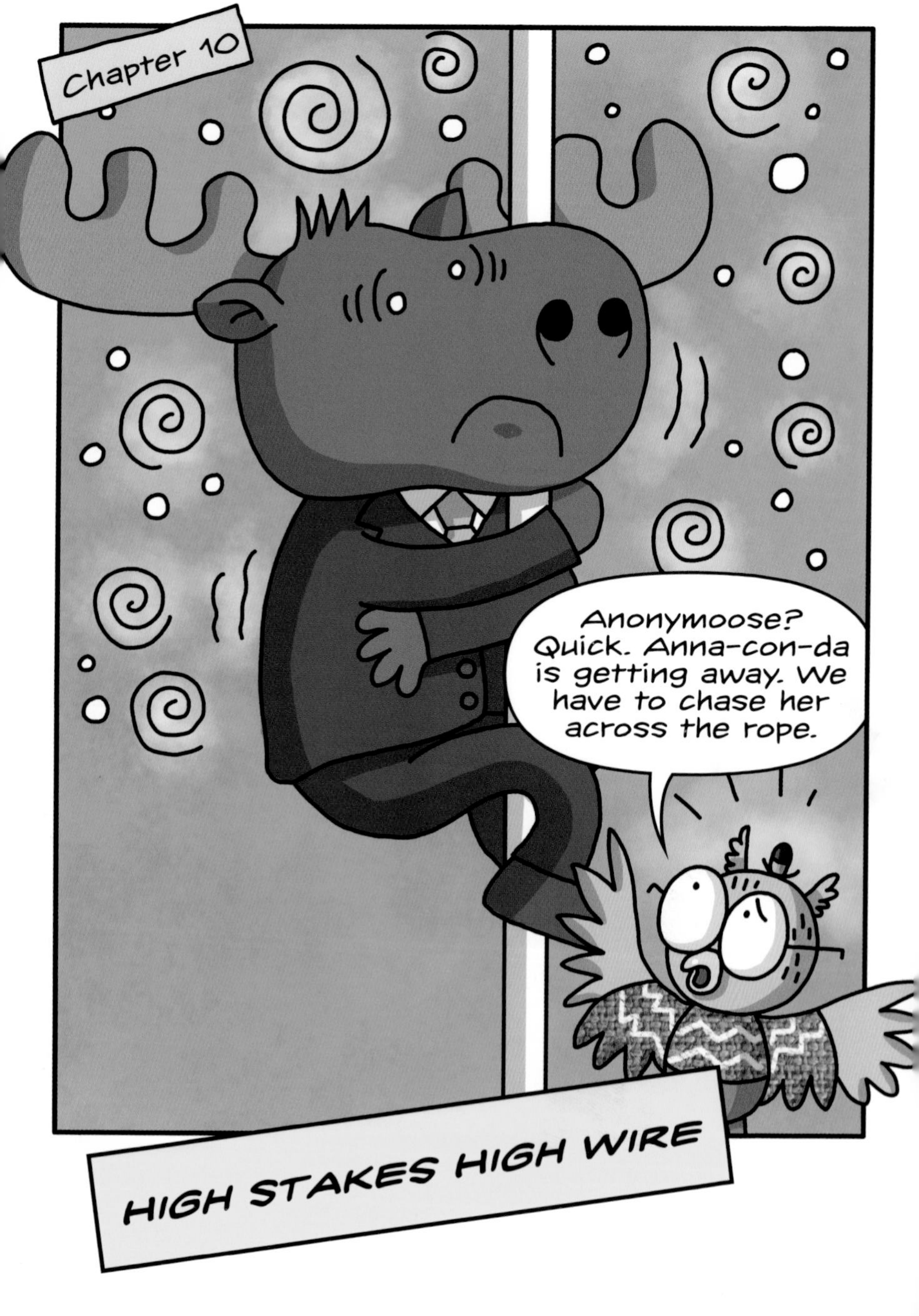
Chapter 10
Anonymoose? Quick. Anna-con-da is getting away. We have to chase her across the rope.
HIGH STAKES HIGH WIRE

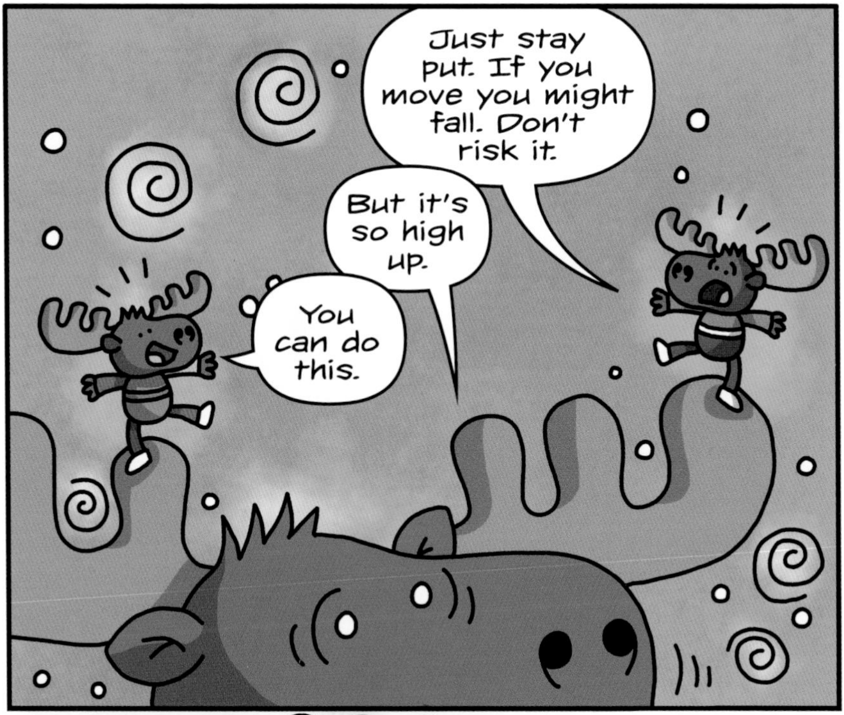
Just stay put. If you move you might fall. Don't risk it.
But it's so high up.
You can do this.

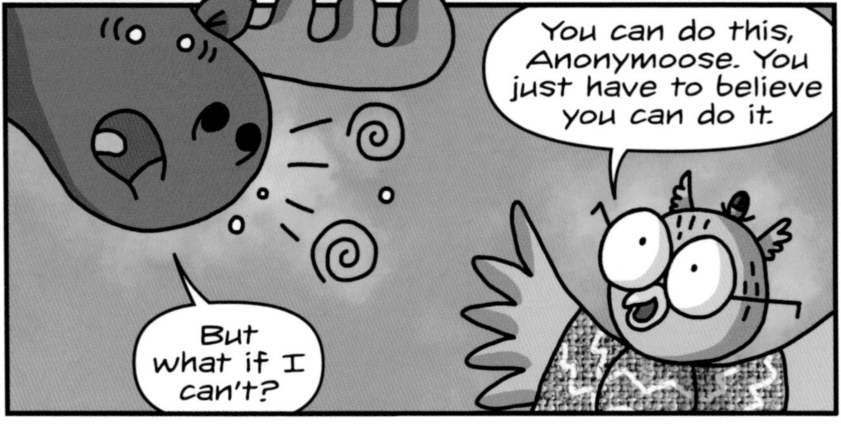
You can do this, Anonymoose. You just have to believe you can do it.
But what if I can't?

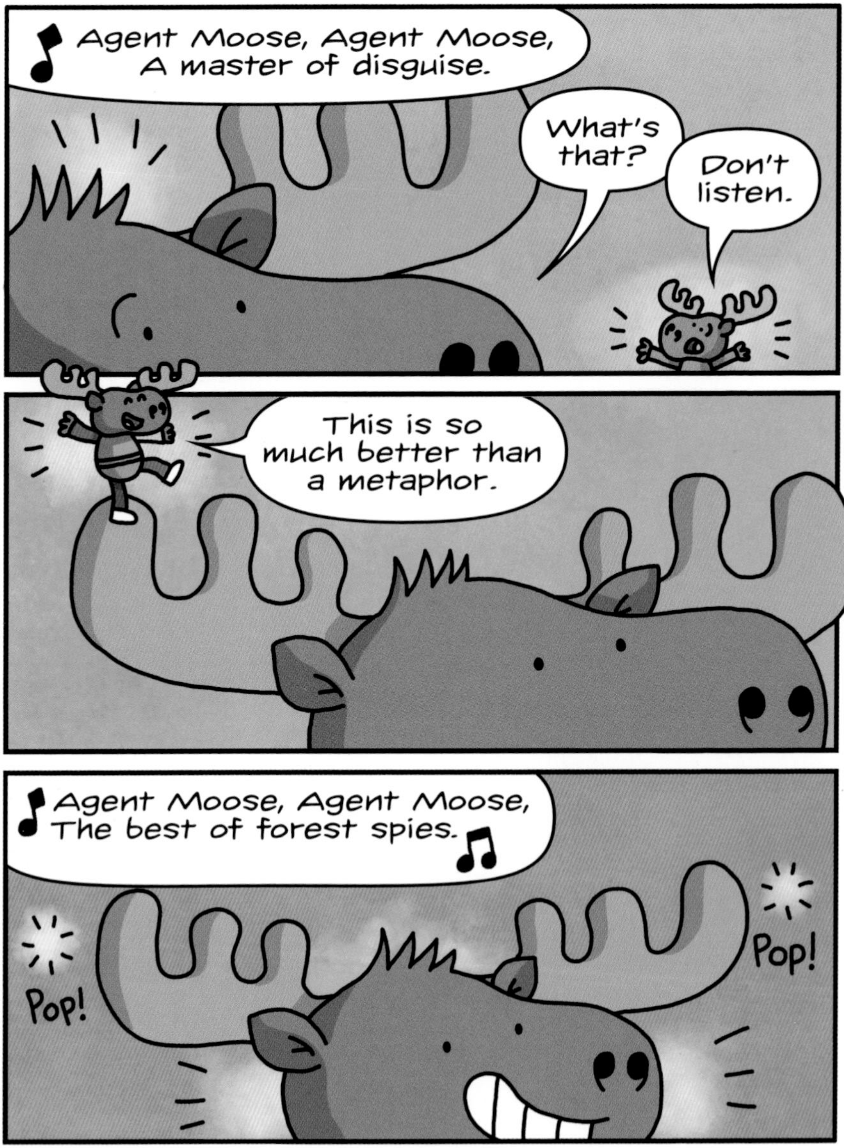
Agent Moose, Agent Moose,
A master of disguise.
What's that?
Don't listen.
This is so much better than a metaphor.
Agent Moose, Agent Moose,
The best of forest spies.
Pop!
Pop!

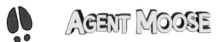

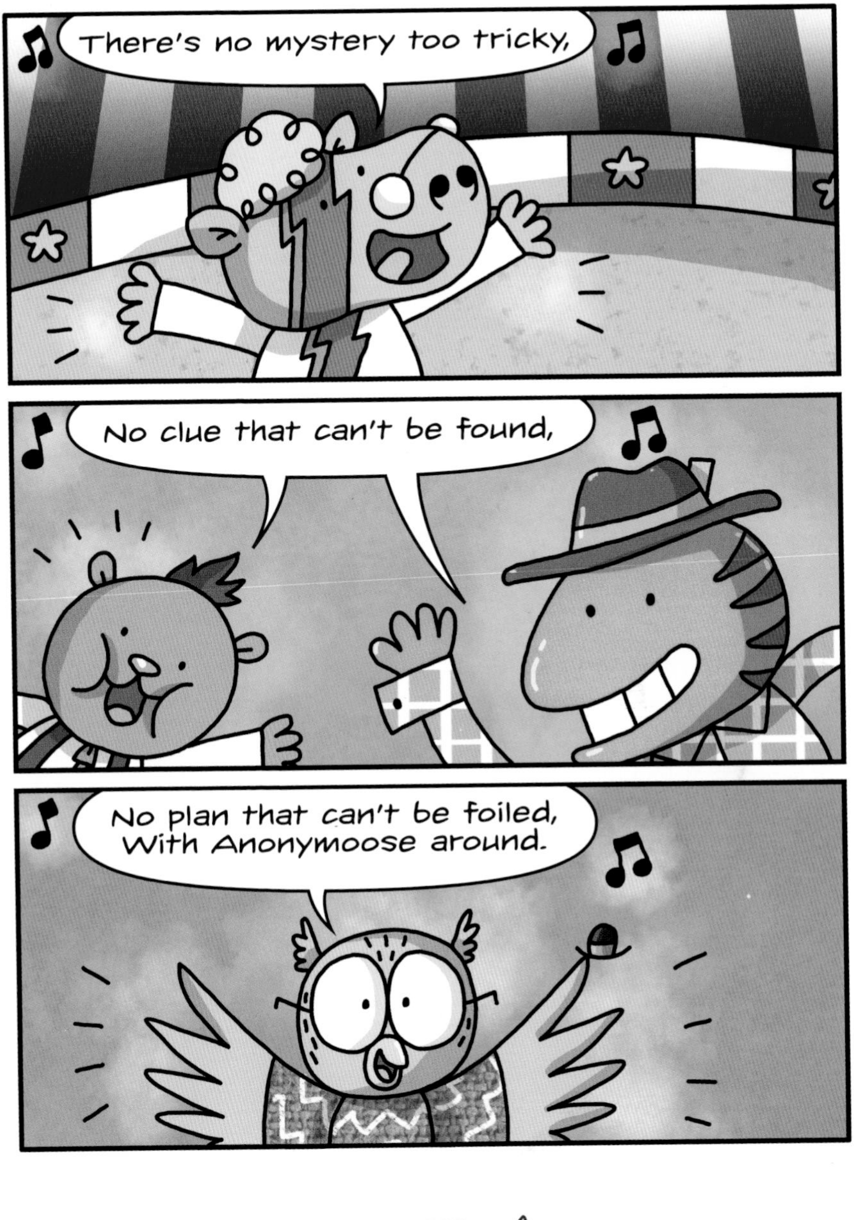
There's no mystery too tricky,
No clue that can't be found,
No plan that can't be foiled,
With Anonymoose around.

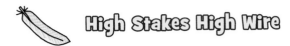

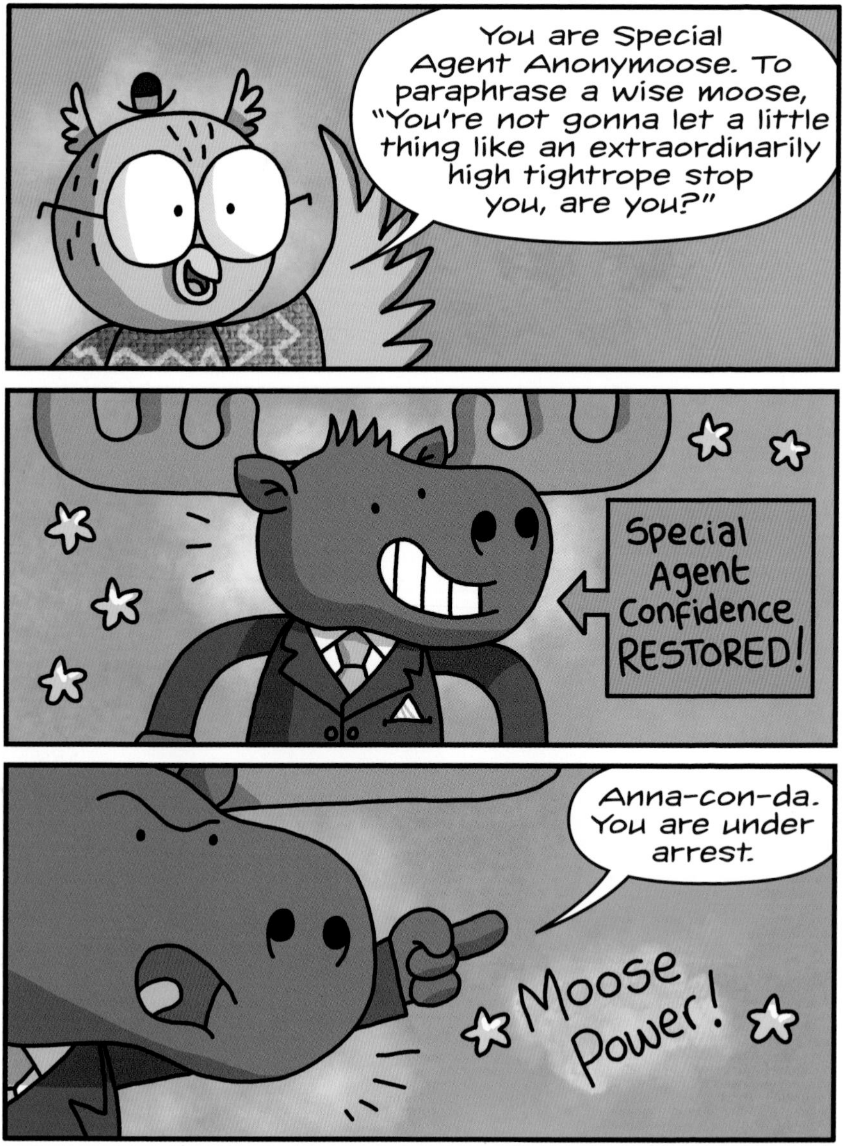
You are Special Agent Anonymoose. To paraphrase a wise moose, "You're not gonna let a little thing like an extraordinarily high tightrope stop you, are you?"
Special Agent Confidence RESTORED!
Anna-con-da. You are under arrest.
Moose Power!

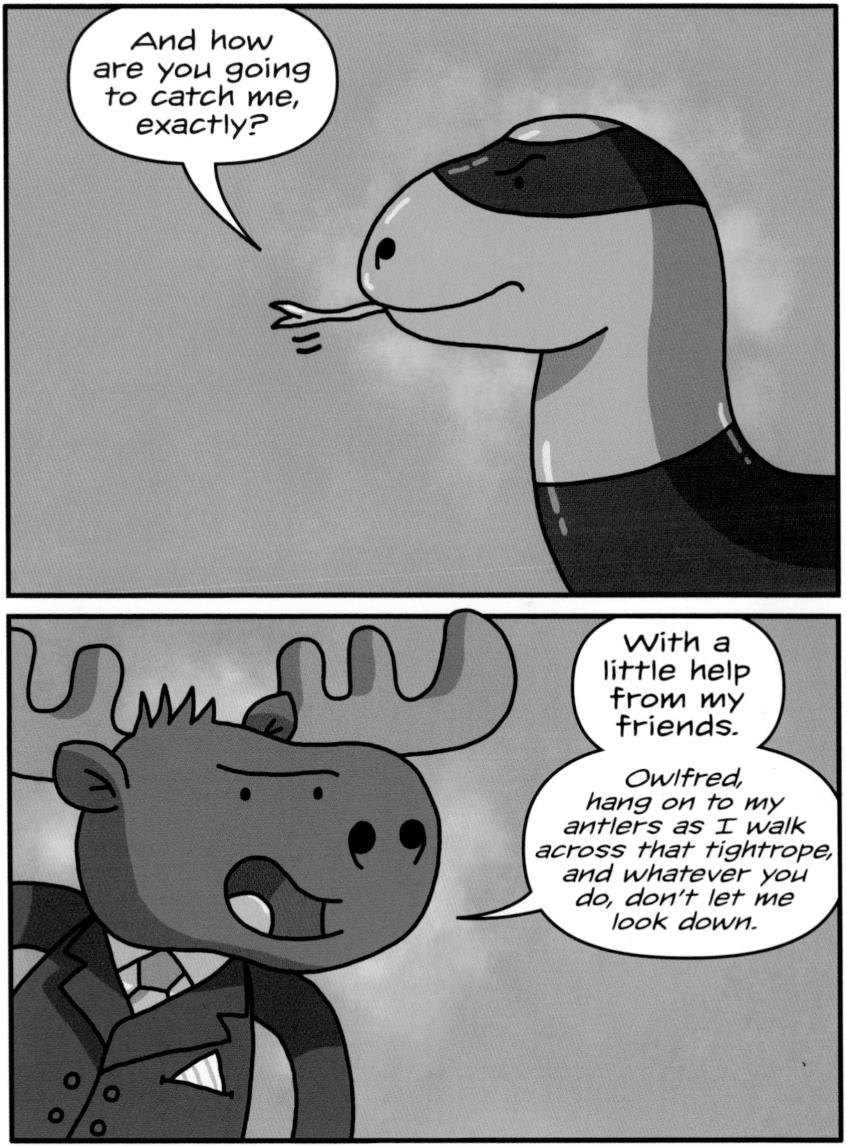
And how are you going to catch me, exactly?
With a little help from my friends.
Owlfred, hang on to my antlers as I walk across that tightrope, and whatever you do, don't let me look down.

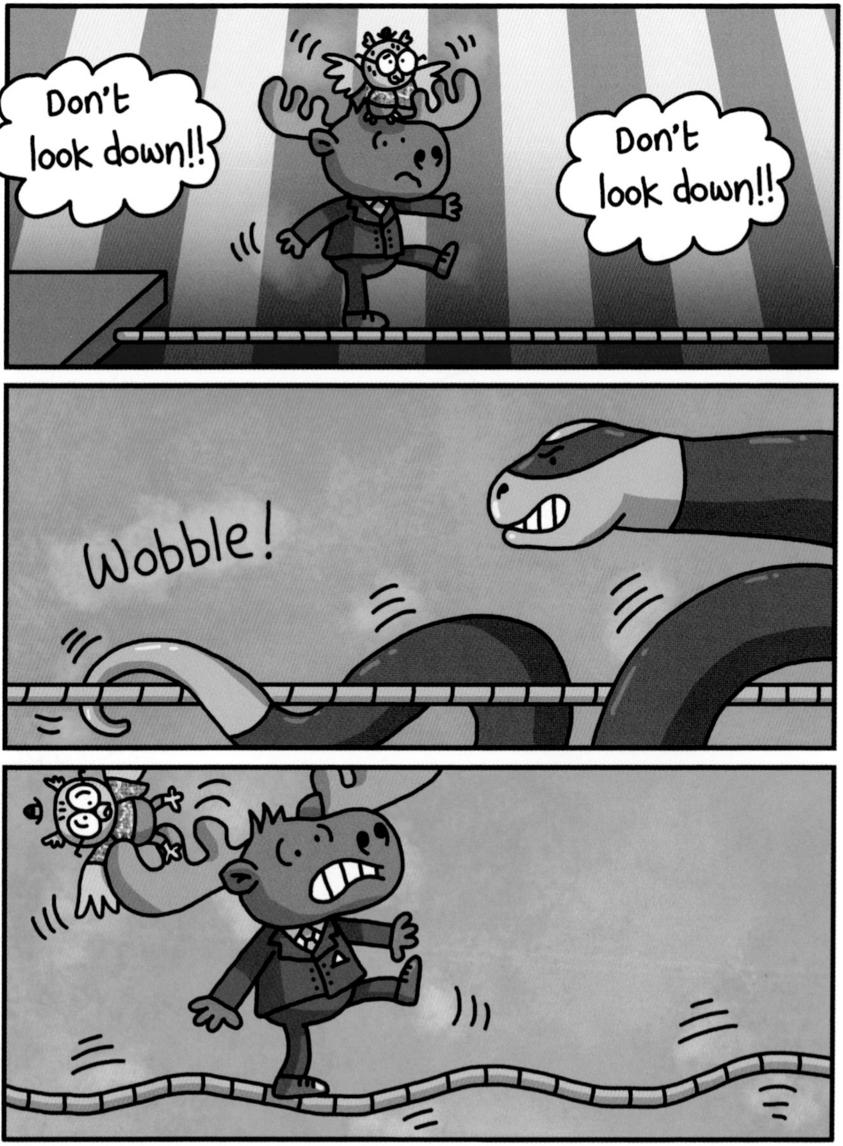
Don't look down!!
Don't look down!!
Wobble!

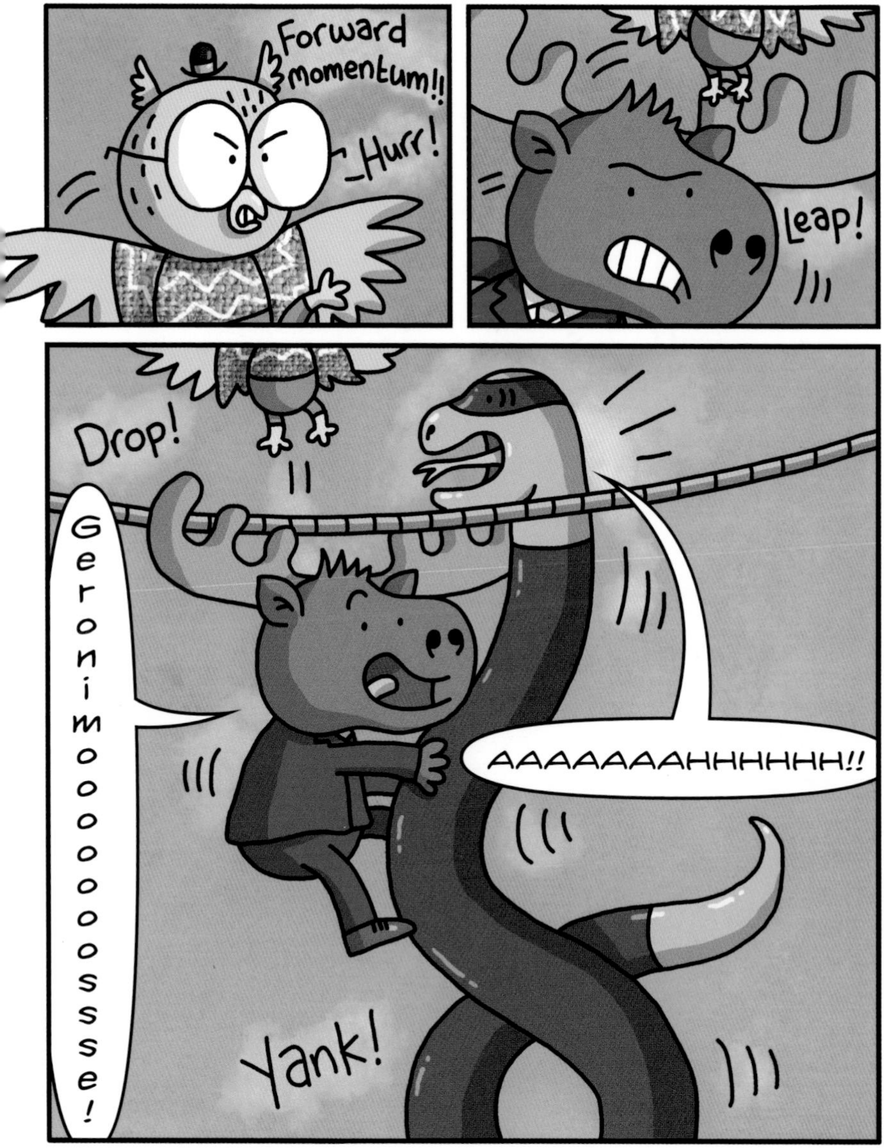
Forward momentum!!
Hurr!
Leap!
Drop!
Geronimoooooooooosse!
AAAAAAAHHHHHH!!
Yank!

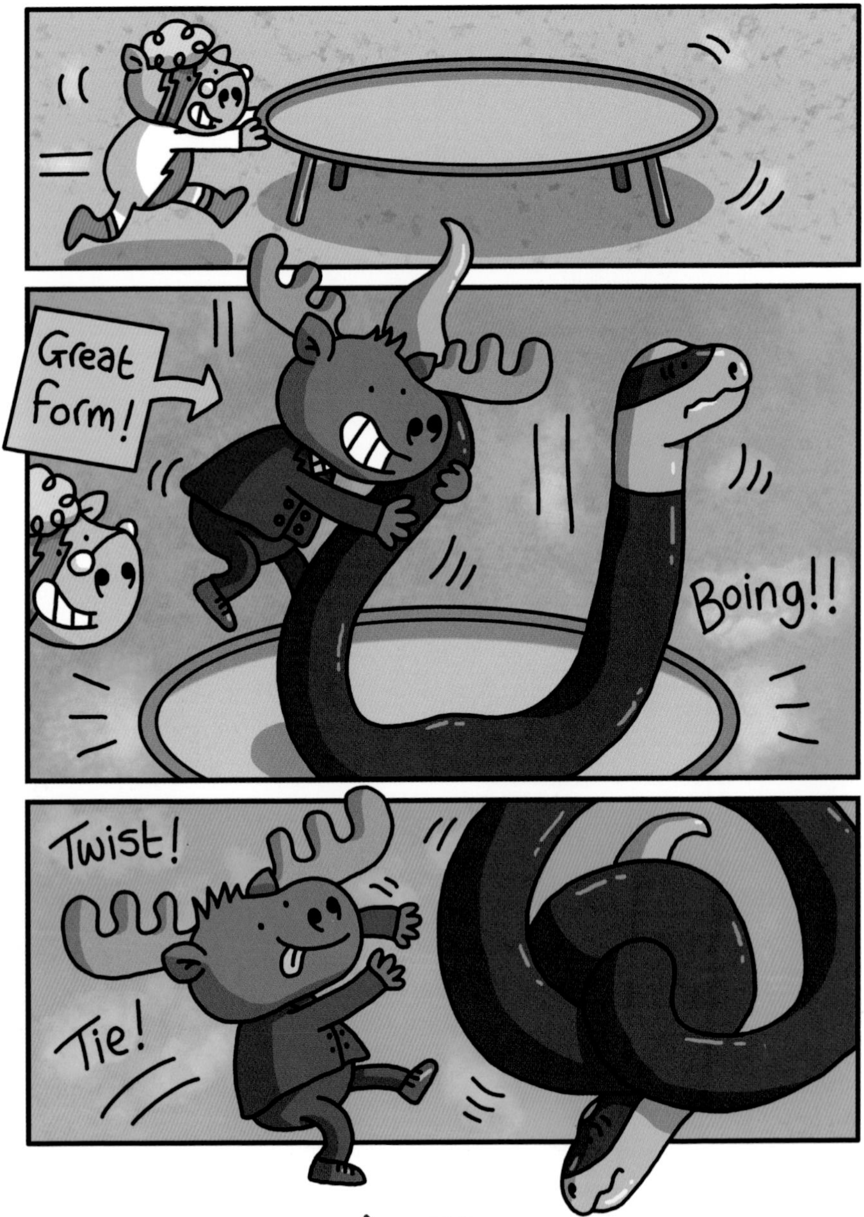
Great form!
Boing!!
Twist!
Tie!

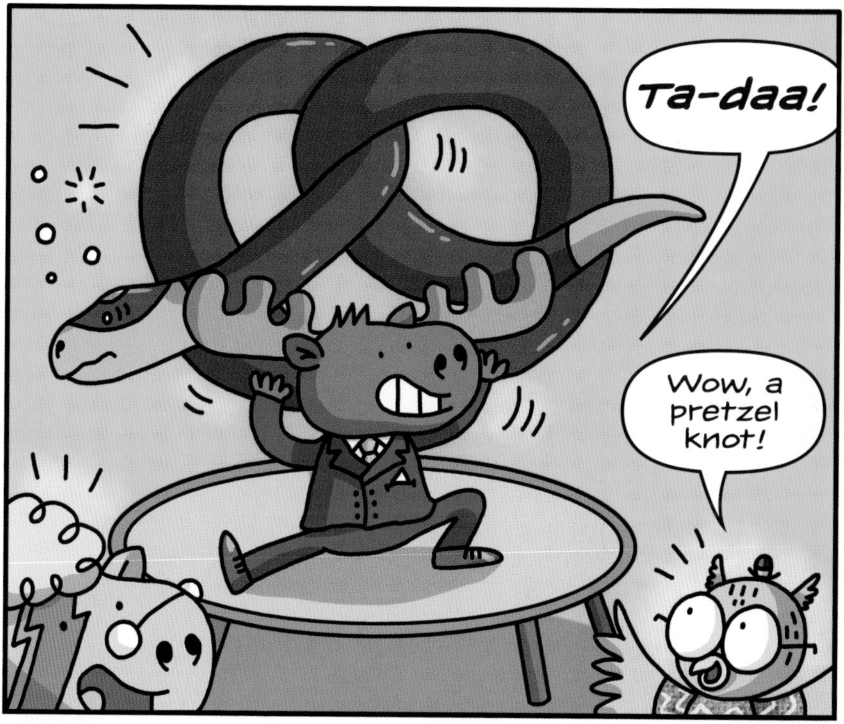
Ta-daa!
Wow, a pretzel knot!

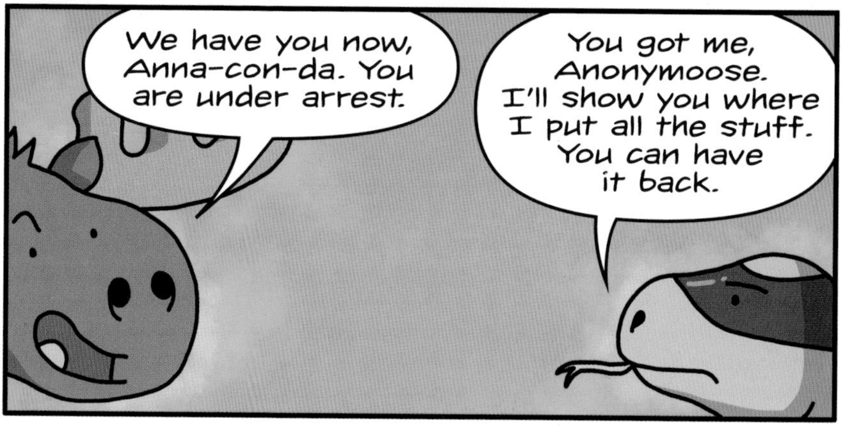
We have you now, Anna-con-da. You are under arrest.
You got me, Anonymoose. I'll show you where I put all the stuff. You can have it back.

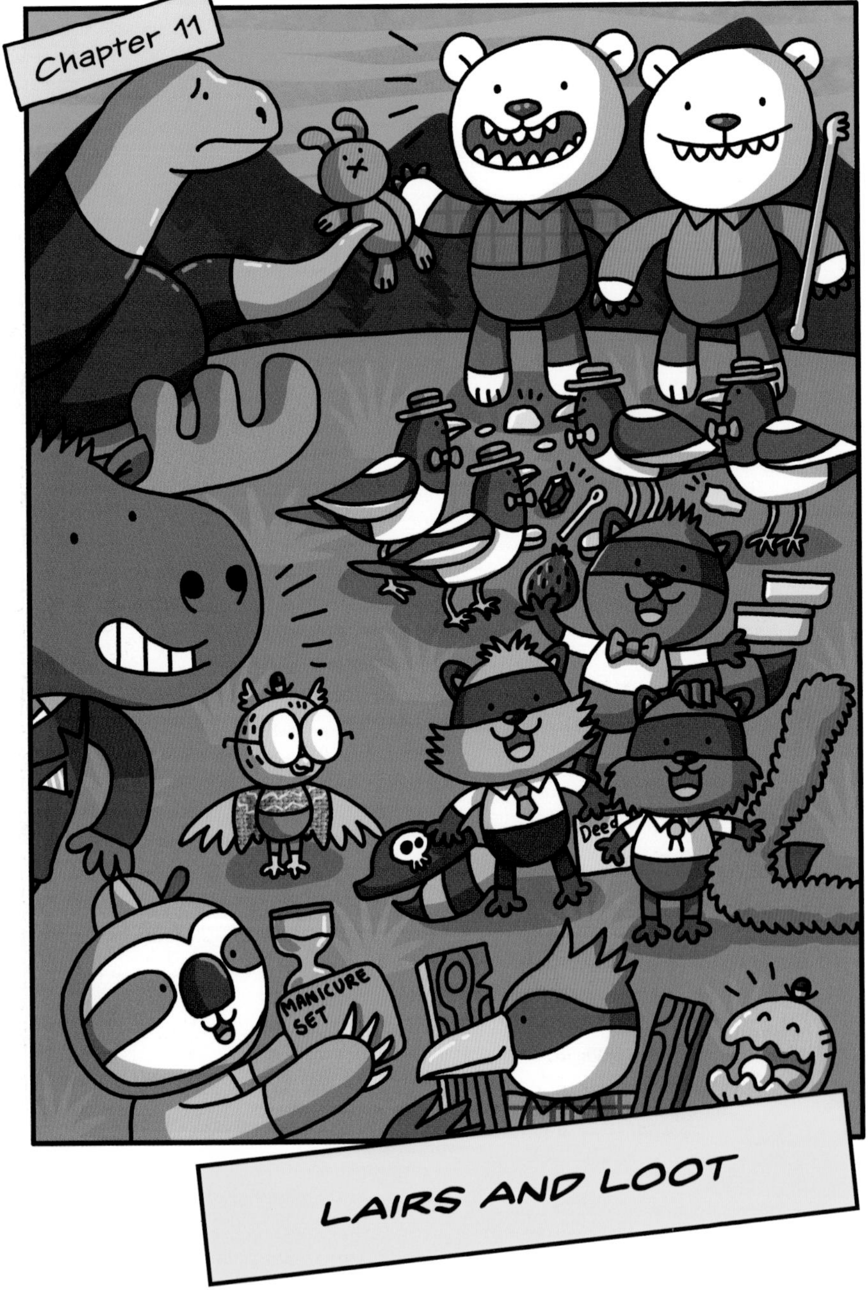
Chapter 11
MANICURE SET
Deed
LAIRS AND LOOT

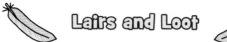

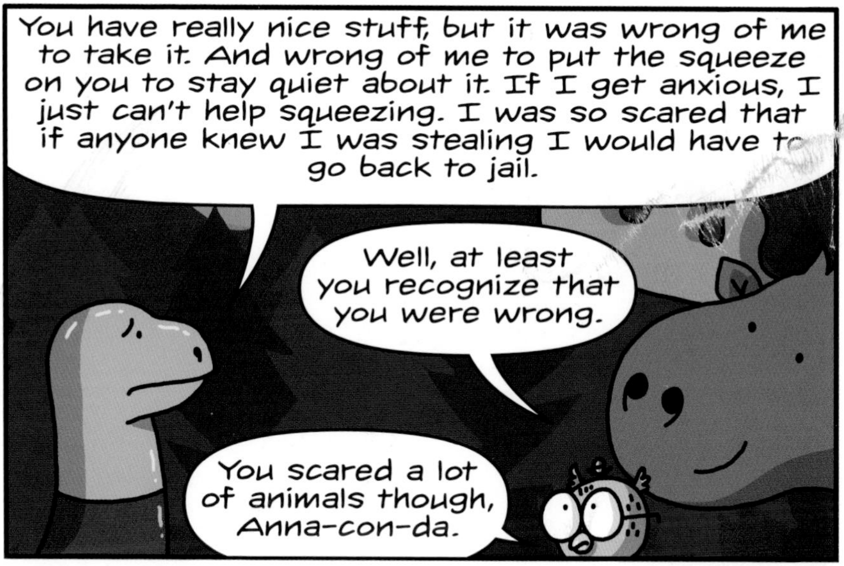
You have really nice stuff, but it was wrong of me to take it. And wrong of me to put the squeeze on you to stay quiet about it. If I get anxious, I just can't help squeezing. I was so scared that if anyone knew I was stealing I would have to go back to jail.
Well, at least you recognize that you were wrong.
You scared a lot of animals though, Anna-con-da.

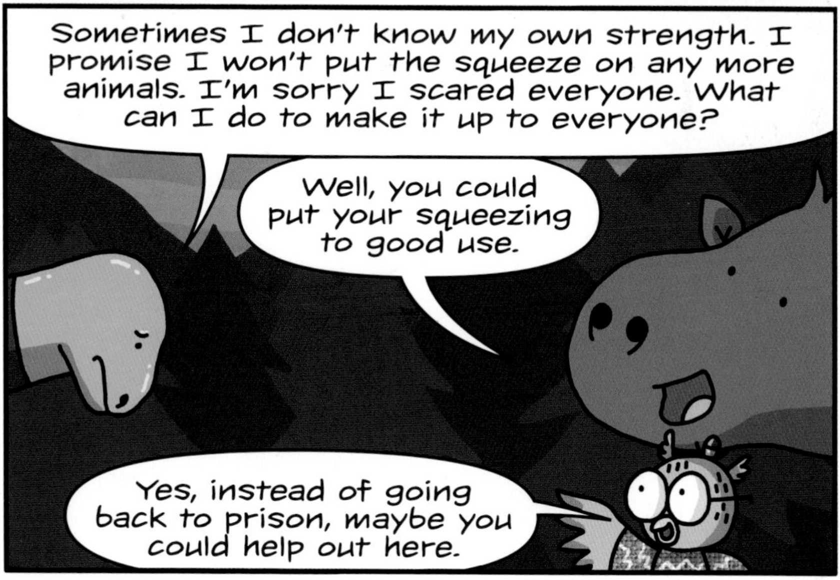
Sometimes I don't know my own strength. I promise I won't put the squeeze on any more animals. I'm sorry I scared everyone. What can I do to make it up to everyone?
Well, you could put your squeezing to good use.
Yes, instead of going back to prison, maybe you could help out here.

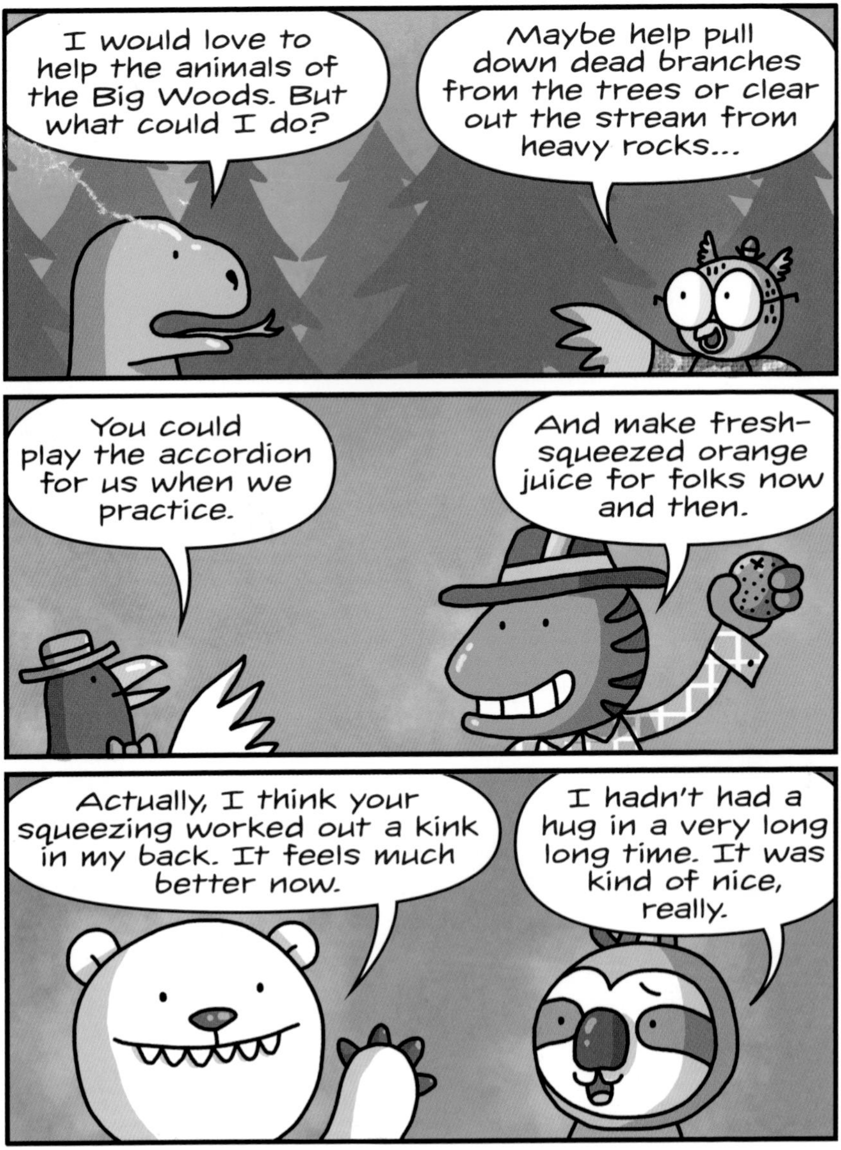
I would love to help the animals of the Big Woods. But what could I do?
Maybe help pull down dead branches from the trees or clear out the stream from heavy rocks...
You could play the accordion for us when we practice.
And make fresh-squeezed orange juice for folks now and then.
Actually, I think your squeezing worked out a kink in my back. It feels much better now.
I hadn't had a hug in a very long long time. It was kind of nice, really.

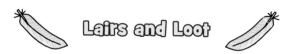

Thanks, animals. I won't scare anyone anymore and when I'm done helping everyone that needs it, I'll head out of the Big Woods and won't cause any more trouble for any of you.

Actually, I might have another idea of what you can do.

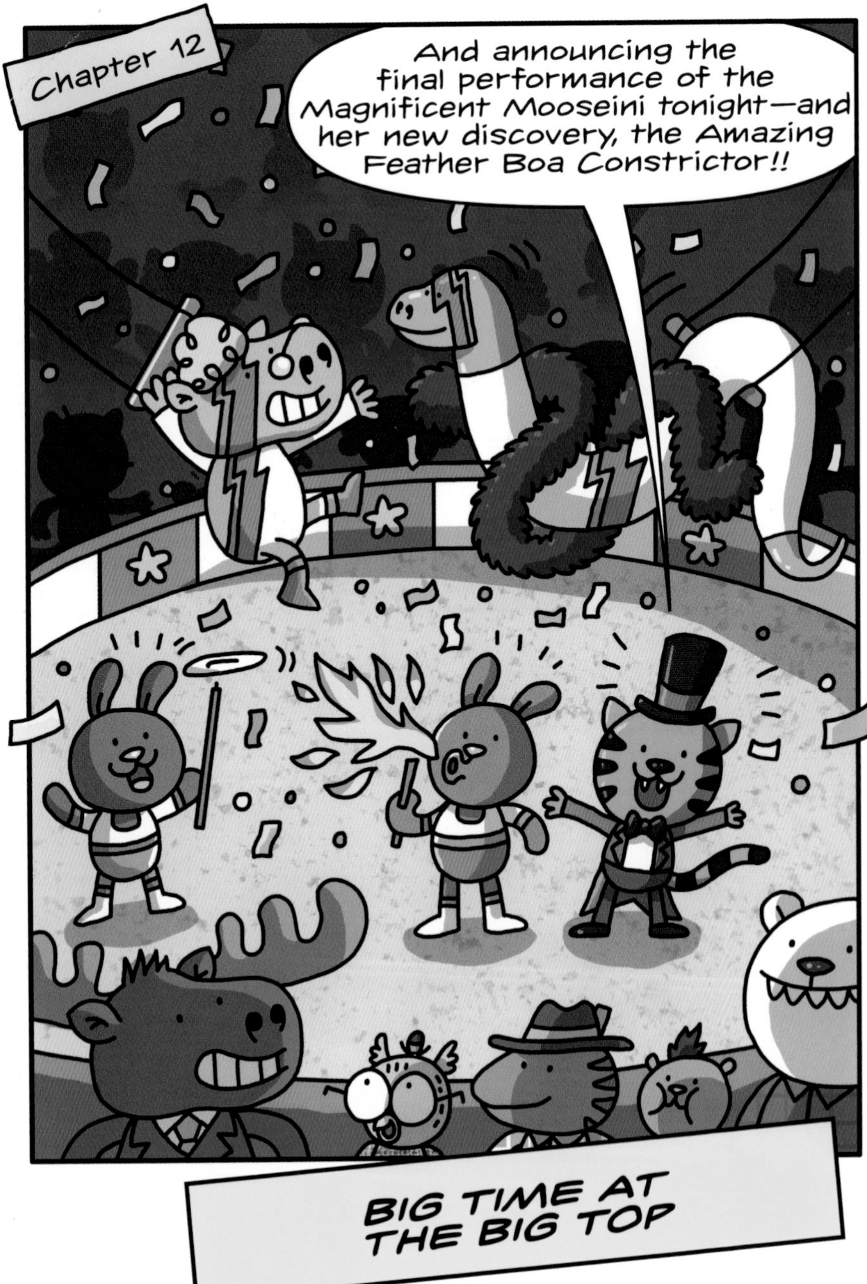
Chapter 12
And announcing the final performance of the Magnificent Mooseini tonight—and her new discovery, the Amazing Feather Boa Constrictor!!
BIG TIME AT THE BIG TOP

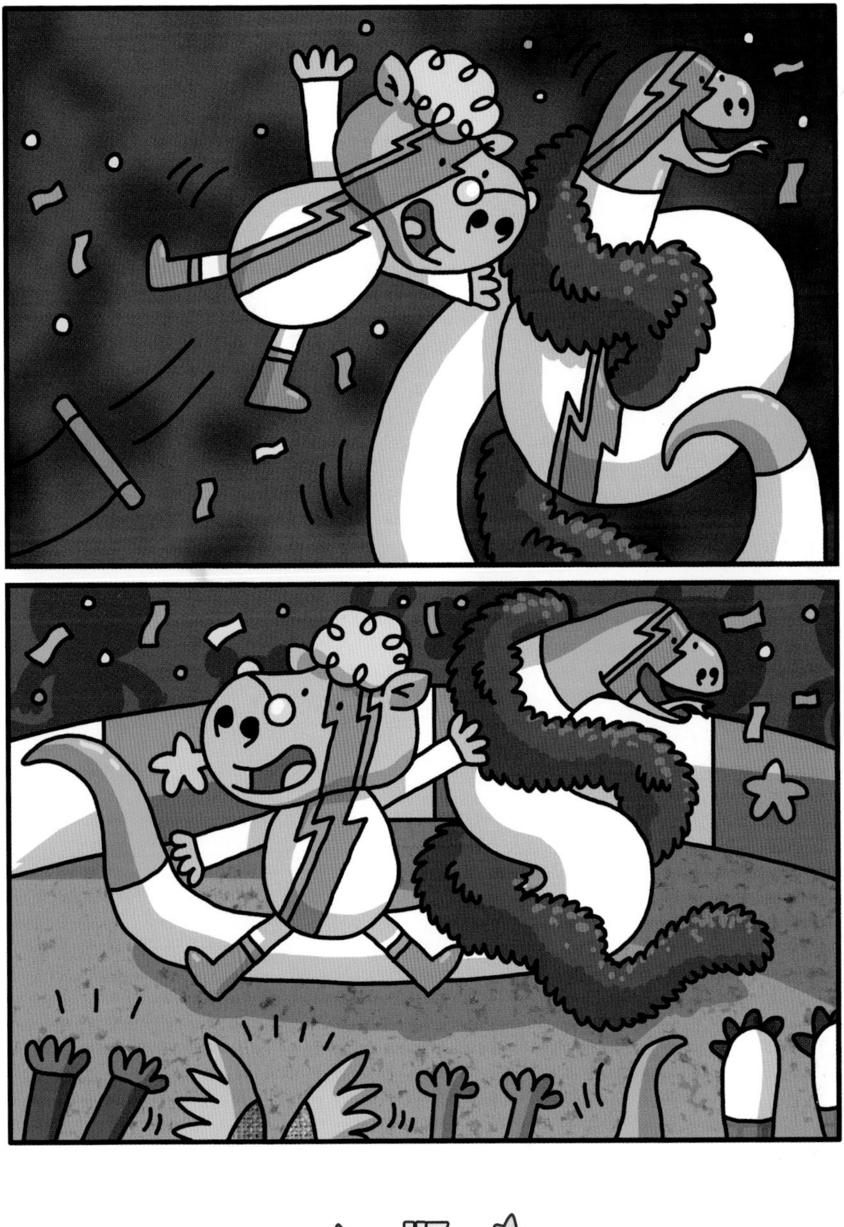

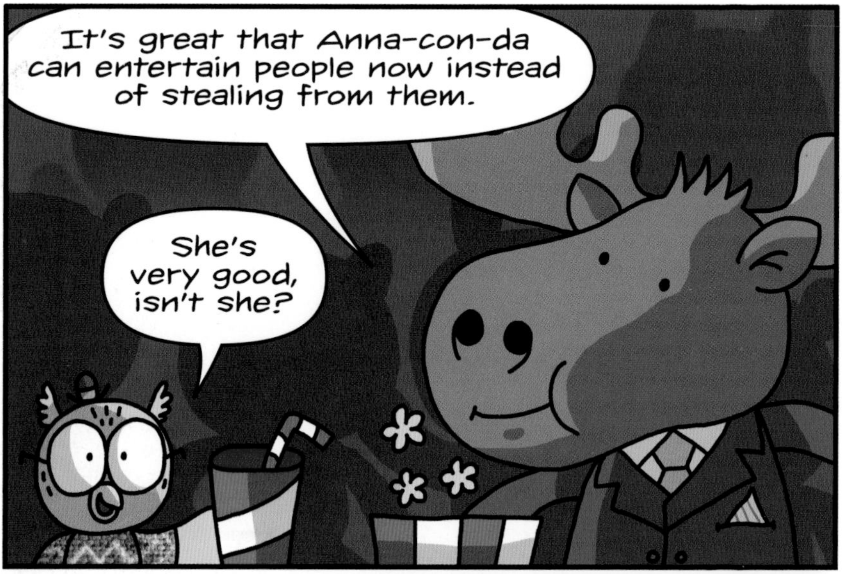
It's great that Anna-con-da can entertain people now instead of stealing from them.
She's very good, isn't she?

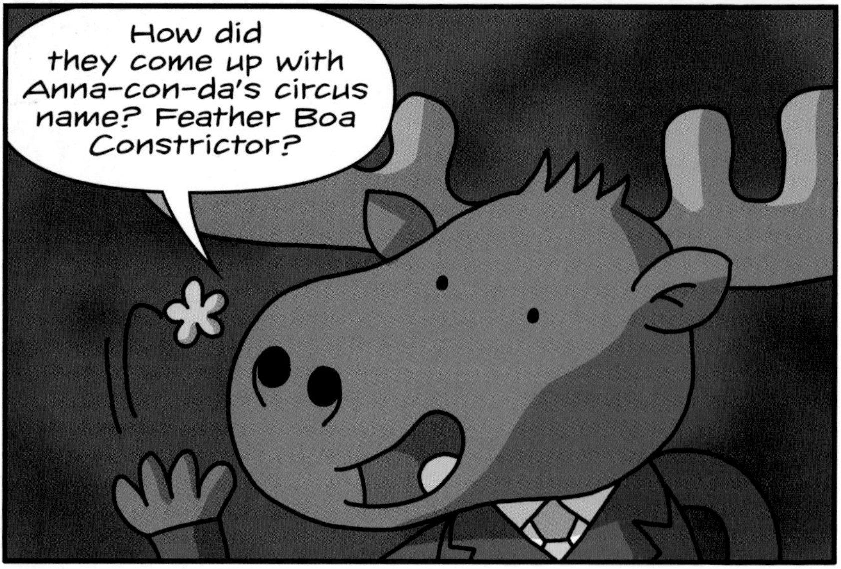
How did they come up with Anna-con-da's circus name? Feather Boa Constrictor?

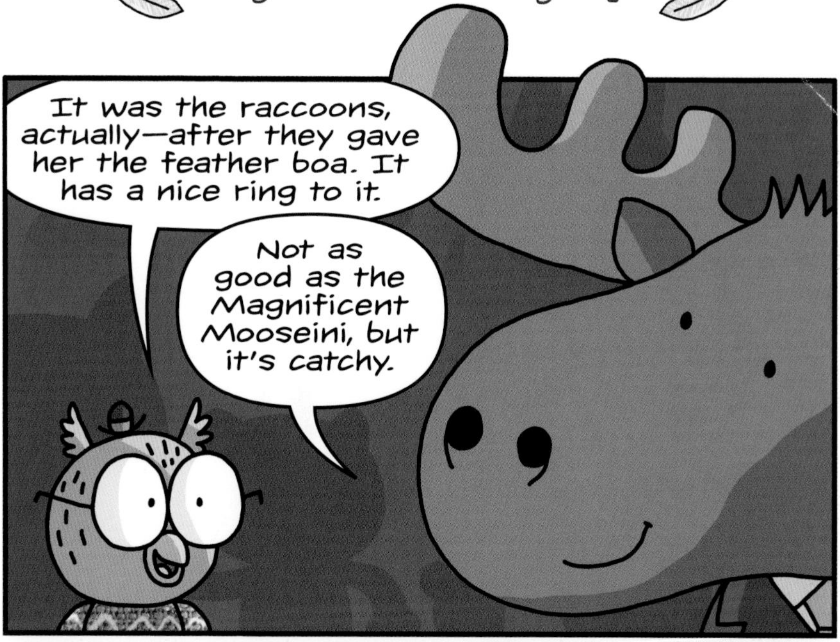
It was the raccoons, actually—after they gave her the feather boa. It has a nice ring to it.
Not as good as the Magnificent Mooseini, but it's catchy.

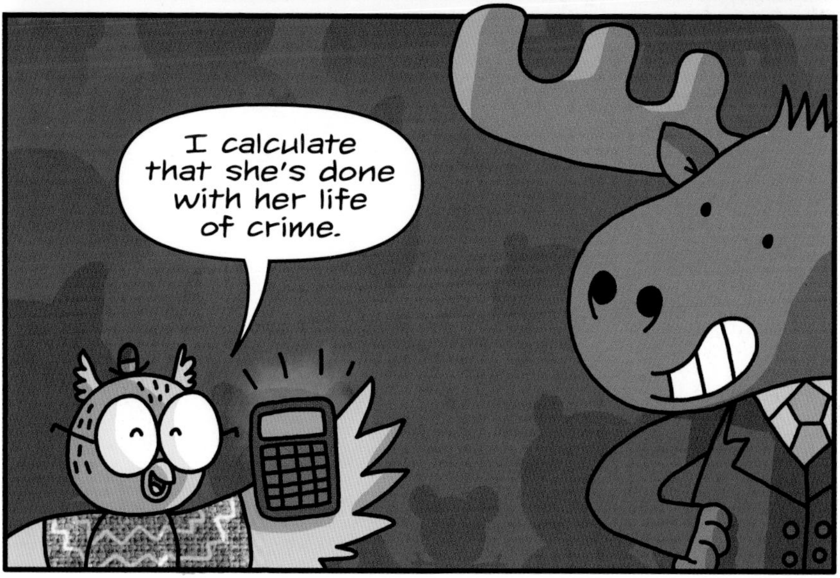
I calculate that she's done with her life of crime.

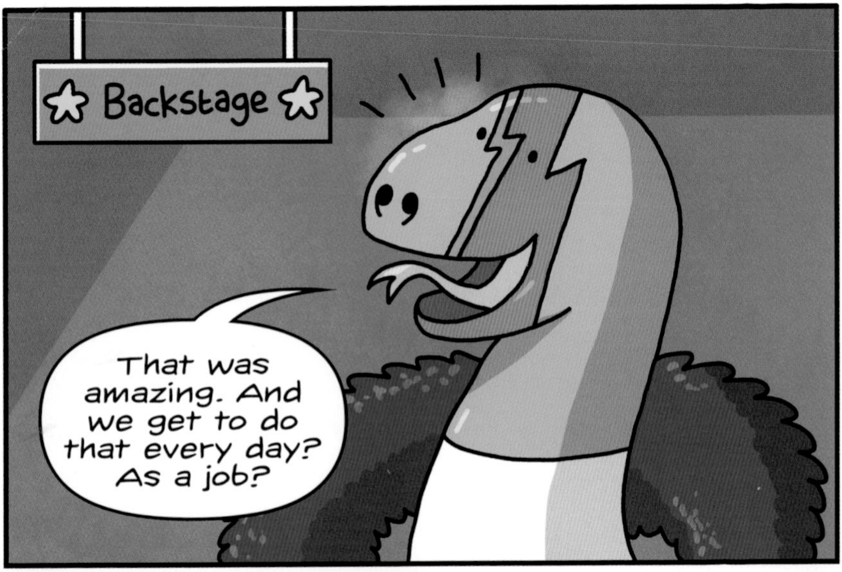
Backstage
That was amazing. And we get to do that every day? As a job?

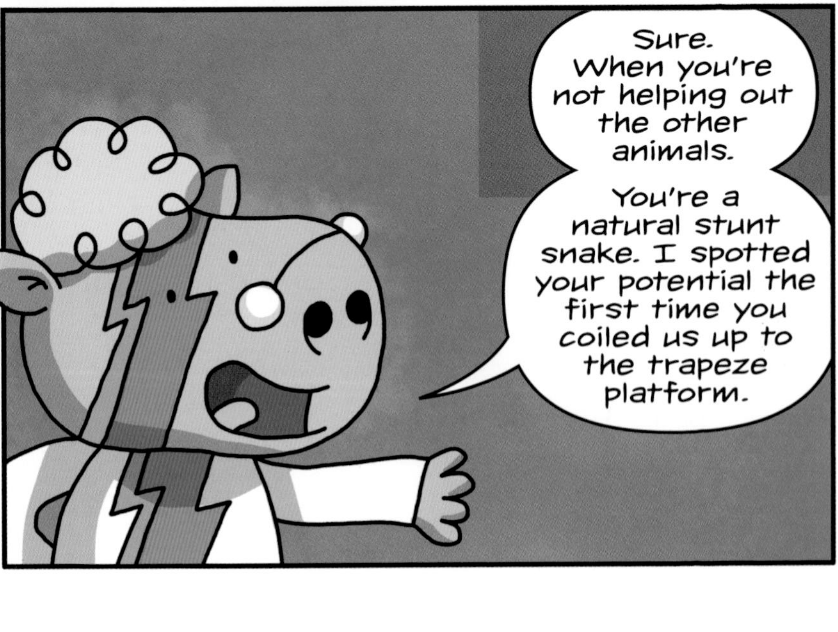
Sure. When you're not helping out the other animals.
You're a natural stunt snake. I spotted your potential the first time you coiled us up to the trapeze platform.

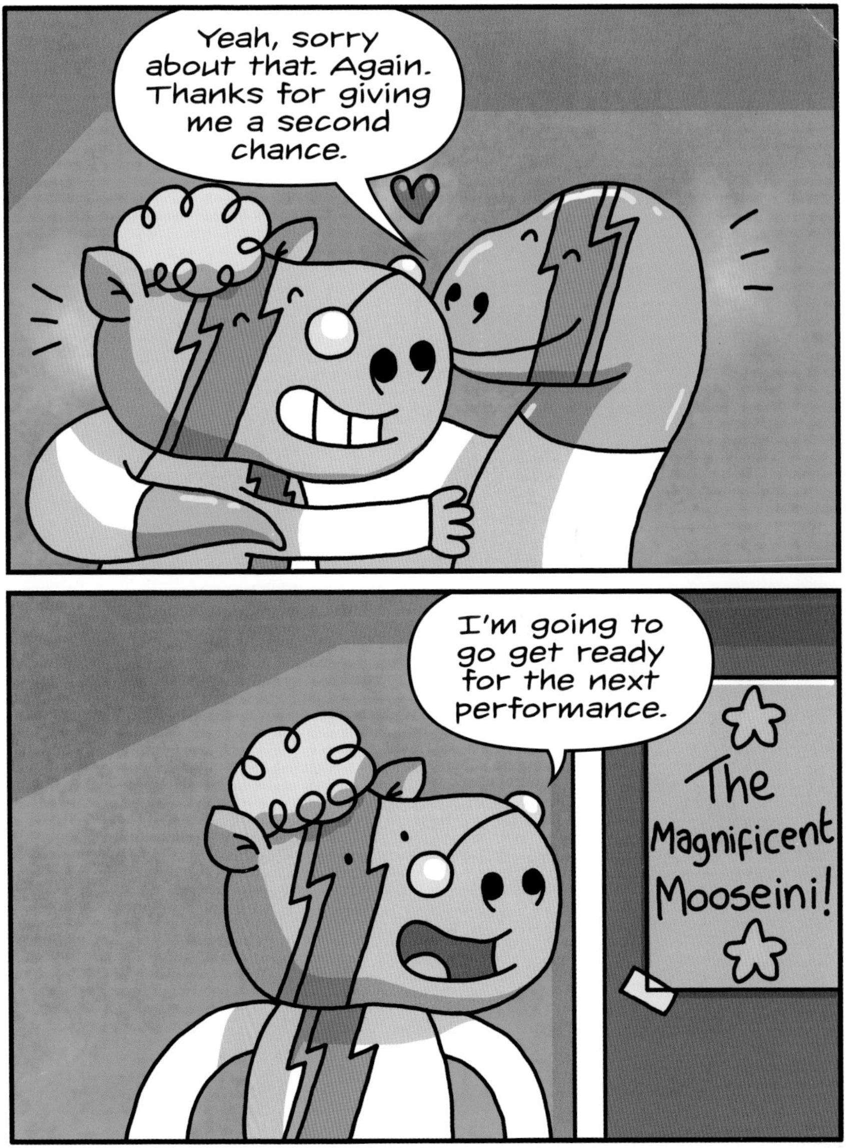
Yeah, sorry about that. Again. Thanks for giving me a second chance.
I'm going to go get ready for the next performance.
The Magnificent Mooseini!

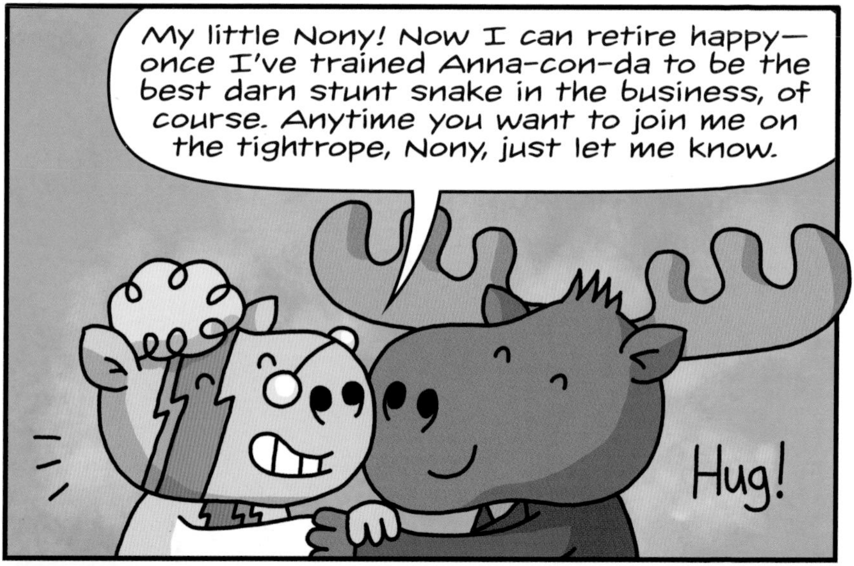
My little Nony! Now I can retire happy—once I've trained Anna-con-da to be the best darn stunt snake in the business, of course. Anytime you want to join me on the tightrope, Nony, just let me know.
Hug!

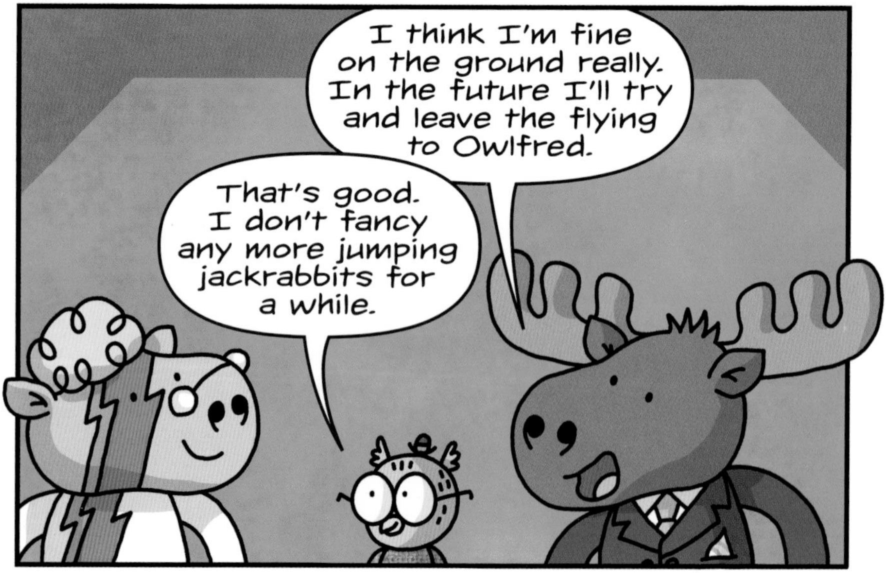
I think I'm fine on the ground really. In the future I'll try and leave the flying to Owlfred.
That's good. I don't fancy any more jumping jackrabbits for a while.

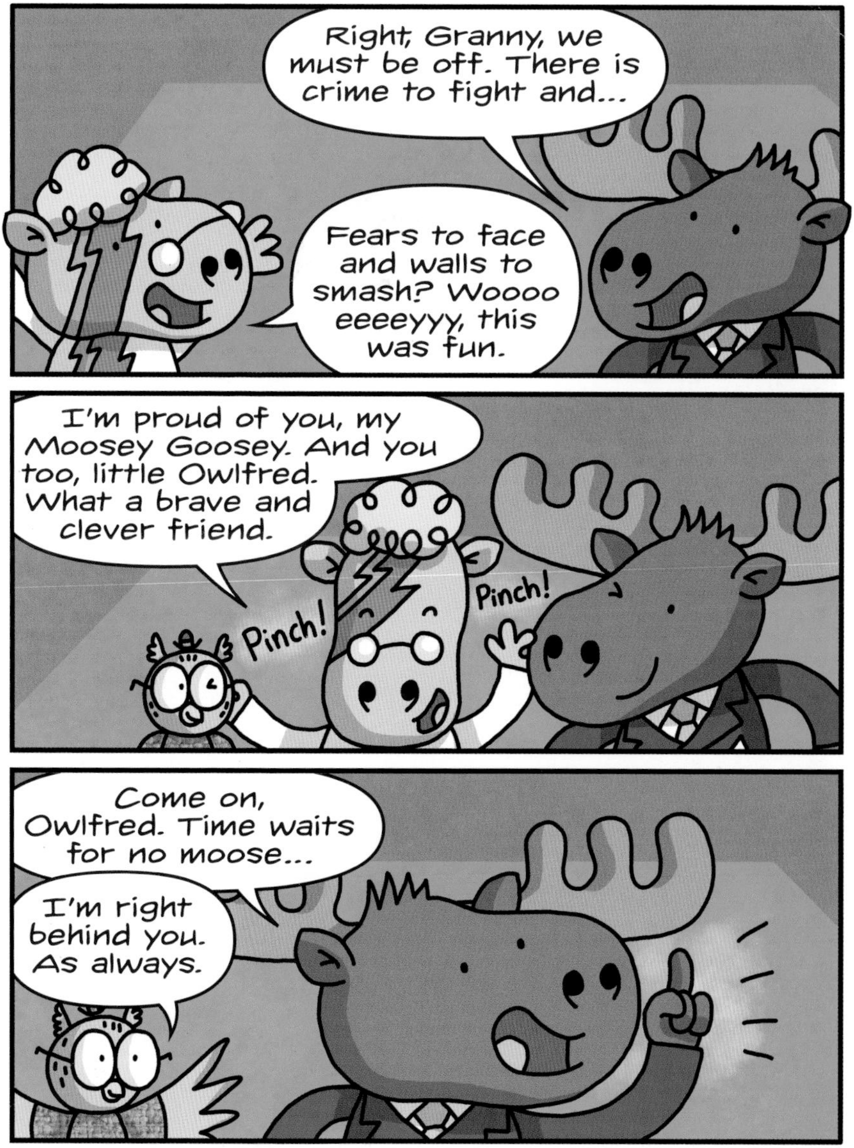
Right, Granny, we must be off. There is crime to fight and...
Fears to face and walls to smash? Woooo eeeeyyy, this was fun.
I'm proud of you, my Moosey Goosey. And you too, little Owlfred. What a brave and clever friend.
Pinch!
Pinch!
Come on, Owlfred. Time waits for no moose...
I'm right behind you. As always.

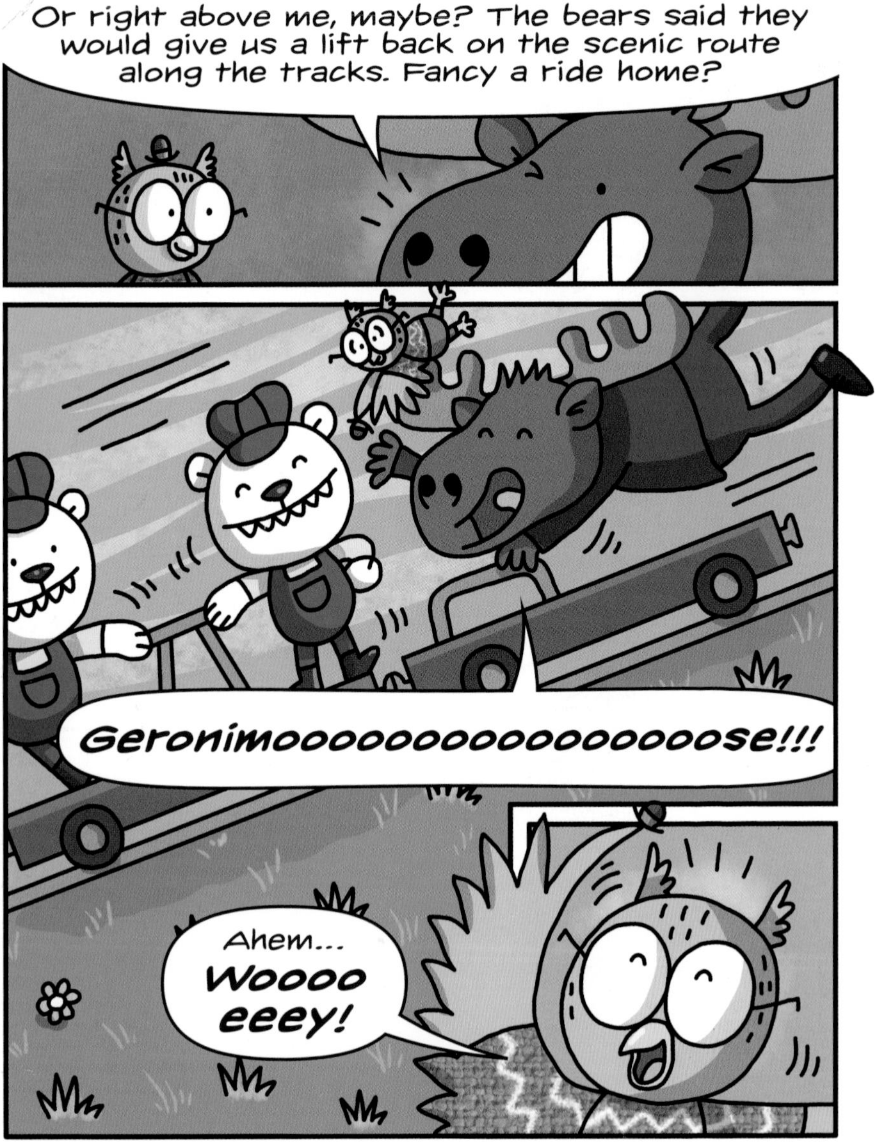
Or right above me, maybe? The bears said they would give us a lift back on the scenic route along the tracks. Fancy a ride home?
Geronimoooooooooooooooooooose!!!
Ahem... Woooo eeey!

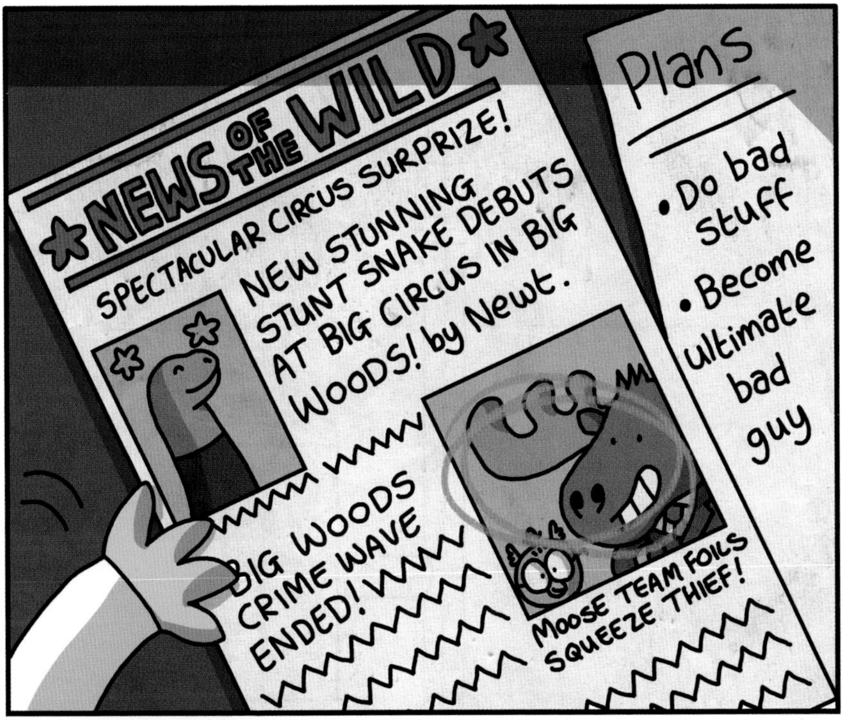
NEWS OF THE WILD
SPECTACULAR CIRCUS SURPRIZE!
NEW STUNNING STUNT SNAKE DEBUTS AT BIG CIRCUS IN BIG WOODS! by Newt.
BIG WOODS CRIME WAVE ENDED!
MOOSE TEAM FOILS SQUEEZE THIEF!
Plans
• Do bad stuff
• Become ultimate bad guy

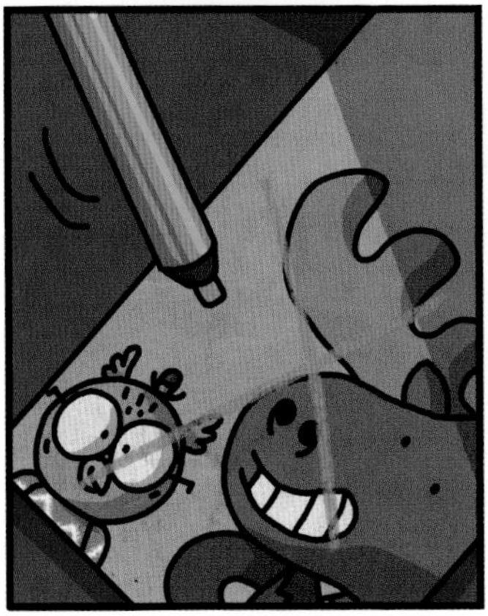

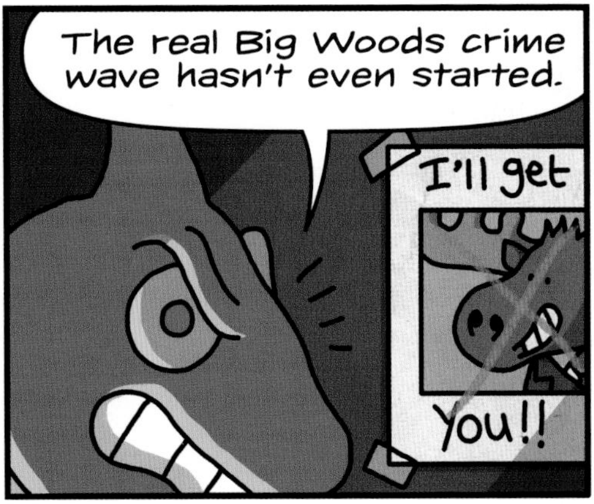
The real Big Woods crime wave hasn't even started.
I'll get
You!!

THANK YOU FOR READING THIS FEIWEL AND FRIENDS BOOK.

The Friends who made

AGENT MOOSE
MOOSE ON A MISSION

possible are:

Jean Feiwel, Publisher

Liz Szabla, Associate Publisher

Rich Deas, Senior Creative Director

Holly West, Senior Editor

Anna Roberto, Senior Editor

Kat Brzozowski, Senior Editor

Dawn Ryan, Senior Managing Editor

Erin Siu, Associate Editor

Rachel Diebel, Assistant Editor

Emily Settle, Associate Editor

Foyinsi Adegbonmire, Editorial Assistant

Kim Waymer, Senior Production Manager

Liz Dresner, Associate Art Director

Mandy Veloso, Senior Production Editor